"No one, in [...]
comes from [...]

"Some spe[...] [...] [...] [...] [...] the ancient dragons that left the realm for the west. Some think it comes from the gods. Or that the land itself has a level of awareness and intelligence all its own. Since we do not even understand the power's origins, certainly no one knows for sure why runes appear on the flesh of some but not others."

He glanced at Rand, who stared back intently, not attempting to conceal his eagerness to hear more of such secrets. "I suspect," the verrik continued, "that the runes are tied to the very nature of the land itself. The power of the runechildren is the might of the land made manifest. Those who find themselves so marked are those who would use the power on behalf of the land. Somehow, the runes seem to know who should have them, and who should not. It is far less a reward than a responsibility."

"A burden, then?" asked Rand.

"That is not the word I choose."

"A manifestation of destiny?"

"More a manifestation of power," said Hvanen. "A bequeathal of the right abilities on the right person at the right time. . . ."

MAL HAVOC PRESS

PROUDLY PRESENTS

MONTE COOK'S
ARCANA UNEARTHED

A variant player's handbook written by one of the designers of 3rd Edition
Dungeons & Dragons®. Features new roleplaying classes, races, skills, feats,
and spells, plus an alternate magic system.

MONTE COOK'S ARCANA UNEARTHED:
THE DIAMOND THRONE

Provides fundamental gameplay support for the variant rules in Monte
Cook's Arcana Unearthed. Includes the basic source material of the setting
plus new prestige classes, monsters, magic items, and more.

MONTE COOK'S ARCANA UNEARTHED:
DM'S SCREEN AND PLAYER'S GUIDE

A three-paneled horizontal screen with all the charts a DM needs to run the
game, plus a separate player reference card. Guide includes eleven different
character sheets, conversion guidelines, and character archetypes.

MONTE COOK'S ARCANA UNEARTHED:
LEGACY OF THE DRAGONS

Provides new adversaries and allies created using the rules from the variant
player's handbook. Also includes important and exciting new nonplayer
character personalities from the land of the Diamond Throne.

MONTE COOK'S ARCANA UNEARTHED:
MYSTIC SECRETS

Expands the magical options available to all characters with new
magic items

MONTE COOK'S ARCANA UNEARTHED:

CHILDREN
OF THE
RUNE

TALES FROM THE LAND
OF THE DIAMOND THRONE
BY
MONTE COOK
ED GREENWOOD
JEFF GRUBB
AND OTHERS

EDITED BY SUE WEINLEIN COOK

MALHAVOC PRESS

MONTE COOK'S ARCANA UNEARTHED:

CHILDREN OF THE RUNE

Children of the Rune is published by Malhavoc Press LLC. This anthology is ©2004 Monte J. Cook The contents of each individual story in this anthology is copyright as listed below, excepting those elements that are components of the *Monte Cook's Arcana Unearthed* and *The Diamond Throne* intellectual properties. Such elements are TM and © Monte J. Cook. All rights reserved.
Introduction ©2004 Sue Weinlein Cook • "Stone Ghosts" ©2004 Lucien Soulban
"How it Works" and "Not Without Cost" ©2004 Monte J. Cook • "Skin Deep" ©2004 Steven Brown
"The Silent Man" ©2004 Richard Lee Byers • "The Fallen Star" ©2004 Ed Greenwood
"Hollows of the Heart" ©2004 Bruce R. Cordell and Keith Francis Strohm
"Child of the Street" ©2004 William B. McDermott • "Clash of Duty" ©2004 Miranda Horner
"The Pebble Before the Avalanche" ©2004 Mike Mearls • "Name Day" ©2004 Wolfgang Baur
"Singer for the Dead" ©2004 John J. Grubb • "Precious Things" ©2004 Thomas M. Reid

Cover art by Mark Zug
Cover and interior design by Peter Whitley
Cartography by Ed Bourelle

ISBN: 1-58846-864-X
Stock #WW16145
First Printing: August 2004
Printed in Canada

Distributed for Malhavoc Press by
White Wolf Publishing
1554 Litton Drive
Stone Mountain, GA 30083

www.montecook.com

MONTE COOK'S ARCANA UNEARTHED:

CHILDREN OF THE RUNE

SUE WEINLEIN COOK

INTRODUCTION

Welcome to the land of the Diamond Throne, home of the runechildren. Since the release of *Monte Cook's Arcana Unearthed* roleplaying game, readers have become entranced with the setting's exotic peoples, arcane vistas, epic history, and—most of all—its ancient magics.

The mysterious runechildren are inheritors of this magic. These chosen heroes are granted mystical powers and the mark of a supernatural tattoo. The runechildren don't know why they're chosen, or even by whom. Is it the gods? The land itself? In any case, their purpose is clear: to shepherd the land and its people through whatever dangers may come.

Some runechildren are unsure of their calling, at least in the beginning. Just making the acquaintance of a runechild can change one's life forever. Often they are asked to take great risks and make great sacrifices for the good of the world. And born of these sacrifices is the freedom the folk of the land enjoy.

Runechildren can spring from any race: the tall and noble giants, known for their battle prowess, ancient traditions, and wise leadership; the reptilian mojh, canny spellcasters who once were human; the three diminutive faen races—tiny winged sprytes, agile and frivolous quicklings, and the magic-loving loresongs; the honor-bound, leonine litorians of the plains; the jackal-headed sibeccai, whom the giants raised to sentience from their once feral status; the strange verrik, with their wine-colored skin and psychic natures; and even the humans, the most populous of all the races.

These select heroes come from backgrounds as diverse as their race. Some are spellcasters like magisters, runethanes, greenbonds, witches, or mage blades. Some are bold warriors—champions, warmains, totem warriors, or the unfettered. And some call upon unique powers, such as the akashics, masters of the racial memory, and the oathsworn, made mighty by virtue of their sworn bond.

In getting to know the runechildren, you will come to discover the exciting land of the Diamond Throne. Three centuries ago, the draconic dramojh held the land and its people captive, subject to their monstrous tyranny and hideous experiments. Then the giants came to these shores, unstoppable in the wardance they called Chi-Julud. The giants freed the people, vanquished the dramojh, and together built a new realm.

This is a realm where one's honor is more important than personal desire, where individual choice can rule over destiny, and where the land is a thing to be protected, not exploited. It is a land steeped in ceremony, upheld by the innate strength of one's sworn oath, and bound together by the burning power of hope.

Some people think the runechildren are only a myth. Others know they're real. But everyone has a different opinion of exactly what it means to *be* a runechild. The thirteen original tales in this book showcase these varied points of view. I hope you enjoy meeting these new heroes, who wield the power of deed and rune.

STONE GHOSTS

Morgain Nai-Barinon strode through the cobblestone streets of Ka-Rone with no interest in the surrounding festivities. Despite her evenly bronzed skin and lustrous black rope of braided hair, Morgain's empty scabbard drew the most stares. Why a warrior such as she carried no weapon added to her mystique. The gazes then drifted back to her unwavering emerald eyes that challenged anyone to make comment. None did. The worn leather attire and the sword scars and arrow nicks on her arms bespoke a veteran.

In all the mystery and beauty of Morgain, never once did onlookers see the rune adorning the back of her hand. They never suspected Morgain as a runechild.

The port city's normally pungent air of brine and slaughtered fish lay masked beneath a sea of new odors: vendors selling roasted chestnuts and spiced chai, taverns serving freshly baked breads and meats. If food didn't delight the senses, then the eyes and ears indulged in other banquets. To the joy of children, performers juggled spheres of colored glass lit from within, while musicians set tempo for the savage movement of litorian war-dancers. Torches of yellow flame lit the streets into the late hours, while dyed cloth and festive banners fluttered from the eaves of buildings.

Morgain, however, stopped for none of these distractions. While the Narasanight Festival was a joyous time, it was once strictly a Hu-Charad celebration. The giants were somber creatures, and their festival was one of words and memories. But, if the giants had learned one thing in these lands they'd conquered, it was that the greatest of human qualities was appropriation. The festival belonged to all now, and had grown far too garish for the understated Hu-Charad. Only in Ka-Rone's giant districts did the noise drop away and the festivities adopt a quiet, more sober tone. Morgain walked past poetry and story circles, where giants sat and recounted their works. Their tales were precise, their passions exact in the measured cadence of rhyming schemes and wordplay. A few distracted giants watched Morgain walk by, curious at the human who seemed comfortable in their hushed streets.

Morgain found her destination, a courtyard park surrounded by colonnaded buildings with pediment-style roofs. The garden's hanging vines and verdant crown of shrubs were spectacular against the alabaster-white structures and toga-clad sculptures. At the garden's center sat a circle of eight giants, while outside that, numerous children played quietly. Even seated, the giants were heads taller than Morgain, but she appeared at ease. The circle listened to one speaker, his voice reverential on this, the Hu-Charad's holy night. A few onlookers roasted corn or boiled chai on a heated brazier at the center of the circle. Morgain, her stride unwavering, marched straight for the giants before stopping. Everyone stared, surprised at this diminutive stranger who now waited for their attention.

"May we help you?" the giantess of the circle asked, her grey eyes curious. Her white hair and eleven-foot stature marked her as eldest, and thus the circle's matriarch.

"*Nasannah Mater*, Hu-Charad," Morgain said, initiating a traditional giant greeting of harmony. "I respectfully ask to join your tale circle." She carefully reached into her satchel and retrieved a large ivory flagon sealed with wax, and three cloth-wrapped loaves. "I offer you this honey mead and coconut bread, in honor of your ancestors' names and memories," Morgain said, concluding her rite of greeting and hospitality.

The giantess looked at her compatriots, surprised. "You're familiar with our customs. What is your name, child?"

"My name is Morgain Nai-Barinon, and my name is my tale," Morgain said.

Again the giants exchanged glances, their curiosity evident.

"Then join us," the giantess said. "Your company is welcome. I am Ia-Tyrrane, and I'm very curious why you have a Hu-Charad name."

Morgain smiled. "When it is my turn, then."

Morgain sat and nearly vanished among her powerful, thick-limbed hosts. She passed her flagon and loaves to her right, as was customary—always away from harm. The giants finished both, in short order, as a show of hospitality and trust in their guest's generosity. The circle returned to its stories, each giant relating his tale and passing the ebony story-stick to the next speaker. Finally, the stick reached Morgain; it was a heavy staff in her hands.

"All tales begin with someone's truth, so know my words are echoed in the Houses of the Eternal and from the lips of the ancestors," Morgain began, using an ancient Hu-Charad custom that few in the circle even remembered.

Ia-Tyrrane leaned forward, infinitely more intrigued by this human who understood giant culture better than her own children did. She studied Morgain in equal parcel to measuring her words, scrutinizing her every movement to determine the precision of her Hu-Charad etiquette.

"Let me tell you of my exploits in the desert city of Khorl," Morgain continued, "where my story ends…."

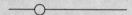

"You seem surprised," the black-robed Vrash said, not looking at Morgain. Again, his voice was flat, betraying no emotion or intention through inflections or changes in vocal timbre. He ran his hand across his bald, deep burgundy scalp.

Morgain studied the children practicing their noon katas in the marshaling square of the gymnasium, the local verrik school. The hot sun over Khorl drew a sheen from the children's faces, their red-wine skin sparkling with sweat.

"That a Nightwalker serves as headmaster of a school?" Morgain replied. "'Nightwalker' is appropriate, is it not?"

"If you draw comfort from such distinctions…."

"A Nightwalker headmaster. I suppose I have seen stranger things in my time."

Vrash didn't reply, but led Morgain under the shade of an adjoining arcade. He stopped and watched the children practice.

"Khorl is a dangerous city," Vrash said, again his gaze elsewhere. "Who else would you entrust your children to than a member of its most powerful guild?"

"With no intended disrespect, a thieves' guild is among the last places I'd entrust a child."

"Thieves are indiscriminate. We are not. And the people of this city feel differently than you. The Nightwalkers serve as headmasters or benefactors for the local gymnasiums. We understand the importance of children."

"I see." Morgain tried desperately to fathom Vrash through a telltale word or betrayed body movement.

Vrash abruptly spun about and walked toward a dark corridor, leaving Morgain to follow. The verrik pushed through a wooden door, one of several in the passageway, and entered a tidy, if dark, chamber. Scroll casings sat in wall niches, while a weathered vellum map of Dor-Erthenos covered the wall behind Vrash's writing table. A bookcase filled with assorted curios adorned another wall.

Vrash sat and studied Morgain; he was waiting for her to sit on the oak chair in front of him. She did, meeting his purple eyes with her own level gaze.

"Who else?" Vrash asked.

"Excuse me?"

"You said the thieves' guild was among the last places you'd entrust a child to. Who else fails your approval?"

Morgain watched Vrash's immutable expression, trying to determine whether her remark annoyed him. It didn't appear to.

"I'm merely curious," Vrash said, "as to your standards. Against whom do you measure the Nightwalkers?"

"Mojh magisters," Morgain said, finally abandoning any lingering pretext at diplomacy. "I wouldn't leave a child under the care of a mojh magister."

"Do you have any?" Vrash asked.

"What?"

"Do you have a child? Are you a mother?"

"No. What does that—"

"Then how do you know your child wouldn't benefit from the mojh, if you don't have the experience to draw such suppositions?"

"I simply do," Morgain said.

"Even if the mojh could teach the child much?"

Morgain inhaled slowly, regaining her composure. This was not the conversation she'd anticipated. "Call it a preference."

Vrash nodded. "A preference, then. But if the Nightwalkers rank equal in favor as a mojh magister, and the mojh rank so poorly in your esteem, then you must be truly desperate to seek my services."

"Desperate? No," Morgain responded. "I'm here for business."

"Indeed."

"I'm told you recently acquired artifacts from an expedition into the Bitter Peaks."

"Yes. In fact, I sold most of them."

"But not all?"

"Trinkets, baubles, and some incomplete pieces. History's waste. Barely worth the mentioning."

"I may wish to buy them."

"Buy them?" Vrash said, a flicker of curiosity knotting his brow. His eyes darted quickly to a corner of the room. Vrash's face became a calm pool again, no ripples to blemish the surface.

Morgain suddenly realized Vrash rarely asked questions that reduced his control over the matter at hand. It placed him on the defensive, which he neither liked nor suffered.

"An associate who bought a piece from you described the remaining lot," Morgain said, hoping to offset Vrash's suspicions. "I wish to see them."

"Why bother?" Vrash said, indifferent. "Nothing remains but scraps."

"I'm a handy judge of something's worth. I'd wish to see them, naturally. Perhaps reach an understanding."

"Why?"

Morgain was taken aback momentarily. Vrash threw questions at her that she didn't anticipate. She adapted as best she could, however. "I thought the Nightwalkers rarely dealt in questions?" Morgain said.

"Rarely… as you say."

"I can resell them."

"That's all? Resale?"

"Yes," Morgain said, controlling her breath and trying to relax the muscles in her face and body. Nothing twitched.

6

Nothing moved. She was a statue. No truth or secret would slip through under the verrik's appraising gaze.

"Very well. Come back tomorrow morning. We'll discuss price then."

"Tomorrow?" Morgain said. "I'd hoped —"

"Tomorrow," Vrash replied, ending the conversation.

Tomorrow wasn't good enough.

Vrash was suspicious, and Morgain couldn't risk him uncovering the potential worth of one particular item, if it was even present. Instead, Morgain retired to her room at the Fell Ox Inn and waited for the laughter and ribald songs from the adjoining tavern to ebb and fall silent in the late evening. During the wait, she oiled her precious athame sword, *Lightfinder*, the mark of her proficiency as a mage blade.

The sword vibrated in Morgain's mind, happy at her touch and immediate presence. Its ability for thought was as basic as its skill to emote sentiment and intent. An akashic ally of Morgain's once called *Lightfinder*'s speech "punctuation," because one derived but a sense of its general mood through the intonations and punctuation normally found in sentences.

"!" the sword said.

"Yes," Morgain responded with a smile. "We have work tonight."

"?"

"You'll see," she said, then realized it was nearly silent in the neighboring tavern. Few people would be wandering the streets now; inns were the best barometer of local life. When they fell quiet, it meant most people were asleep or unconscious.

Morgain sheathed her blade and slipped out the window of her second-floor room onto the sturdy wooden overhang. From there, she moved to the awning of an adjoining building with a small leap across the bordering alley. Morgain had chosen this inn because it lay near the verrik gymnasium and because the neighboring structures were packed closely together, their awnings nearly touching over the alleys. They formed a canopy of paths above the patrolled streets. Quickly darting from building to building, Morgain made her way to the gymnasium.

The oasislike compound in the otherwise dusty city lay behind high walls. Morgain maneuvered her way to the darkest edge, where the street's wash of meager lamplight waned most heavily. She drew *Lightfinder* and brought it up with a flourished fencer's salute, pressing the cool flat of the blade against her forehead; orange runes briefly lit the blade with their gentle glow before vanishing. Morgain's eyes flew open, but gone was the emerald green, now replaced by shadows that streamed forth. Tatters of this darkness engulfed her, encasing her in its own night. She became a dark spot on an already dark wall. Morgain sheathed her blade and scaled the wall, proficiently stuffing her fingers into niches and wide cracks.

Up the wall and over, Morgain found herself in a small, dark grove of palm trees worn smooth by the climbing of adventurous children. There was nobody in sight, however, neither on the dusty marshaling field nor across it at the two-story gymnasium with its shuttered windows. Morgain moved along the wall, a darting shadow in the night. Upon reaching the gymnasium, she ran from column to column under the covered arcade that had sheltered her earlier that day, and down the passage to Vrash's study.

Careful not to touch the door, Morgain leveled *Lightfinder* horizontal, the flat of the blade facing her, and stared into the reflection of her own eyes. Her reflection dissipated, however, and the blade mirrored the doorway behind it, as though the sword were translucent. Morgain could now see anything of an arcane nature within her line of sight; but of the door and lock, neither possessed any apparent magic.

Morgain slipped her lockpicks into the door and, after considerable effort manipulating the tumblers, finessed it open. She entered Vrash's dark study and immediately went for the bookshelf. A collection of prayer stones, funeral statuaries, and meditation beads covered the shelves; otherwise, Morgain could not find her quarry. She investigated the corner of the room and a small trunk where Vrash had glanced during their conversation, but it was empty. The desk likewise held nothing of interest for Morgain. Nothing behind the wall map, either, or in all the nooks one would think of hiding such wares. Morgain swept the room with *Lightfinder* in hand, hoping to unearth objects of arcane craft, but the attempt proved fruitless.

Morgain sighed, her fears validated. Her questions earlier had likely fueled Vrash's suspicions, and now the wastrel items were ensconced elsewhere, under scrutiny. And while Morgain's prize would escape casual inspection, it would surely pique interest under a more diligent search. That was, if Vrash possessed what she sought.

". . ." *Lightfinder* said.

"Patience then," Morgain replied. "Tomorrow it is."

Morgain sighed quietly, again seated before Vrash, again waiting for some semblance of normal conversation. It was not forthcoming. Instead, the morning sun already promised a hot, grueling day, and Vrash administered to his duties by reviewing documents. To Morgain's side stood a young, black-haired verrik girl, no more than twelve years of age. The girl cast a quick, sidelong glance at Morgain, then looked forward again. Her back was straight, Morgain noted, rigid with experienced discipline.

"Well, Ndleeta," Vrash said, his gaze fixed on the document, "why are you in trouble?"

"I—" Ndleeta began, but Vrash interrupted with a raised finger; he pointed to Morgain and never looked up.

"Explain it to our guest, please," Vrash said, reading.

Unabashed, the young girl faced Morgain, and the mage blade found herself unintentionally straightening in her chair.

"I fought with Radiir outside of the sparring circle," Ndleeta explained with militialike punctuation to her response.

"You broke his arm," Vrash said, distracted by his work.

"Yes."

There was an uncomfortable pause in the room. Morgain realized the two verrik awaited her comment.

"Well," Morgain said, unsure of what to ask, "why did you break his arm?"

"He mocked me," Ndleeta said simply.

"Has he done it often?" Morgain asked.

"No. He's my cousin and best friend."

"Then he angered you?" Morgain asked.

"No. I hurt Radiir because if I hadn't, my classmates would think they could mock me as well."

"You broke his arm to warn the others? Threaten them?" Morgain asked, her eyes wide.

"Yes," Ndleeta replied.

"So," Vrash asked Morgain, "how would you punish her?"

"Punish her?" Morgain said with a genuine laugh. "I think I like her."

A slight smile escaped Ndleeta's lips, but it was fleeting.

"Your reaction," Vrash said to Ndleeta, "has costs. I admire your foresight and motivation, but we must all heed consequence. Consider the form of your punishment. We'll discuss it later."

Ndleeta spun on her heel and left the office. Silence lingered a moment longer before Vrash finally raised his head.

"We have business to conclude," he said. Vrash reached down and produced a satchel. He unhooked the fasteners, and unfurled the flaps, revealing two rows of bulging cloth pockets. He removed the items, one by one, producing a medley of broken and discarded articles: urn handles, brightly colored mosaic fragments, bronze scales, and several pieces too ravaged or broken to identify.

"May I?" Morgain asked, motioning to the items. Vrash nodded.

Morgain filtered through the objects, careful not to pay undue heed to any one or another. Unfortunately, what she sought was not present. Her heart sank.

Could my information have been wrong? she wondered. *Or is he hiding it from me? I must rethink this.*

"Well?" Vrash asked. "Shall we discuss price?"

Morgain was silent a moment before responding. "No, and I'm sorry to have wasted your time. You were right. This is all obviously worthless." Morgain stood and nodded. "Good day."

"And to you," Vrash replied, without a shred of disappointment or regret.

The verrik compound had a single entrance, so it was easy to track the students and teachers who passed through its gates. Morgain began her vigil on a rooftop neighboring the gymnasium immediately following her meeting, and kept watch into the late evening. By then, it appeared as though everyone had left . . . except Vrash.

Morgain summoned the darkness again to shield her movements, and she remained in the shadows upon dropping down into an adjoining alley strewn with heat-fetid refuse. Nobody detected her swift passage through the maze of unlit alleys, or her vault over the gymnasium's walls.

Once sheltered by the grove of palm trees, Morgain watched the empty marshaling square. She slipped across.

Under the arcade, she waited, listening. The gymnasium was quiet.

Down the hallway, Morgain found herself at Vrash's door again. She knelt and peered under the door, spying only darkness beyond. Nobody appeared within. Morgain removed her picks and gently inserted them into the lock, anticipating an easier time opening it than last night.

The clack of footfalls echoed inside the halls of the gymnasium. Someone was about, the steps the unmistakable shuffle-slap of sandals against floor and heel. It can't be Vrash, Morgain thought; he wore boots beneath his black robes. Still, someone approached Morgain's corridor from an intersection farther up the hallway. The growing cast of torchlight against the walls intensified; the footfalls echoed throughout the stone passages, obfuscating direction and immediacy. Morgain had precious few seconds to act. Despite night's cloak resting on her shoulders, someone walking past her would likely notice her in the corridor's confines.

Morgain tried retrieving her picks, but they snagged in the lock. She pulled harder in the moment's desperation, then realized that whoever approached was almost at the intersection. Morgain abandoned the picks in the lock and moved toward the arcade, her back against the wall. . . .

. . . Too late.

A custodian entered the hallway, bringing Morgain's retreat to a halt. He was an old verrik man, draped under brown robes and carrying a lantern. He couldn't see Morgain in the darkness of the corridor, but the mage blade knew that if she moved to the open archway, the moon-lit marshaling square beyond would betray her silhouette to the custodian. If she didn't move, however, he would stumble across her, or the picks in the lock, soon enough.

Momentary indecision overtook Morgain, which only increased the likelihood of discovery. At worst, she could silence the custodian; but she was not indiscriminate and he was not deserving of injury. At best, she could flee and risk exposure, meaning any future attempts to retrieve the item would prove all the more impossible.

And all this, Morgain thought, *for an assumption.* She didn't even know if Vrash possessed what she sought, but the slimmest possibility demanded this venture. Morgain acted. She slowly withdrew *Lightfinder* from its sheath.

"!!"

I know, Morgain thought. The custodian was several feet from Vrash's door and her exposed picks, and Morgain was another twenty beyond that. The skirt of the lantern's wash was almost upon her heels. Morgain concentrated on her spell and channeled its release through gentle flicks and twists of her wrist.

The custodian approached the door.

Morgain's craft with *Lightfinder* rested in the minutia of her movements. Most mage blades relied on the overt dances of their spell-katas, but Morgain favored subtlety in her motion to reflect her choice of magic: obfuscation, redirection, and divination. In this case, Morgain appeared to be moving her blade with the same swishing movement of fencers loosening their wrists. In actuality, it was a distraction ploy, one that allowed Morgain to conceal an audible illusion in that one simple action.

The custodian failed to notice the picks in the lock, and instead walked past them. Fifteen feet away from Morgain . . . and he heard phantom shuffling behind him. He spun around and peered down the corridor, drawing up the lantern to see better.

The corridor was empty.

Take the bait, damn you, Morgain thought.

The custodian listened intently a moment, concentrating.

Morgain knew the verrik capable of extraordinary feats with their senses; thus, this one needed further incentive to investigate, and Morgain was only too willing to comply. She focused on the sound of a pebble hitting stone, and heard the resulting echo dance through the halls. The custodian shuffled quickly, back down the corridor, past the door and the way he arrived, his steps surprisingly lithe despite his age. He rounded the corner.

Racing as quickly as silence allowed, Morgain reached Vrash's door as she sheathed *Lightfinder*. She set upon the picks, trying to unhook them. The custodian's light still illuminated the adjoining corridor; he was within feet of the intersection, but not moving.

Morgain retrieved the picks and reinserted them into the lock. She cast quick furtive glances back down the hallway.

The light moved again . . . toward the intersection. Morgain hissed a curse; she didn't want to generate any more sounds, lest the custodian call for help.

The tumblers fell into place. The door opened. The custodian was rounding the corner.

Morgain slipped through the door and quietly closed it. She waited in the dark chamber, slowing her breathing, trying to calm her stammering heart.

The shuffle-slap of sandals approached. They stopped at the door. A pause. The footsteps continued again, fading down the corridor. They vanished into the marshaling square.

Morgain rested her back against the door a moment, lost in relief. She stood and retrieved *Lightfinder* from its sheath.

"Ready to search anew?" she asked.

"." *Lightfinder* responded.

"I know we didn't find anything, yesterday," Morgain replied, "but we didn't have the proper spell."

"?"

"You know the one," Morgain said with a smile. She brought the blade up again and peered into the reflection. Her mirror faded, revealing the room beyond.

Morgain's suspicions were well founded. The spell whispered in her ears . . . the room held a hidden door somewhere, which was why she hadn't seen Vrash leave. Morgain searched the chamber carefully, and the spell eventually tugged at the blade, drawing her gaze to the wooden floor beneath Vrash's desk. She waited for her magics to reveal the door's triggering mechanism. Her attention fell on the vellum wall map, particularly, the glow from four Zalavat ruins. She needed to press those locations to unlock the trapdoor.

Morgain's brow wrinkled in obvious confusion. Her attempt to unveil magic here yesterday proved fruitless, so how had this arcana escaped her notice? Unless . . . Morgain lifted the map's skirt and studied the bricks beneath. At least eight seemed loose in their sockets. It was an intricate locking mechanism that would either reveal the trapdoor or unleash harm if she pressed the wrong bricks.

With the map properly back in place, Morgain studied the Zalavat ruin markers, trying to determine which to press first. None of the four sites glowed with any particular shine or diminished cast, however, so Morgain simply pushed the four together and, thus, the bricks beneath them. With barely a grated whisper, well-oiled pulleys shifted their counterweights, and a lock unlatched, opening a small floor hatch beneath the desk. Wooden stairs vanished into the darkness.

Morgain crept down the stairs into another unlit chamber. With a simple wave of *Lightfinder*, she could suddenly see her environment clearly, her world reduced to stark blacks and whites.

The chamber was a storage room, with barrels, sacks, and chests of various designs and sizes. Two workbenches split the room, with items left outside for inspection alongside appraising tools like tiny brushes and picks. A simple door waited opposite the stairs, reeking of dank sewage; Khorl's sewers likely lay beyond, for hidden travel and escape.

Morgain moved to the tables first, unraveling wrapped cloth pieces and examining everything carefully. Incense clay from De-Shamod, rare dyes from Ravadan, litorian battle claws of exquisite design, Navael crystals, and other valuables caught Morgain's brief attention, but none held her interest. Finally, she found one cloth the length of a long dagger bound by red string. A surge of anticipation shot through Morgain, down to her stomach; this moment was almost holy in its implications. She unraveled the string and carefully unrolled the cloth on the table. And there her prize lay, two stone fingers . . . male, broken off at the knuckle, but connected down their center.

Morgain inhaled sharply and studied the piece. The fingers belonged to a giant statue, the workmanship divine by its details, from the fingernails to the wrinkles and ribbon-creases along each joint. Morgain removed her glove, revealing her rune badge of station, and gently grasped the two fingers. Her eyes glowed a soft white, an affirmation of her commitment to the world around her. The whispers of yesterday filled her thoughts. As a runechild, she called upon her ability to reveal the item's past, to authenticate it as that of her quest.

Hushed voices unraveled in Morgain's mind, revealing images and sounds from the statue's three hundred fifty years of existence. Morgain felt the statue's body as her own, cracking and falling away under time's hammer and the callous blows of thieves and crypt robbers. Finally, her consciousness dwindled with each piece that dropped into the mists of her thoughts . . . body falling from arm; forearm from elbow; hand from wrist, and finally, her perceptions shattered down in scope to two fingers. . . .

"I assume you found what you wanted?"

Morgain spun around to meet the voice; Vrash stood in the corner, his appearance sudden. Morgain barely controlled her combat-honed impulse to draw *Lightfinder*. Vrash would not appear if he didn't already possess the upper hand.

Am I surrounded, Morgain wondered, *or outclassed?*

"That must be quite the experience, to draw a tear from you," Vrash said.

Morgain realized she'd been crying. She wiped the errant tears from her cheek.

"And, you're a runechild, at that," Vrash said with his typically flat aplomb. "I must say, this makes matters more interesting."

"Interesting?" Morgain asked.

"I was willing to dispose of you for such a predictable and short-sighted attempt at thievery, but . . ."

"But, I'm a runechild," Morgain said, understanding. Her actions and purpose now held more weight and merited greater consideration. Vrash evaluated her conduct in light of her nature as rune-chosen and not mere thief.

"What are the fingers to you?" Vrash asked.

"I cannot say."

"You've said plenty already," Vrash said. "To risk incurring the wrath of the Nightwalkers is, in itself, a statement of intent and dedication."

"Name your price," Morgain said, going on the offensive.

"I cannot ask a price for something I do not appreciate," Vrash replied. "I've studied the fingers and, aside from the remnants of some arcane crafts, they appear worthless."

"Appear," Morgain said, agreeing. She had learned long ago that no artifact or item possessed an established value. Its worth was a measure of prevailing circumstances and someone's desperation to claim it. Value was always a matter of timing, and Morgain's moment was desperate. Vrash knew that and, thus, could demand almost any price.

"Do you seek the fingers from personal interest? Or in relation to your duties as rune-marked?" Vrash sat atop a barrel, studying Morgain's posture.

"Yes," she said, allowing a concession. "As rune-sworn, personal interest and duty are the same."

Vrash nodded. "I understand. You share much with the Nightwalkers."

"I doubt that."

"Indeed. There are some runechildren who operate within our ranks."

"Impossible," Morgain said. "We've sworn to champion the world around us. We serve no other interests, selfish or otherwise."

"And some rune-sworn recognize the advantages we offer to that end. But then what of these fingers?" Vrash asked. "How does their recovery benefit the world?"

Morgain said nothing.

"Then, if I destroyed them?" Vrash asked.

"That's a hollow threat," Morgain said. "You wouldn't destroy something you don't yet understand. It would be . . ." Morgain paused for the sheer drama, "short-sighted."

Vrash smiled. "That is supposition. You already know the fingers' worth and believe them too valuable to destroy. And, while I can only guess at their value, all I have are assumptions. Thus, I'm far less invested in protecting the two fingers. So, yes, I could destroy them, because sometimes . . ." Vrash said, adding his own irony to the moment, "ignorance is bliss."

Morgain tried formulating a retort to Vrash's comments. She had nothing to offer, however. The verrik was right. The items meant little to him. She was at his mercy, unless she attacked, but she had little inkling as to what she faced. Vrash, however, knew her to be a runechild and remained self-assured enough to face her, seemingly unarmed and alone.

"So, then what?" Morgain asked. "Destroy the fingers, but that would net you little in the process."

"True," Vrash said. "Let's dispense with the verbal sparring. I'll negotiate for purchase of the two fingers . . . if you answer one question."

"Can I hear the question first?"

"Certainly, but if you refuse to answer, I destroy the fingers."

Morgain thought about it for a moment. "Ask."

"What is so important about the fingers that they hold a runechild's devotion?"

Morgain mulled over the question, searching for the best response without revealing a necessary truth. Finally, she said "My duties as rune-sworn are no less valid if serving one person or helping a hundred. What matters isn't the nature of my service to the world, but the intent with which I carry forth my obligations."

"Well evaded," Vrash said. "What will you sacrifice for the two fingers?" he asked.

"Sacrifice?"

"Come now, you didn't think this would come down to money?"

"I had hoped. . . ." Morgain said.

"We've both invested too much in this moment to reconcile it with coin or bauble. And there's little you could offer me that would truly improve my fortunes. So . . . what are you willing to sacrifice?"

Morgain shook her head, not knowing what she could sacrifice that would mean much to the Nightwalker.

"You said you wouldn't trust your child to a mojh or Nightwalker?" Vrash said.

"What?"

"Yesterday," Vrash replied, offering Morgain context that the verrik themselves so rarely needed or used in their conversations. "Would you entrust your child to a mojh or Nightwalker for the two fingers?"

"The point's moot. I have no child to offer," Morgain replied, suddenly uneasy.

"Indulge me," Vrash said. "Would you offer your child?"

Morgain thought about her possible responses, but she knew there was no right answer save the truth. "No."

Vrash smiled, a slight upward tilt of his lips. "What of your athame?"

"What?!" Morgain asked

"Your blade. Would you sacrifice it for the fingers?"

"Is that what you're asking? Is that the price?"

Vrash sat on the corner of the workbench and watched Morgain a moment. "Yes," he said.

"But," Morgain said, stammering, "it's worthless to you!"

"No more than the fingers," Vrash said with a shrug. "But I am curious. Which of the two items is worth less in your esteem? If you won't tell me their cost, then I'll make you impart a value. Your athame for the statue's fingers and an oath that you will not create a new athame . . . nor summon this one back . . . nor make any attempt to steal it from me. That is my price."

Morgain paused, the weight of decision heavy on her heart. *Lightfinder* was her companion, her friend. The fingers, however, were part of a cycle greater than she. And for the moment, Morgain discovered she couldn't speak. . . .

Ia-Tyrrane and the other Hu-Charad were silent, waiting for Morgain to whet her parched lips with mead. Morgain, however, stopped drinking and quietly watched the fire. Ia-Tyrrane realized they had their answer. Morgain's scabbard was empty.

"So you surrendered your athame?" the giantess asked.

"How could I not?" Morgain whispered. She reached into a pouch and withdrew a cloth wrapping, which she opened carefully. Hidden in the deep folds rested the two stone fingers. "Vrash believed I surrendered *Lightfinder* because it was a lesser prize. He was wrong."

"You loved *Lightfinder* more," Ia-Tyrrane said.

Morgain merely nodded and stared at the fingers.

"What obligation do you carry that demands such sacrifices?" a young giant asked.

"Centuries ago," Morgain said, "the dragon wizards, the dramojh, enslaved my ancestors. Your people freed us from slavery."

"Your family name. . . ." Ia-Tyrrane said, understanding Morgain's story more clearly.

"We changed our name to Nai-Barinon, to that of our giant liberator," Morgain said. "We swore an oath to serve Nai-Barinon for as long as our family still bore his name."

Ia-Tyrrane motioned to see the statue's fingers. Morgain passed them to her. The giantess studied them, gentle in her touch and tender in her gaze.

"Several of my ancestors fought alongside Nai-Barinon when he ventured deeper into the lands of the dramojh . . ." Morgain continued.

A sad smile crossed Ia-Tyrrane's face; she realized the fingers were too delicate and perfect in their details.

". . . but the dramojh were powerful. They had many allies."

The fingers, Ia-Tyrrane realized, belonged to no statue . . .

"My ancestors saw Nai-Barinon fall to a medusa," Morgain said.

. . . the stone fingers were once flesh.

"One of my ancestors survived that battle," Morgain said, "but she lived only long enough to tell us of Nai-Barinon's fate. Since that time, my family has sought his now shattered remains—to offer him proper burial and a shrine where his stone body may rest."

"How long?" Ia-Tyrrane asked. "How long has your family carried this obligation?"

"Three hundred and fifty years," Morgain said, "and we are far from finished. Each generation is lucky if it finds a single fragment of Nai-Barinon, and I will not live long enough to see my family's debt repaid." Morgain passed the storyteller stick to her right. "My story is done and holds no truths left to tell," she said, completing the Hu-Charad rite.

"May I ask why you privileged us with this?" Ia-Tyrrane asked, returning the fingers to Morgain.

Morgain stood up and folded the cloth over her bitter prize. "Every year, at the Narasanight Festival," Morgain replied, "my family shares its tale with one circle of Hu-Charad. So that you might know of Nai-Barinon and his deeds. So that you bear witness when we renew our oath to him . . . and to you. Will you bear witness?"

Ia-Tyrrane stood. The other giants followed suit, each of them towering above the small human in their company. The giants beckoned to their children with outstretched hands and quick whispers, drawing them into the circle to witness this moment and hear Morgain's words.

"From the Houses of the Eternal, I speak for my ancestors," Morgain said, reciting a Hu-Charad prayer. "Their blood shall never run dry for as long as it flows in my veins. Their words shall never fall silent for as long as I utter them. Their oath is my truth, and I accept no truth other than this promise . . . I swear on the very blood and breath of those who have passed on before me to honor the Hu-Charad for their deeds against the dramojh and to make whole again the spirit of Nai-Barinon."

"On behalf of my kind," Ia-Tyrrane said, "we accept your oath."

Morgain offered a deep nod in thanks, then gathered her belongings. She still had a long journey ahead. She reached down, to touch the pommel of her athame, but *Lightfinder* wasn't there. Her assurance, her friend, was gone. A heavy sadness eclipsed Morgain's heart and she remembered her own words to Vrash.

What matters isn't the nature of my service to the world, but the intent with which I carry forth my obligations.

And how dearly she paid for those words.

Morgain left the giants and vanished into streets of Ka-Rone.

HOW IT WORKS

When Jynnie Folus found herself marked with a mystical rune one bright morning in Fourthmonth, the people of Bluehaven thought their troubles were over. Jynnie was only in her sixteenth year. She was plain and quiet, with hair the color of wet straw and a warm smile that showed itself too infrequently, as far as her father was concerned. A miller by trade, Jynnie's father, Erlen Folus, claimed the respect of most every one of the two hundred souls that called Bluehaven home. Just as important, folks liked Erlen. He was quick to pull out a joke or a good story from the days of the rebuilding after the great fire of 1720, and he seemed to have an endless supply of them—or at least, no one had ever noticed him retelling one they'd already heard.

Erlen always tried to bring a little laughter into his daughter's day, usually in the morning before he would head off to the mill or at night when he would return, looking like a ghost from the flour that covered him from head to foot. Jynnie would smile at her father's jokes or funny antics, but it was as much to please him as it was from true enjoyment. Jynnie's heart had broken the day her mother died two years prior.

It was still hard to smile, even now.

On that cool spring morning, when Jynnie came rushing out of the room where she slept and found her father cutting up some bread to take for his lunch, neither of them knew what to do about the rune. Erlen would be late to the mill that day, no doubt about it.

Jynnie had the rune right on her face. It was red and green—a swirling pattern that ran down her cheek and onto her chin. Parts of the curving lines framed her right eye in a way that made it seem as though she was looking at you very intently, whether she was or not.

She was plain no longer.

Now Erlen, as the best kind of fellow who likes to tell tales, also liked to listen to them. Thus, he'd heard the term "runechild" before and thought he had an inkling of what it meant. He'd never seen one, though, or known of anyone who had. But folks understood that the rune-mark was a good thing, not a bad thing. He knew that young Jynnie's appearance wouldn't frighten anyone. Just the opposite, in fact.

Still, his first instinct was to devise a way to hide the rune.

"But why, Daddy?" Jynnie asked him.

"I'm just afraid that folks won't understand."

Erlen was right.

Of course, there was no way to disguise such a thing. Jynnie went out to the market that day, and everyone she saw gasped. Mavish Nauton the seamstress fainted dead away. And word spread quickly.

"Little Jynnie Folus is a runechild," they would say.

"Erlen's girl?" would come the reply.

"None other."

"My word!"

Eventually, the conversation would take a predictable turn.

"What is a runechild?" someone would ask.

"Why, it's a person with a rune on their face," came the answer.

"I've heard tell it can also be on their hand," someone would add.

"But what's it mean?"

"It's a good omen," was always the triumphant answer. "It means that no harm will come to Bluehaven. She'll be able to take care of all our problems!"

Everyone had little trouble agreeing that this was a good thing. No one could ever give a more specific answer, however, so folks took away from the discussion what seemed to make the best sense to them, personally.

The day after the rune appeared, there came a knock on the door of the Folus house. It was early in the morning, but Erlen had already left for the mill.

Jynnie answered the door and saw Old Tam Bacon standing there. Now, of course, Old Tam Bacon wasn't really his name, but most folks couldn't remember what he was rightly called. Tam was a pig farmer who kept his stock down by the river. He supplied the village with pork and, since his herd was large and Tam knew what he was doing, the bacon he sold in Bluehaven enjoyed a reputation for two villages in every direction. Tam said they even talked about his pigs in faraway Mi-Theron. "Those giants, they know good pork when they've had it," he would say.

Tam held a squirming piglet in his arms, and—as usual—was covered from head to toe in pig stink. However, his grin ran from ear to ear. "Jynnie, I'm so glad to see you," Tam said.

"It's nice to see you, too, Tam," Jynnie lied, trying to breathe through her mouth.

"Jynnie, what with you havin' that rune and all," Old Tam said, still smiling. "Would you bless my newest little pig, here?"

Jynnie didn't have the slightest notion of how to bless a piglet. She didn't know how to bless anything. Other than the change in her physical appearance, she hadn't learned anything or felt any different than before the rune appeared.

She told Tam that. He smile lessened, but did not fade altogether.

"Ah, c'mon, Jynnie. Just put your hand on the little fellow and give him some of your rune power. Make him grow up big and strong."

"I do want to help you, sir." Jynnie shook her head. "And I would like to see him grow up well, of course. But I don't know what I can do about it."

Old Tam's smile was gone now. "Just put your hand on the pig and give it your blessing, girl."

Jynnie was a little startled at the change in Old Tam Bacon's tone. She did as she was told. She grabbed the struggling animal and said, "Grow up big and strong, little pig."

Nothing happened, of course. Not that Old Tam Bacon noticed. His big grin returned immediately and said, "Thank you, girl. This little village doesn't have anything to worry about now with you here." With that, he walked off with his blessed pig.

"But I've always been here," Jynnie said, too quietly for anyone to hear. "I'm still just the same girl."

However, that wasn't entirely the truth. Her encounter with Old Tam Bacon and his pig started something churning within her. She felt something begin to come alive. It was an idea—the kind of idea with a great deal of potency to it. She began to get a picture of what it was that a runechild was supposed to do. It was still unclear, but it was more than she'd known before.

And she was certain that it wasn't blessing pigs.

But Old Tam Bacon was just the start (which was surprising, because, except for knowing what to feed your pigs or when to butcher one for meat, Tam wasn't likely to be thought of as the smartest fellow in town—it wasn't often that he got an idea before anyone else). Soon folks were coming up to the Folus house in droves.

Tabor Finch wanted Jynnie to assure him that the late spring rains would be enough for a good crop this year. She just smiled, but Tabor took that to be a yes and walked away happy.

Mavish Nauton the seamstress came to ask Jynnie to help her with her sewing. Mavish had been sick with river fever for a month, and everyone in town knew she was so behind in her work that she'd never catch up. Jynnie agreed to help the woman, as soon as she'd finished her own work at home. Since her mother's death, Jynnie had the responsibilities of the Folus home, and she took them very seriously. But she kept her word and went to Mavish's house to help her with the sewing.

Mavish would later tell her friends, "I don't know what all the fuss is about. She sewed just like a regular girl. No magic. Nothing special."

And it was true. The rune gave her no magical sewing powers. When she tried to explain that, Mavish insisted that runechildren were there to help folks in need, and she was in need.

Finally, Jynnie just told her, "I don't think that's really how it works."

Nitell the smith asked Jynnie if she could conjure up some gold for him to use in a project he was working on.

"I don't think that's really how it works," she told him.

When Draven Mullet came calling to ask Jynnie if she could please restore a jug of milk that had gone sour, she told him, "I don't think that's really how it works."

Emish Caulton, the mayor of Bluehaven, told Jynnie that he wasn't going to ask her for anything specific, just that she help the town in general. She said she would try.

Word soon got around that Jynnie the runechild wasn't providing anyone with the help they needed. "She doesn't deserve all that power," they would say.

"Why'd *she* get that rune, anyway?" Someone else would ask.

"I would certainly help you all if I had the rune," an indignant soul would respond.

"You couldn't have got the rune. It only goes to the young. That's why they're called rune*children*," someone might add. Usually Old Tam Bacon.

"I don't think that's true," would often come the response.

Mavish tried to call a town meeting. She told everyone that she'd had enough of Jynnie's refusals and excuses. If they couldn't get her to agree to do what they needed her to do, she proposed that they make Jynnie give the rune to someone else. And wasn't Mavish's daughter, Gealia Nauton, a fine choice? She was prettier and friendlier than Jynnie and would be willing to give any kind of help to anyone who asked.

Fortunately, no one else in the village thought that was a good idea, and most figured it wasn't even possible, to boot. Of course, it helped Jynnie's cause that Gealia, while perhaps prettier than she, wasn't, in fact, friendlier, and everyone knew it. Oh, she was friendly enough to some of the young men in the village, but that kind of friendly wasn't what they were talking about. So the matter died, and folks began thinking about other things.

Weeks passed, and summer arrived. The warm rays of the sun played across the Central Plains, and the nomadic litorian tribesmen stopped at Bluehaven, as they always did, seeking the comforts the river could grant them. The folk of Bluehaven got along well with their leonine neighbors, and news of Jynnie's rune came quickly to their lips when they were talking to their nomadic friends.

One day in early summer, Jynnie was taking in the wash outside her house when a litorian warrior approached. His mane braided with thorny vines, his furry body clad in thick leather armor covered in metal studs, the warrior was an imposing figure. Jynnie was more than a little afraid.

"Runechild," the litorian said in a deep, resonant baritone.

Jynnie just stared at him.

"My name is Charnerost. May I speak with you?"

Jynnie nodded, still a little nervous. But the litorian's manner, unlike his appearance, was gentle and careful. He smelled of leaves and grass. So much so that it almost made her sneeze.

"You have recently acquired your rune," Charnerost said.

Again Jynnie just nodded. Suddenly, she began to wonder— is this litorian going to ask for a blessing or a favor as well? How would he react if she had to turn him down?

"It is difficult, I understand, to know what you should do next," he said.

Jynnie stared at him. He wasn't going to ask for her help. Was he offering his own? "Do you know anything about runechildren?"

"A little. There was a runechild in our tribe when I was very young. He told me things."

"Then can you tell me what I'm supposed to do? Or what the rune does?"

"All I can really tell you is that you'll know when you need to know."

Jynnie's heart sank a bit. She was hoping for a real answer.

"I can also tell you that you got the rune for a reason. This isn't the kind of thing that happens by accident, or randomly."

That did make her feel a little better. "But how will I ever learn the reason?"

"Do you feel anything inside you, guiding you, even just a little bit?"

Jynnie hadn't really explained this to anyone, not even her father. "Yes, sort of. I can't really describe it. Mostly it just tells me that the things folks around here expect of me—that's not really what being a runechild is about."

Charnerost nodded. "Follow that feeling, child. It won't steer you wrong." It was difficult to tell when a litorian smiled, but Jynnie thought he was smiling now. Just in case, she smiled back.

Erlen came home from the mill that night as he always did, covered in flour. While he washed up, he listened to Jynnie's retelling of the day's strange visitor. He nodded sagely and said, "You should listen to him, Jynnie. Those folk have a wisdom about them. Why, I remember once . . ."

Jynnie didn't listen to that night's story. She wasn't in the mood. Instead, she tried to think about what Charnerost had told her. She reached deep inside her, searching for a voice that would tell her what she needed to know. The rune-voice, she called it. But she found nothing.

The next morning, Averil Tunstan, the brewer, came to the Folus house while Erlen was still packing up his lunch before leaving for the day.

"Erlen, I've come to ask for your girl's help," Averil told him. Jynnie stayed in the next room, but she could hear what they said.

"What kind of help, Averil?" Erlen asked slowly, with a bit of a sidelong glance.

"It's my boy, he's sick. Real sick."

"Oh," said Erlen, obviously a bit startled.

Sick? That actually seemed like a legitimate problem. Like something proper for a runechild to do. Jynnie came into the room. "What can I do to help?"

Both men looked at her. It would be untrue to say that Erlen didn't beam a little with pride.

"Well," Averil said in his gruff voice, scratchy from too many years of smoking the blue tobacco leaves that grew along the riverbank. "I don't rightly know. I don't know what it is that you do, now."

He paused. "What is it that you do, Jynnie?"

She frowned, flattening her face. She stammered a bit.

"She does what's right," Erlen said with a smile.

Averil grabbed Erlen by the arm with his big sausagelike fingers. "I knew you folks wouldn't let me down."

Jynnie went with Averil to his home, where his young son—only eight years old—lay in bed, obviously burning up with fever. This was the river fever, the same one that had taken her mother from her. She knelt by the boy's side, but he gave no sign that he knew she was there.

Averil watched over her shoulder.

She requested some cold, wet cloths for the boy, and asked Averil if he had any hunch root that she could brew. Averil just stood there.

"Cold cloths? Hunch root tea?"

Jynnie nodded at him.

"No, girl. I asked you to come here to use some of your power."

Jynnie gulped. "I don't think that's really how it…" But then she stopped and wondered. Could she do that? She had no idea. It seemed like the kind of thing she should be able to do with the rune. Something told her that the rune, and the power it granted, was there for important things. And what's more important than healing a sick little boy?

She turned back to the child and laid her hands on his hot, damp forehead. Closing her eyes, she delved down deep inside herself. She sank into her own soul like a rock tossed into the deep part of the river. She grasped for any kind of special healing power, some sort of potency within, and tried to bring it up with her, channeling it through her hands and into the sick child.

She felt nothing. She'd found nothing. Oh, it wasn't that her soul was empty; it's just that it held nothing that could cure a fever. She wondered whether anyone had that kind of power. She'd heard stories—from her father, of course—of people with magical power greater than that. But those people seemed far away. She wondered what would have happened if one of those people had been on hand when her mother lay sick in her own bed.

Having produced no power to heal the sick, she opened her eyes. She saw now that Averil knelt beside her, his head atop the little boy's body. He looked up at her expectantly.

She knew all too well how he felt, looking for any kind of answer. Before she could stop herself, she heard her own mouth say, "All right, I did it. He's going to be fine now. But he still needs good care."

Averil's eyes lit up like flares. "Really? Is it true? Oh, Jynnie—you are a blessing for this town!"

Jynnie ignored him. "Now, you've got to get me those cloths, and the hunch root."

"Of course," Averil said, nodding violently as he stood. "Of course."

Jynnie didn't leave the boy's side for four days. She tended him, with Averil obeying her every command and fulfilling her every request. On the fourth day, the fever broke. Averil's son would be fine.

Walking home, Jynnie knew she was in trouble, now. She didn't have any special healing touch. The rune didn't grant her that power. The child got better because he was well cared for and lucky. But the folk of the village wouldn't see it that way. What would she do the next time someone got sick? Pretend to heal them as well? Eventually, that lie was going to turn sour.

And what about that lie in and of itself? She was no regular liar—not beyond the little fibs that all children tell once in a while, but she'd outgrown even that. Still, a lie's a lie. Is that the kind of thing that could make her lose the rune? Could that happen? Who was the judge of such things?

She shook her head. Too many questions, and she was so tired after helping Averil and his son. She hoped the inner voice that Charnerost had told her about would get busy and start explaining itself soon.

A few more days passed and, surprisingly enough, they were uneventful. Folks seemed content knowing that Jynnie would use her power to help them when she could. They stopped asking her for ridiculous or petty favors. They'd learned, after all this time, that she would refuse such things anyway, saying, "I don't think that's really how it works," like she always did.

Late one afternoon, a tolling bell interrupted her preparations for dinner. As Jynnie ran outside, she heard shouts and a lot of commotion. She ran a short way down the path and spotted Old Tam Bacon about the same time that he saw her.

"Jynnie," he shouted. "It's the mill. There's a fire!"

Her father!

Time began to move very slowly. Jynnie, despite her fear for her father and the others in the mill, grew very calm. She began to run down the path toward the river and the mill. She noted with casual ease that everyone else moved as though they were underwater—or perhaps suspended in syrup. She breezed past the villagers, often having to jump to one side or the other to do so.

She saw the burning mill, surrounded by black smoke as impenetrable as a stone wall. She knew that there was no greater danger to a flour mill than fire, for the flour dust that choked the air inside could carry the flames so quickly, the place would seem to explode.

Jynnie was surprised by how quickly she reached the door, but she didn't spend any time thinking about it. She did wonder why it was closed, and why the workers inside weren't running out. She tried the door and couldn't open it. It felt warm.

Jynnie grabbed the handle with both hands and drew in a deep breath. With a mighty heave, she pulled the jammed door open. Black smoke belched out of the doorway, and she could see that it was blocked by timbers and flour sacks.

A warm tingle played across the skin of her cheek as she tossed flour bags out of the burning building, one or two in each hand. She didn't take the time to dwell on it. With some of the bags cleared out, she pushed at the timbers until they gave way and forced her way inside the mill.

The entire interior of the mill was aflame.

She stepped back in horror, coughing in the smoke. A voice within her told her that it was all right. She could go in.

"I'm afraid," she whispered aloud.

Something within soothed her, calming her again. She closed her eyes and walked right into the flames.

She could feel the heat, and feel the fire drawn into her throat and lungs as she breathed, but the sensation never went beyond that. It was uncomfortable (and disconcerting, to say the least), but the flames didn't burn her.

Inside the burning building, she looked around for her father and the two people who worked with him. Unfortunately, while she could ignore the burning of the fire, she still couldn't see through it. She knew she had to act fast.

Jynnie thought about her father and how smart he was. It was he who had told her about the dangers of a mill fire—he would have known something brilliant to do in case of a fire, but what would it have been?

Then it came to her. The water tub. That's the only place where they could be if they were still alive. She couldn't see it, but she'd been inside the mill hundreds of times. She knew where it was, next to the far wall, and she struggled through the flames to get there.

"Daddy!" she called out, her throat full of fire.

When she could feel the sides of the tub, she knelt down and thrust her face into the water. She saw her father and the others crammed into the water, submerged and trying to hold their breaths.

But surely they would run out of air before it was too late! How long had they been in the water? There was no time to figure out the answers.

The folk of Bluehaven tell the tale over and over again. If you ever go there, you'll hear it more than once. They'll tell you of the day they saw little sixteen year old Jynnie Folus smashing her way through the back wall of the mill toward the river. They'll tell you how she came out of the burning mill covered in flames (which had burned away all her clothes, although they rarely tell that part, because that's not the point and it is, well, a story told in mixed company). This young slip of a girl, they say, emerged from the hole in the wall she made carrying a tub of water six feet across and dumped three adults and the water out of it and into the river.

Most of the storytellers will go on about how the mill blew apart just a heartbeat later, exploding in a bright flash you could see for at least two miles. Others will mention that her rune was glowing like a beacon in a storm, outshining even the fire's flames. The good storytellers, like her father Erlen, will mention that detail for certain.

Jynnie discovered amazing powers granted her by the rune that day. She was hailed as a real hero for saving her father and the others. She enjoyed their adulation quietly, as was her way.

Only a few days later, after much of the excitement had died down, she spoke with her father as he got ready to go off to help rebuild the mill. She explained that, now that she knew what she could do, she knew what she had to do.

"I kind of figured on something like this," Erlen told her.

He wasn't surprised when she said that she had to go. The world was a big place, she told him, and the land needed her kind to keep it safe. There were wrongs to be righted and deeds to be done.

Erlen nodded and kissed his daughter on the forehead.

The people of Bluehaven brag about Jynnie to this day. They'll tell you that, just knowing she's out there doing what needs to be done, well—they know their troubles are over.

RICHARD LEE BYERS

THE SILENT MAN

The dead men shambled about the benighted cornfield, tearing up the knee-high stalks. Though still bruised and sore from the previous evening's battle, Galen Bock and Avard Syler led the charge down the rows. Since they were the only greenbond and totem warrior in what was otherwise a village of farmers, it was their responsibility.

Crawling with green phosphorescence, a reeking corpse pounced at Galen. Wispy white curls still clung to its scalp, enabling him to identify his own Aunt Benna, whom he'd buried three winters ago. The sight was horrifying, but he'd passed the point where such moments of recognition made him falter. He scrambled back, away from the corpse's raking nails, and jabbered an incantation.

He felt the power of the Green—the pure heart of Nature, fountainhead of all life and vitality—surge in the plants around him and the earth beneath his feet, then gather as a coldness in his hand. He thrust out his arm, and jagged ice shot from his fingertips to bury itself in Benna's wormy chest. The corpse collapsed. Galen looked for his next opponent.

Behind him, metal clinked. He whirled to behold a hulking stranger in mail, with a broadsword in one hand. This was a living man, not an undead, though he carried a round shield bearing a skull emblem, and his dark surcoat and other items of his regalia displayed the same macabre device. He'd lost his helmet, and his right profile was black with blood. He raised his blade and stumbled forward.

Agile and lightning-quick, Avard lunged out of nowhere. Like Galen, he was a lean man in his late twenties, clad in homespun and leather. Though the totem warrior's hair was black and long, worn loose, and the greenbond kept his own sandy locks cropped short, they still looked so much alike that strangers sometimes mistook them for brothers by virtue of blood as well as from their innumerable shared hardships and endeavors.

Avard drove his spear into the stranger's back. The swordsman fell on his face, then struggled to lift himself up again. Contact with the earth had swiped some of the gore from his features, exposing the sigil on his cheek.

At its center, the mark was another image of a grinning skull, but surrounding that was a circle radiating curving, tapered blades, like a stylized picture of the sun. As far as looks went, it was nothing particularly special. When travelers passed through the area, Galen had occasionally seen intricate tattoos that put this brand to shame. But the power he sensed in it jolted him and made him catch his breath. It wasn't the touch of the Green, but neither was it akin to the crawling corruption he sensed inside the undead. It was unlike anything he'd ever experienced before.

Avard pulled back the spear for another thrust. "No!" Galen cried.

Like many settlements in Verdune, Kebrel's Crossing had a palisade to keep out the undead. In recent years, folk had sometimes asserted that the wall was no longer necessary, that they ought to tear it down and give the hamlet room to grow. As Galen and his fellow defenders passed through the torchlit gates into the cramped, muddy streets beyond, the greenbond reflected that no one was likely to make that argument anymore.

Folk clustered around to find out which of their loved ones had survived the latest attack, and which had not. Some babbled questions when they spotted Galen and Avard's burden. Answering tersely, without pausing, the pair pressed on to the greenbond's bungalow, where bundles of medicinal plants hung from the rafters. Goldeyes helped them make their way through the crowd. Many people hesitated to approach the grey wolf too closely, even though he never bit anyone unless Avard, his "brother," wished it.

"Let's put him on the bed," Galen panted, feeling the swordsman's weight.

"Why?" Avard asked as they lay their burden on the straw tick. "Why fetch him here at all? Why wouldn't you let me finish him off?"

"There's a pitcher in the corner. Pour some water into the bowl." Galen stooped to open the chest in which he kept bandages and other supplies.

Scowling, Avard picked up the ewer; Goldeyes watched the stranger with an unwavering stare. "I asked you why you're wasting your skills on this wretch when some of our own folk need healing," the warrior said.

"I checked them. They'll keep. This man won't. I cast a restorative charm on him in the cornfield, but he needs further care. The spear wound isn't as bad as it could be—you're getting sloppy—but I don't like the look of his head."

"Damn it, you know what I'm getting at. What kind of warrior uses a conjured shield and sword that melt away after a time, as his did a while ago?"

"A champion." Galen dumped medicinal powder into the bowl of water, stirred it, and dampened a cloth.

"And what kind of champion has a skull on his targe, surcoat, belt buckle—"

"A champion of death, I imagine."

"Right. Now, stay with me. Our fathers and grandfathers pretty much cleared this patch of Verdune of undead. Until recently, we only had to deal with three or four a year. Now, suddenly, they're returning by the dozen, and nobody knew why until we ran into this bastard. He's got to be the necromancer calling the corpses out of their graves."

"Ordinarily, I might have jumped to the same conclusion, but look at the mark on his cheek."

"So?"

"He's a runechild."

"Oh, come on! You've never seen a runechild, so how would you know what the sign looks like? That's likely just a common tattoo."

"I have a strong feeling about it, and the Green speaks through my feelings."

Avard snorted. "You're claiming your hunches are better than mine? Who found Moll's little girl when she was lost in the woods?"

Galen sighed. "You did."

"Yes. I know you've always liked tales of runechildren—"

"I like the one about how a runechild purged this region of a great evil a hundred years back. Our village wouldn't even exist if not for that. I also enjoy the story of how a runechild aided Wallendin when he was a reckless young wanderer and needed it most." Wallendin had been the Crossing's greenbond before Galen. He was also the foster father who'd taken him in, raised him, and trained him after his parents died of the weeping fever. "What would have become of me, if not for that?"

Avard shook his head. "Nobody's saying that runechildren don't exist, or that they don't do heroic things. But they're rare. Very rare. So do you really think the power that anoints them would select a champion of death in preference to all the selfless oathsworn and wise magisters alive at the same time?"

"I certainly wouldn't have thought it, but I tell you, I feel something strong and special inside this warrior. If it's not the power of a runechild, I can't imagine what it could be, and if I failed to help such a person to the very best of my ability, it would be a betrayal of everything Wallendin taught me."

Avard ended the discussion with an irritable swipe of his hand. "Enough of this. Where's that rope you traded for? If you insist on keeping an enemy alive, let's at least tie him up. Maybe that way, if we're lucky, he won't do any harm before you figure out that your imagination's running away with you."

Galen bolted up from the blankets he'd spread for himself on the rush-strewn earthen floor. Something had disturbed his sleep, but for a moment, his thoughts muddled, he couldn't make out what. Then he realized the champion had awakened to shout and thrash in his bonds.

Galen hurried to his patient's bedside. Just enough moonlight leaked through the carved wooden screen on the window to reveal the swordsman's wide, rolling eyes.

"It's all right," Galen said. "It's true, you're bound, but I'm not going to hurt you."

The champion left off struggling to glare at him.

"My name is Galen," the greenbond said. "I'm a healer. Who are you?"

The stranger only glowered.

"I think you're both a runechild and death's champion. Am I right? Can that be possible?" He paused to give the big man a chance to answer. "Why did you come here?"

No reply.

"I healed you a bit already," Galen said. "I'm going to do it again." He reached to cradle the swordsman's head in his hands.

The champion clenched like a defiant prisoner determined not to flinch from a torturer's touch, and Galen understood why. The contact stung him as well. A force lived inside the champion that was antithetical to the wholesome energies Galen sought to channel. Still, he kept his hands in place for long enough to direct the regenerative power into torn flesh and broken bone.

It did some good, but, Galen sensed, not as much as it should have. The warrior's unswerving devotion to death dampened the magic of the Green, even when exerted in his benefit. The gash on his head remained, and the healer could feel deeper, more serious damage stubbornly enduring as well, an insult to the brain that clouded the champion's reason and deprived him of the ability to speak.

Galen would keep trying, though, and continue applying mundane remedies as well. He opened his chest and rummaged through the medicinal powders.

Prenda Lome was one of the best cooks in Kebrel's Crossing, and as she silently set the tray on his table, Galen reflected that the breakfast was scarcely up to her usual standards. It was just a bowl of greyish mush and a heel of untoasted and butterless brown bread.

But he supposed it would be unreasonable to expect a feast after the anxieties of the night just concluded. No one had gotten much rest. "Thank you," he said, "but I should have come to your house and told you: I need you to fix two trays for the next few days."

Prenda scowled. The expression looked out of place on her round, pleasant face. "It's true, then. He's here."

"Someone is. I'm not sure who or what he is yet."

"Danette lost her oldest last night. She's been my best friend since we were girls."

"I know. Jon's wound killed him instantly. There was nothing I could do."

Prenda sniffed.

Galen didn't know what else to say. After a moment, he settled for: "You'll bring a second breakfast?"

"If I must." She didn't bring even one supper, though, and that night, the dead stalked into the apple orchard to claw into the sapwood and so poison the trees. Somehow they understood that, if they threatened the village's food supply, the living had no choice but to come out and fight.

Had Galen wished, he could still have seen the interior of the bungalow, where he sat cross-legged on the floor, but it wasn't what he wanted to see. He'd entered his trance to behold the primal essence of the Green. To his senses, a fragrant, rustling riot of verdure seemed to rise all around him. Vines coiled and creaking branches shifted, weaving themselves into cryptic patterns. Spirits with leaves and flower petals for hair and long, gnarled toes like roots flitted about.

Tied to the bed, the sleeping champion of death lay in the middle of it all. He was the one aspect of mundane reality Galen had carried into the dream.

Gradually, a long shadow thickened in one portion of the grove. The spirits shied away from it. Galen peered at it intently as it seemed to thicken and take on definition. Perhaps he was finally on the brink of receiving a revelation.

Then, however, Avard and Goldeyes stepped from behind a massive oak. Galen had ties to a host of spirits. His friend and the beast that followed him were bound to only one, the wolf totem, but that sufficed to imprint them on the vision.

Still, they weren't supposed to be here. Galen's meditation was a private thing, and the spirits would disclose nothing with other mortals bursting in and blundering about. The shadow evaporated.

Exasperated, the greenbond willed the dream to end, and the walls and furnishings of his home snapped into view around him. "What is it?" he asked. "Another attack?" Then he realized it was a foolish question. It was still daylight. If the dead came, it would be after sundown.

"Do you know," Avard said, "people are watching this house? Wondering what you're doing. Why you don't come out. They think we should be making preparations for the next fight."

"You're the one who understands tactics and all that. I'm trying to help in a different way."

"With another trance."

Galen rose and stretched. His spine popped. "I know it didn't tell us anything useful the other times I tried it, but I hoped that if I carried the runechild into the vision . . . no luck, though." Despite his frustration, he saw little point in complaining that Avard's untimely entrance might well have ruined his attempt to gather information. The last thing he wanted to do was provoke another argument with his friend.

Although it seemed inevitable in any case. "Including the stranger in the vision didn't help," Avard said, "because he's not the answer to our problem."

"I still feel he is."

"Piss and spit, Galen! You have to abandon these fancies. Nobody would cheer louder than me if the land itself really did birth a hero to save us. But if it did, the man wouldn't be a servant of death."

"He might. You and I work to keep our folk alive, and we should. It's our proper role in the scheme of things, and naturally, it leads us to think of death as the enemy. But Wallendin taught me that death isn't the same thing as evil—or as greenbonds name it, the Dark—and the Dark's what spawns undead."

"I don't know about that, but I do know that a good many champions of death have consorted with the things."

"I don't think this is one of them."

"Are his brains unscrambled yet? Is he talking?"

"No."

"Will he ever?"

"I'm trying to mend his wounds by every means at my disposal, but truly, I can't say."

Avard shook his head. "I don't know if that's good or bad. But I do know it would be wise of you to let the rest of the village see you making yourself useful. Go check on the other wounded folk."

"I just did that a couple hours ago, but if it'll make you happy, fine. I'll get my satchel."

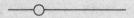

By the time Galen made it back to his house, the light was failing, and thus, he smelled the stink of the manure smeared on his door before he saw it. At first, he was more surprised than angry, though he could feel that anger would come. The defilement was a traditional way of expressing scathing contempt, and he was used to his neighbors holding him in high esteem.

Telling himself it only took one fool to make this sort of mischief, he opened the door. Just in time to see the champion cast off the last of his bonds and scramble up from the bed.

"Easy," Galen said. "You don't want to be tied anymore, I understand, but it's too soon for you to be up."

A broadsword, its pommel cast in the shape of a skull and the cross guard in the form of bones, shimmered into existence in the champion's grip. He rushed Galen.

The warrior's balance was impaired—otherwise, Galen could never have jumped back in time to avoid the cut. The blade whizzed through the air scant inches short of his flesh. He tried to take a second retreat and backed into the wall. The champion lifted the blade for another stroke.

Galen cried out to the spirits. A thick green tendril erupted from the dirt floor and lashed itself around the big man like a constricting serpent. Even so, he nearly managed another cut before the plant wrapped around his sword arm. He thrashed, trying to break free.

Galen grabbed the swordsman's throat and squeezed, cutting off the flow of blood to the brain. Eventually, the champion slumped to the floor, unconscious. The greenbond hoped that the choke hold hadn't done the warrior any permanent damage.

Although perhaps he was a dunce to care. He didn't entirely know why the champion had attacked him. Was it simply because the swordsman was still addled, or because he was in fact the enemy that Avard—and many others, apparently—believed him to be?

A sentry's ram's-horn trumpet bleated. Galen ran out into the street and peered about.

An archer on the wall-walk atop the palisade loosed an arrow. He was shooting almost straight down, which could only mean that, for the first time, the dead were trying to storm the settlement itself.

45

Squinting against the dark, Galen peered over the wooden points comprising the top of the wall. Nimble as a squirrel, its claws biting into the logs, a shriveled form clambered up the outside of the barrier. "Kill it!" Frejam the shepherd barked, pointing with the pitchfork he was using as a weapon.

"I can cast only so many spells," Galen said. "I'm trying to save them for when we need them most."

"Or are you just worried your new friend wouldn't like it?" Frejam jabbed at the corpse's upturned face. It lost its grip and fell.

Moments later, several undead started up the palisade all at once. Galen conjured a clot of mud into his hand, hurled it, and knocked a corpse from its perch. He rattled off a second spell, and his fist tingled and glowed red. He snapped a punch into the face of another decaying husk as it tried to squirm over the top of the wall.

The magically augmented blow rocked the dead thing, but that was all. Contrary to Galen's expectation, it failed to tear its mushy head off, or even send it tumbling backward. Points of green light flared in the creature's eye sockets. It grinned, exposing long fangs unblemished by decay.

Some undead were stronger and craftier than others. Galen just had time to comprehend that this was the most dangerous specimen he'd yet encountered, and then it hurled itself at him.

He recoiled and nearly toppled off the wall-walk. The dead man grabbed him, though, smashed him down on the ledge, and threw itself on top of him. It leaned down to sink its fangs into his throat, and he struggled to hold them away. "Help!" he cried.

Frejam hesitated for what seemed a long time, then edged in, thrusting with the hayfork. The wounds in the slimy, withered flesh started closing as soon as the tines pulled out. Eventually, though, Galen managed to fumble the knife from his belt and rip at the corpse's belly. Fighting in concert, he and

46

Frejam drove their weapons into the creature again and again, until finally its recuperative powers failed it, and the corrupt power animating it bled out the cuts and punctures.

Avard called through the door. When, yawning, Galen opened it, he was surprised to see that this time, his friend and Goldeyes hadn't come alone. Van, Dunlas, and Oda stood behind them. The trio of elders was the closest thing the village had to a ruling council.

"Come in," Galen sighed, and everyone did, to glower at the warrior now once again tied securely to the bed.

"I'm sure you know," said Van, "we can't endure many more attacks." His baritone voice was slurred from the stroke he'd suffered the previous year. Galen had pulled him through, but the affliction had left one side of his face stiff.

"I do know," Galen said. His head still felt thick from his interrupted sleep. He dipped his hand in the water pitcher and scrubbed his face with the tepid liquid.

Galen's expression of agreement didn't stop Dunlas, stooped and leaning on his walking stick, from elaborating on Van's point. "The dead come every night. More and more. Stronger ones. Now they're attacking the town itself."

"The reason," said Oda, wrapped in the handsome scarlet cloak she'd woven and embroidered for herself, "is that fiend on the bed. He's calling his creatures to set him free."

"I doubt it," said Galen. "For one thing, his mind is still too cloudy to use such a tactic."

"Do you know that for certain?" Dunlas replied. "Do you understand the limits of his powers? Perhaps he has a way of making you believe he's sicker than he is."

"If he is controlling the cursed creatures," said Van, "and we silence him, maybe the things will go away."

"You're talking about killing him," Galen said. "But I've explained, he's a runechild, come to help us."

"And we've explained," Avard retorted, "nobody believes that but you. Where's the proof?"

"I feel something extraordinary inside him," Galen said. "But if you won't accept that, consider this: How did he come by his head wound if he wasn't fighting the dead the same as we were?"

"Easy," Avard said. "He attacked one of our folk, one of the pair who didn't survive, and Jon or Rogeth landed a lucky blow before the bastard cut him down."

"You can't kill him simply because you suspect he's an evildoer and you're afraid. It would be unjust. It's likely to bring the worst kind of luck down upon us all."

"It's his life against the lives of everyone in the Crossing," said Van. "If killing him is a sin, we three will carry the burden. All you have to do is step aside."

"I can't."

"Young man," Oda said, "everyone here respects you for your skills, but you're not our mayor or lord. You have no authority, no right, to defy the will of the entire town."

"You and I have been friends all our lives," Avard said, "and seen one another through many a danger. You trust me, don't you? Well, I'm begging you, please, let this go, for your own sake and everyone else's."

Well, curse it, why not? Galen felt worn down. Exhausted. He was sick of his neighbors' mistrust and disdain, and the truth was, he didn't know for certain the champion was a runechild. Indeed, the warrior had tried to kill Galen, his benefactor, which scarcely argued for a heroic nature. The green-bond drew breath to give Avard and the elders leave to do as they would.

Then, however, he thought of Wallendin, who'd been a second father to him. Who'd owed his life and soul to a runechild's heroism in the face of a terrible evil. Who'd taught Galen to trust his own instincts and perceptions, because they were the foundation of everything a greenbond was. And after the younger healer pictured his master's face, he couldn't force the words of acquiescence out.

Instead he said, "I can't let you throw away what might be our only chance, nor ignore what I take to be the counsel of the Green."

"The counsel of madness, more likely," Dunlas growled.

"We've spoken our piece," Avard said. "Galen, promise me you'll at least ponder what we said."

"I will."

"Then we'll go." And to Galen's surprise—he'd expected the argument to drag on—they did.

The pounding and shouting jarred Galen from the first sound sleep he'd enjoyed in three days. He groped his way to the door.

A lad named Triven was on the stoop. "Moll fell!" he said. "She's bleeding! You've got to come."

"All right." Galen grabbed his satchel and dashed off into the street. The bag bounced against his hip. The feeble grey light of the hour before dawn made the footing treacherous. It was hard to see the ruts in the mud.

He was halfway across the village before it struck him as odd that Triven wasn't running along beside him. Then, abruptly, he understood. He sprinted back the way he'd come.

When he turned down his own street, Avard and Goldeyes were waiting to intercept him. "I had a hunch the trick wouldn't fool you for long," the warrior said. "But at least it pulled you away from the necromancer's bedside."

"Let me by," Galen said.

"No," Avard said. "See, I figured it out. Death's agent bewitched you. It's the only explanation for the way you're acting."

"You're wrong."

"I'm sorry for this, but you'll thank me later." Avard glided forward, gripping his spear like a quarterstaff, plainly intending to pummel Galen into submission with the butt end. Goldeyes stalked along beside him.

Giving ground, Galen commenced an incantation. Avard charged and swung, and the greenbond sidestepped. The spear missed his head but still clipped his shoulder with brutal force. Refusing to let the pain balk him, Galen gritted out the final words of power and thrust out his fist.

A ray of dazzling brightness flared from it into Avard's eyes. Temporarily blinded, the warrior struck again, but missed. He pivoted, caught his foot, and stumbled. At the same instant, something jerked Galen's leg out from under him, slamming him to the ground, and clamped down with excruciating pressure.

Goldeyes had him. Avard had surely instructed the snarling wolf not to harm his friend, but the animal was agitated now, alarmed by his human comrade's incapacity. Galen feared Goldeyes would rip him apart.

Panicked, he responded with an attack of his own. Ice exploded from his fingers to batter Goldeyes. Bone snapped, and the wolf went down thrashing and screaming. When Galen saw the animal's forelegs, bent where they ought to be straight, and the spur of rib jabbing through a bloody rent in his furry chest, he realized just how badly the barrage had hurt him.

"What did you do?" Avard howled, sounding as if he himself had taken the wound. "What did you do?"

"I'm sorry!" Galen said, but the statement was so inadequate, such a pale reflection of the remorse that wracked him, it seemed, in a nightmarish way, laughable. He panted as if he'd run twenty miles without a rest, not from his exertions, but from horror at the harm he'd wrought.

Yet even so, something—conviction, perhaps, or instinct—held him to his purpose. He conjured a gigantic spider web to hold Avard in its sticky strands even after his sight returned, then ran on to his house. He suspected he was already too late.

But he wasn't. Though still tied, the champion had managed some manner of arcane attack that left one of his would-be executioners writhing on the floor. Appalled, the others hesitated, none eager to be the next to carry his dagger with arm's reach of the bed.

"Get back!" Galen yelled. Two of his neighbors pivoted and reached to grab him. He slashed his hand through the air and left a trail of floating, glowing green blobs in its wake. The illusions were harmless, but the assassins didn't know that. They flinched back, and Galen scrambled to the side of the bed.

"You can't do this!" Galen said. He jerked loose the knots securing the champion's bonds. "It's murder! If you don't want him here, I'll take him away."

"Take him away to lead his creatures against us?" asked Morkan the shaggy-bearded smith. His big, grimy hands curled into fists. "No." He and the others surged forward.

Galen thumped one attacker on the chest, invoking a magic that filled the man with an overwhelming terror. He turned to contend with the next and saw the champion's conjured broadsword shear into Morkan's neck. The smith fell, his head half severed.

It was as if Galen split into two people at that moment. One stood aghast, frozen with shock and grief at Morkan's death. The other, however, summoned a blast of wind that staggered the attackers. He grabbed the champion and manhandled him outside, then filled the air with mist. The obscurement enabled them to slip out of the village without having to fight anyone else.

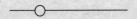

The grass and earth erased Galen's footprints. Branches bent themselves out of his path lest he break a telltale twig. He even managed to use the Green to hide the champion's trail as well.

But he didn't know why he bothered. Eluding pursuit wouldn't fix the things that had gone so hideously wrong. Goldeyes maimed. Morkan slain. As a result, Galen was surely outlawed, hated and hunted by the only friends he had in the world.

He struggled to cling to the conviction that he'd done only what he had to do to save everyone in the Crossing, but found little comfort in the thought. Even if he was right, he'd thrown away his whole life, and had no idea whether, at this point, there was even any use in it. Suppose, arrogant as it suddenly felt to do so, that he was right and everyone else was wrong, and the champion truly was a runechild. That didn't mean the warrior would ever recover sufficiently to play a savior's role. Perhaps his brain was crippled forevermore.

In any case, Galen despised himself for not spiriting the champion out of town before the situation there erupted into violence, even though he knew he couldn't have given the swordsman adequate care in the wild. He gradually realized he hated the big man, too. He reckoned his fellow fugitive had had to strike Morkan, in self-defense, but had it really been necessary to kill him? Couldn't an expert warrior employ a less drastic way of protecting himself?

Maybe, if the warrior reverenced life as greenbonds did, but Galen had known from the start that the stranger had pledged his service to an opposing principle. The healer just hadn't wanted to believe how dire the consequences of that fealty could be.

Such was the tenor of his brooding, twisting thoughts as he fled from the only home he'd ever known. Grief, guilt, and doubt tormented him, gnawing away at the belief and resolve that had brought him to this pass. He might have fallen utterly into despair, except that then, finally, the warrior spoke. "East," he croaked. "I need to go up into the hills."

"My name is Phenalath Trel," the champion said, the yellow light of the campfire flickering on his coarse features and the mark on his cheek. He spoke haltingly but coherently. Judging from his accent and diction, he was an educated man from one of the great cities beyond the mountains to the east.

Galen leaned forward. After insisting they make for the high country, Phenalath had said nothing more for the remainder of the day. Galen had feared the champion had fallen mute again, that the one declaration had been a fluke. But now it seemed Phenalath was ready for an actual conversation, which meant Galen might finally learn the truths he both craved and dreaded. "How much do you remember?" the greenbond asked.

"Enough. An undead hurt me in the cornfield. You tended me. Kept me tied, too, but since I was out of my head, I suppose it was necessary."

"We villagers all took you for a champion of death."

Phenalath smiled a crooked smile. "You were right. I'm surprised that, having recognized me, you were willing to nurse me back to health. Even in the best of circumstances, greenbonds generally don't like me."

"I helped you because my instincts told me you're a runechild as well as a champion."

"Ah." Phenalath fingered the mark on his cheek as if it were sore. "My instincts have been suggesting the same."

"You mean you don't know for sure?"

"When I was eleven years old, I started hearing death's voice. Perhaps you have some inkling of what that's like."

"Maybe. I have my own connection to the Green."

"Death told me I was its hand, and from that day onward, I strove only to enact its will. If anyone had said a time would come when I'd serve two masters, that such a thing was even possible, I would have laughed. Then one day I awoke with the brand, and heard a new voice speaking inside my head."

"The voice of the land. You are a runechild."

Phenalath shrugged. "If you say so. Why the land would choose me, when I was already sworn to another power, I can't say. Maybe because I've devoted so much of my time to destroying undead. I do it because they cheat and affront death, but I imagine other entities have their own reasons for disliking them.

"Be that as it may," the big man continued, "I live in dread of the day when my two masters will pull me in opposite directions, but so far, it hasn't happened. The rune has simply made me stronger and faster, better able to do my work."

"What work brought you here?"

"Isn't it obvious? I came to stop the undead from rising up in such profusion."

Galen slumped with relief, finding a shred of comfort in the confirmation that he'd been correct about his companion, even if it wasn't sufficient to erase his feelings of guilt over what had happened to Goldeyes and Morkan, or his grief at his estrangement from everyone he cared about. "Do you know why the dead are plaguing us?"

Phenalath frowned. "Not the dead. The undead."

"Call them what you like. Why is it happening?"

The champion pointed uphill, toward the mountains looming unseen in the night. "There rise the Bitter Peaks. Perhaps you're aware of their reputation."

Galen gave a weary chuckle. "You're in Verdune, runechild. Every hillock and stand of trees has a part in some grim legend."

"Well, the Peaks deserve whatever ill folk speak of them. They spawn black streams, manifestations of the power you call the Dark. Flowing across the land like invisible rivers, they cause sickness and raise undead."

Galen remembered the long, twisting shadow he'd glimpsed in his trance, before Avard's untimely intrusion caused it to disappear. His instincts told him the spirits had been trying to show him a vision of the same phenomenon Phenalath had described. "One of these streams has burst forth hereabouts."

"Yes. I am trying to track it to its source, where I can destroy it."

"I'm glad to hear it. Now that we've shaken Avard and the rest of the village off our track, we can pick up the trail in the morning."

Phenalath shook his head. "I appreciate all you've done, but this is my task."

"It's mine as well. It's the lifelong task of any greenbond to purge corruption. Besides, you can use me. Now that I know what to look for, I think I can sense this black stream where it taints the land. I can also fight. Maybe if you have an ally, the next pack of undead you meet won't bash your head in."

"With your greenbond sensitivities, you won't find me pleasant company."

"Maybe not, but it doesn't matter. This errand is my duty. It's also my only chance. My work, my friends, my life in Kebrel's Crossing . . . they're all lost to me, and rightly so. Maybe my intentions were good, but I still hurt a friend, and sided with you as you killed one of my neighbors. My only hope of atoning and winning forgiveness, little as I may deserve it, is for the two of us to save the village as I promised."

"Sleep, then. You'll need it. I'll wake you when it's your watch."

"This is it," Phenalath said. He discarded the crude spear he'd fashioned—a length of wood with a fire-hardened point—and, with a thought, summoned his magical broadsword and shield into being.

Galen peered about the sloping shelf on the windswept mountainside. All he saw were stones, scraggly weeds, and gnarled brush. Yet he knew Phenalath was right, because he could feel the concentrated vileness in the air, stinging his skin like lye. This was surely the place they sought.

It had taken five days to reach it, a trek punctuated by periodic encounters with the undead. Roused from their resting places, the corpses and skeletons instinctively followed the course of the black stream down toward the lowlands and Kebrel's Crossing in search of prey. Fortunately, Galen and Phenalath hadn't encountered more than two or three of the creatures at a time, and had proved equal to the task of destroying them.

Galen could only hope they were capable of meeting the ultimate challenge as well. "What now?" he asked.

"Now," Phenalath said, "I use the strength the rune gives me to draw the pure essence of death into this place. When I finish, nothing else will be able to exist here, even a manifestation of the Dark."

Galen winced. To scour even the possibility of life from a place seemed a terrible act indeed. Yet he sensed that even such annihilation was preferable to leaving the Dark in control here to poison the lands below. "It's that easy?"

The big man laughed without humor. "No. The invocation is really just a ploy to make the evil take on tangible form. Since it can't afford to let me finish the spell, it will have to come out and fight, and then we complete our task by killing it. You keep watch. Don't let it creep up behind me while I'm conjuring."

"Right."

Phenalath stared into space and murmured under his breath. Galen peered about while working a spell of his own. Rustling vines grew from the air to twine around his body, forming a protective layer that would armor him like mail.

After a minute, he sensed death approaching, answering its champion's call. It felt like an avalanche rushing to sweep him away, and he had to steel himself against the terror of it. Then the Dark, or its minion, appeared, and it was more fearsome still.

The spirit was a shapeless, shifting mass of vapor or shadow, of long, snaky limbs and pale, luminous eyes. But its form, hideous though it was, wasn't the most dreadful thing about it. Rather, it was the sense of infinite malice and uncleanness emanating from its seething core. For a second, Galen froze, but when the entity pounced at the oblivious Phenalath, he managed to shout a warning.

Abandoning his invocation, Phenalath whirled, caught the blow of a hooked appendage on his targe, and slashed with his sword. The spirit recoiled. Evidently it could be hurt, and, heartened, Galen hurled daggers of ice into its boiling mass.

Over the next few minutes, though, he started to wonder if their attacks were merely paining it without doing actual harm. For surely Phenalath had landed a hundred sword strokes, while Galen had assailed it with blasts of wind, missiles of compacted earth, and psychic thrusts to its mind. No matter what they did, it wouldn't slow, bleed, or drop a length of severed tentacle on the ground. Rather, it attacked as viciously as ever, with a ferocity certain to prevail when Galen ran out of spells, Phenalath's weapons vanished, or fatigue leeched away their agility.

Then Phenalath shouted, "We're winning!"

For a moment, Galen didn't understand. Then he saw that the spirit was shrinking. Drawing in on itself. He laughed, then cast a spell to sheath his hands in corrosive jelly. He raked them through the entity's semisolid body, and it diminished again.

57

Phenalath charged it. Maybe the prospect of victory made him reckless, for the spirit finally hit him squarely, swinging a thick limb, whacking him across the chest, and flinging him through the air. He slammed down hard and lay motionless.

But perhaps Galen could finish off the entity by himself. He started another incantation, and the shadow-thing extruded something resembling a human head. Its two eyes met Galen's gaze.

Galen killed the creature by splitting it in two with a mass of ice, then healed Phenalath one final time. After that, they went their separate ways. On the hike back to the Crossing, Galen pondered how best to tell the tale of the black stream, and how to plead for his friends' forgiveness.

As it turned out, he never had the chance. He didn't see who threw the rock, but after it hit the back of his head, he couldn't speak coherently, or fight or run, either. The other villagers surrounded him, chopping with hoes and axes, hammering with shovels and mallets, everyone clamoring and shoving for the chance to strike a blow.

The vision only lasted an instant, and then Galen was looking into the spirit's eyes again. "Now you understand," the shadow crooned.

Horribly, he did. It didn't matter if he destroyed the black stream. No one back in the village would believe it or accept him back, not after what had happened to Goldeyes and Morkan, not when the undead the Dark had already spawned would remain to trouble the settlement for a time. No matter what, Galen was still kinless. Friendless. Outcast.

A terrible feeling of loneliness and futility welled up inside him. The spirit extended a dozen smoky arms as if to gather him into a comforting embrace, and though he knew that wasn't really what it wanted, it didn't seem to matter anymore.

But then, suddenly, it did. Galen drew power into his fist till it blazed with scarlet light, and, an instant before the spirit could bind his limbs with its own, he punched into its squirming heart.

The Dark's minion screamed, writhed, and, in the course of heartbeat or two, dwindled away to nothing.

"You didn't realize," Galen gasped. "It doesn't matter that my folk have turned against me. I still have a duty, to them and to the Green." He stumbled toward Phenalath, to help him if he could.

"It's good you came," Phenalath said, his tone even more gruff and grudging than usual, the late afternoon sunlight striking highlights in his black hair. He and Galen still occupied the same high shelf where they'd done their fighting. With the Dark driven out, it was no more noisome than any other place. "I couldn't have done it alone."

"Neither of us could," Galen said, binding the warrior's bruised ribs with strips of cloth.

"What will you do now, if you can't go home?"

"It's a big world. There must be another village somewhere that can use a greenbond." Galen tried to feel some enthusiasm at the prospect of looking for it, but he couldn't manage it. The thought of leaving behind everyone and everything he cared about to fare among strangers was simply too daunting and dreary.

"Travel with me, if you think you can stand it."

Galen blinked in surprise. "A healer and a killer wandering together? How long before we find ourselves at odds?"

"But I'm not only a champion of death. I'm a runechild. Something you respect, apparently. And if we see things differently, perhaps our two ways of thinking will lead us to a deeper wisdom than either could discover on his own."

Perhaps they would at that. For as Galen had told Avard, life and death weren't truly foes, but partners in the vast design. The greenbond felt his bleak mood lifting. "I will travel with you," he said. "Gladly. My foster father was a rover when he was my age. He always said it was a great adventure."

BRUCE R. CORDELL &
KEITH FRANCIS STROHM

HOLLOWS
OF THE HEART

The dramojh once enslaved humanity and faen. As much demon as dragon, they fielded vast armies of spellcasting warriors. Only the furious power of the giantish armies could conquer them.

Centuries after the giants hunted these despicable "dragon scions" to extinction, they are troubled by the appearance of the mojh, a race that seeks to emulate the power of the vanished dramojh.

—Collected Histories of the Diamond Throne

Hope is a song sung in the heart.

—Au-Navan, Lorekeeper of Navael

The invaders came at the height of Sunshadow, when winter's claws raked the heights of the Bitter Peaks, freezing the very sap-blood of the trees. Wind raged across the face of the mountains, while needle-sharp darts of ice sought skin and scale and unyielding stone. Wrapped tightly within a woolen cloak, a solitary sentinel kept vigil upon the frost-rimed walls of the ancient citadel, peering into the void of night.

Ignoring the lash of the wind, Dagath leaned on an ivory-white staff. The mage cast a weary eye upon the flickering campfires in the valley below. For three straight days and nights Dagath had used magical power to track the path of the ragged army as it struggled forward. Avalanches, snow-demons, and the savage predations of deadly frost cats had exacted a terrible toll upon the force as it marched up from the treacherous mountain pass. But they soldiered on, perhaps yet four hundred strong. They huddled in their encampment below the ruined walls of the fortress. They seemed intent on watering the dark roots of the Bitter Peaks with their own blood.

All because of the giant.

The fools! Can't they see they've lost before they've begun? The army was no match for the arcane might assembled within the mojh citadel. Even fully rested, the invaders would inevitably fall beneath combined skill of the Fleshrunes. Death would be their lot.

The keening wind renewed its assault, piercing Dagath's clothes as if they were nothing. While the mojh's thickly scaled hide offered more protection from the elements than human skin, it could not compensate for the wretched wind. Extending arcane senses honed from decades of study, the magister channeled a minute portion of the energy contained within the citadel's core to ward off the chill. The dragon scions, in their wisdom, had built this stronghold over a deep power cyst, and the most practiced of the Fleshrune brethren fueled their magic at one time or another with this additional energy. There was only one other among the brethren who could claim greater facility with the deep cyst, but Dagath had been working secretly on a new technique . . . .

Dagath sighed wearily, sending a plume of breath into the moonless night. It—for the mojh people gave up all gender when they abandoned their humanity for their powerful new forms—had little wish to kill anyone else, but the Fleshrunes were so close to their goal. Years of sacrifice, spent toiling in the shadow of ruined temples, dark dungeons, and ancient libraries gleaning fragments of old knowledge, were about to bear fruit.

Dagath reflected on the position of the mojh Fleshrunes here in the citadel; the magister and its brethren were a resurgence of the old Fleshrune order founded nearly two thousand years ago. The Cult of the Fleshrunes had nearly disappeared in recent years, but now Dagath and the others had been recruited by the Master of Claw to fill out the ranks.

Above all else, the Fleshrunes revered the runechildren.

Not exactly true, Dagath self-corrected. We just want the foundation. From what source do the runechildren channel their power? Some uber-cyst, perhaps? Some sea of energy that makes the deep power cyst here seem but a tide pool?

The akashic would no doubt give up his knowledge soon, and the secret would be theirs. The Master of Claw had decreed that the secret of the runechildren lay with the giants.

It is inevitable. Not even an army of misguided heroes can stop us. All they can do is die. But that thought left the magister feeling unaccountably empty.

The wind ebbed, its rabid howling falling to a mournful wail. As sometimes happened, Dagath heard within it the gentle voices of childhood, of a time before the love of arcana had become a white-hot need burning inside like dragonfire. A time when Dagath was still human and happy simply to play with his older brother, Jerem. A time when his mother called him in from a day filled with fun, to sit at the table where she'd prepared supper. Such memories were painful. They made Dagath recall, quite involuntarily, that it was once not so different from those who made up the army below. Would Dagath have done any less if Jerem had been taken from him? No doubt the giant, too, had family. . . .

The mojh was still listening to the siren song of the wind when the summons came. A single mental command from the Master

of Claw sent mojh-born kobolds scurrying from their post within
the shelter of an old tower. There was much to do before the inevitable attack upon the morrow, and the Master of Claw wanted
a report from Dagath. Channeling more power from the citadel's
core, the magister lifted the staff with both scaled hands. Eldritch
force ran along its runescribed length. The liquid fire grew
brighter, burning away darkness, frost, and even scaled flesh.
When the light faded, no one remained upon the crumbling wall.

The giant's bones snapped like dry tinder in the shadowy cell.

Na-Devaon screamed, a deep-throated, bull roar of pain that
shook the rusted metal bars that had marked the edge of his
world for . . . he knew not how long. Time had fled the decaying stone walls of his prison, even if he could not. He wondered
how much longer he could hold out. Would anyone come to
rescue him? He was a popular figure in the city of De-Shamod,
known by many. Perhaps they were looking for him even now.

Perhaps.

But hope was a distant song in this cold mountain fastness,
and Na-Devaon's heart an unsure instrument.

Familiar russet- and black-cloaked figures shifted around
him. They were his constant companions, harbingers of pain.
Scale and claw gleamed dully in the gloom of dim magefire as
the mojh interrogators drew close again.

Needles of agony shot from Na-Devaon's ruined hand. Gasping from the pain, he had little time to react before the hammer
fell a second time. Darkness rose up to envelop him, but it was
driven back by the raspy touch of a scaled hand and a spear of
flame thrust into his mind.

"Do not think to leave us so soon, my friend," a sibilant
voice chided from the shadows. "Our conversation is something
I anticipate. It has become the highlight of my day."

The owner of the voice resolved into the brown-robed form whom the mojh called the Master of Claw. In the deep watches of the night when they thought Na-Devaon asleep, the other mojh and their kobold servitors whispered a name, like a benediction or curse: Verthrax.

Where his other captors were cautious—and even a bit nervous—about holding and torturing a giant, Verthrax reveled in the opportunity. The cult leader displayed a heartless arrogance; it was clear to Na-Devaon that every mark upon his body, every indignity he had endured at the hands of his captors, had been precisely orchestrated at Verthrax's command.

The giant was numb. They had played out this exchange so often that it was almost comforting, a familiar ritual in the midst of an ever-changing array of pain and suffering.

"And what," Na-Devaon asked finally, "would you like to talk about?"

Spindly, silk-gloved fingers traced across Na-Devaon's once-handsome face. "I seek that which your race, in its arrogance, chooses to hide from the rest of us—the secret of the rune-children!"

Verthrax continued, "You will tell me what I need to know, or I will make sure you spend an eternity in such exquisite agony that mere words falter in the description."

The giant's gaze slipped from the furious eyes of his captor to the pulped flesh of his tortured hands. Gone were the days of harp and lyre, when his fingers ran like water across strings of gold, spinning gossamer threads of melody to bind the hearts of lord and beggar. Broken things and pain were all that was left to him. Na-Devaon shed a single tear—not for the pain he had already endured or the agony his next response would no doubt elicit, but for that single, crystalline realization of loss, now woven into the tapestry of akashic memory.

May those who have gone before me to the Houses of the Eternal watch over me. He knew what would come next. "The

Hu-Charad have no such knowledge of the runechildren," he said at last.

"Lies," Verthrax responded, on cue. Blue-green energy arced from the mojh's raised hands, raking the giant.

Big as he was, the arcane blow slammed Na-Devaon against the cold stone wall. Rings of eldritch power encircled him, burning through his ragged clothes to sear the exposed flesh. The pain of the attack drove his sight inward, thrusting open akashic doorways normally sealed by mental discipline, unleashing a vortex of memory and consciousness. The giant was pulled along, tumbling through a barrage of emotion, sight, and sound—unmoored in a sea of collective memory.

From the vantage of memory's skein, the malice of his mojh captors was like the fury of the long-defeated dragon scions. The skies filled with the whirling mass of the dramojh battle host while, below, the land thundered with the defiance of the Hu-Charad. Caught in the blood-red tide of war, Na-Devaon was the fulcrum of a thousand battles, each more brutal than the last. Steel and claw, flame and spell—the rhythm of the Wardance reached out to him.

Chi-Julud beckoned.

Na-Devaon felt the battle rage rise within him, sweet and hot and potent. He focused that energy, galvanized the iron will of his people, and ripped himself from the akashic reverie. Who would he kill first?

He was surprised to see the willowy form of a mojh bent over him, assessing whether he yet drew breath. It would be simple to lash out at the unsuspecting mojh and crush its skull. Though the cultists were strong enough to overpower him on a lonesome road outside the city of De-Shamod, the giant still possessed enough strength in his injured body to kill this one, and perhaps several more, before they brought him down.

He tensed. Rage ran as blood. His heart cried out for vengeance—and, with a sigh, did nothing.

The drums of Chi-Julud fell silent.

Memory's purveyor he might be, possessed of the ability to experience the glories of every past victory, but as an akashic, he was also heir to the suffering of an entire world. The streams of collective memory were awash with blood, and he'd vowed long ago not to add any but his own. *Which,* he realized in retrospect, *is probably why the cult chose me in the first place.*

He would not resort to that which he'd pledged never to choose. He let out a long, deep, cleansing breath, attracting the attention of the nearby mojh, one he did not recognize

"Do you perhaps wonder," said this one, who suddenly leaned over him again, feeling for his pulse, "if this giant truly does not possess the knowledge you seek, Master?"

"And what if he does not, Dagath?" came the sibilant voice Na-Devaon had learned to hate.

"Then, you are torturing him to no end, except for your own pleasure."

"And what of that?" laughed Verthrax. "If joy in the giant's pain is all I reap, then I'll not count it as a complete loss."

Satisfied that the giant yet breathed, the one called Dagath pulled away. Na-Devaon thought the hand was oddly gentle.

The solicitous mojh faced Verthrax, saying, "You called for a report on our defenses, Master of Claw, so I know you but play with me. Attracting an army to rescue this singer of songs is the only thing that his kidnapping has accomplished for us."

Na-Devaon opened his eyes, hope born anew within him after Dagath's words. *An army? For me?*

"Your last report indicated that we should defeat them," said Verthrax.

"But at such a cost! They will throw away their lives and accomplish nothing."

Verthrax squinted at the subordinate. "Should we care about the lives of those opposed to the Fleshrunes?"

"Not just their lives—many kobolds will fall in this conflict, maybe even a few brethren. How will these deaths lead us any closer to our goal? I fear that we have set upon a course of gratuitous conflict." The kobolds, the giant had learned, were born of mojh flesh; despite their pathetic physique and servitor status, these mojh-born were entitled to full lives.

Verthrax laughed again. "This rabble of an army is only more grist for the Fleshrunes' magistry. We may sustain our own losses, but they are acceptable, even useful for training some of our younger brethren, as your own report indicates. Trouble me no more with your misguided concerns."

"But . . ." began Dagath.

"Return to the defenses," commanded the Master of Claw.

Dagath glanced at Na-Devaon with a look the giant could not read, then disappeared in a glare of eldritch fire.

The giant considered. All in all, he was glad he had not smashed Dagath as he'd first proposed.

"It seems I did you no permanent damage," Verthrax's voice cut into his thoughts. "A shame," the cult leader added. "Unfortunately, other matters press their claims upon me. But do not hope that I shall fail to return. Next time, I will not be so . . . gentle."

With a final hiss, Verthrax turned and departed the cell. The steel door clanged shut. Days earlier, the giant had tried his strength on the door, to no effect. It was apparently ensorcelled against his prodigious might. Darkness descended upon the room like an overturned ink bottle. Na-Devaon collapsed in a heap upon the chilly floor, cradling his broken hands against his shivering body.

He had not known about the army—Verthrax had kept that from him. The other one, Dagath—that mojh's words gave him sudden hope, though his pain made it impossible for him to even smile.

But hope is a song sung in the heart.

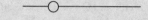

Dawn brought little clarity.

Despite the gathering light, fog blanketed the valley, choking the narrow pathways leading up to the citadel. Dagath stood upon the crumbling battlements, peering into the greyness. Neither spell nor mundane eye could pierce the murk, so the mojh had sent a detachment of mojh-born and two Fleshrune magisters to serve as sentries. They would guard the trails and give warning, should the invaders attack. Dagath felt the surrounding, enveloping stillness of the morning—as if the whole world held its breath.

The full-throated braying of horns split the air. The mountain walls rang with the echo. A hissing storm of arrows fell upon the fortress. Most clattered harmlessly off the castle wall, their force spent and tips blunted or shattered. A few, however, bit flesh. Wounded kobolds squealed as they tumbled from rocky perches. One of the other brethren Verthrax had assigned to the citadel's defense erected eldritch barriers to deflect further arrow flights.

Lifting the ivory staff into the air, Dagath chanted magic-laced words. As the staff began to glow, the magister whirled it in a swift circle. The air hummed, and the air gusted. Dagath summoned the wind itself, always a tricky task. The gusts grew in strength, swirling around the citadel, growling with pure, elemental fury. Dagath beckoned with the staff, and the wind streamed into the valley below. Within minutes, the shroud covering the valley had blown into scattered tendrils.

The magister then saw that the citadel's lower sentries lay dead, their positions overrun. The enemy streamed up each of the trails, intent on reaching the wooded plateau that would allow them to consolidate their force for a final assault upon the fortress. Human, sibeccai, litorian, and even faen warriors marched up the slope. Clearly, the invaders had not misspent the opportunity provided by the cloaking fog. A clever plan, but ultimately hopeless. They still had far to go before they would reach the relative safety of the plateau.

The magister barked quick commands to the kobold archers remaining upon the wall. Chittering, they launched a volley with the advantage of height on their side. Feathered shafts flew from the battlements, becoming a sleet of darts among the invaders. Scores went down beneath the hail, screaming in pain.

Dagath wondered at the pity those cries awakened in its heart. They died according to the forces the mage had orchestrated. *The fallen would yet live if they'd left well enough alone. Why have they risked so much for one giant?*

The enemy advanced slowly, paying an awful price for each step. The frozen ground grew slick with gore; the snow-covered slopes blushed pink under the weight of the fallen. Their cause was hopeless, yet they carried on. *Why did they not simply retreat?* The mojh wondered at the foolishness of it all.

The invading force pressed forward, its success measured in the bodies left unmoving behind on the trails.

When the rays of the setting sun enflamed the tips of the Bitter Peaks, Dagath surveyed the battlefield. Fully a quarter of those who'd started up the trail this morning lay dead or dying. Despite their loses, the enemy had managed to capture the plateau.

And was that goal worth it? Dagath knew that, while the plateau offered some advantage, it would not be enough. The Fleshrune brethren had yet to extend their full power in defense. More would die tomorrow, and the magister knew the enemy could not sustain another day of such losses. Bone weary and faintly sickened by the smell of death that hung over the valley, Dagath set the night watch and walked carefully down from the vantage point on the battlements.

The high-pitched keen of faen mourning songs filled the valley below.

The one with the gentle hands was back.

Na-Devaon ceased his placid song. He'd been humming a simple doggerel, but one favored by the brave knights who traded songs for tales of their heroic exploits. The song kept up the giant's spirits. Perhaps some of those very knights were among the army that now approached? Na-Devaon hoped it was so.

The mojh said nothing. It merely studied Na-Devaon through the narrow bars of the cell. *What had Verthrax called this one? Oh yes.*

The giant said, "It is a little soon for more 'questioning,' Dagath."

The mojh started slightly at hearing its own name. Then it said, "I do have questions. I would like answers. But I am no torturer."

"I'm glad to hear that."

The silence stretched again. Dagath broke it once more, saying, "Why…"

The giant waited.

Dagath spoke, "I want to know why these hapless humans, giants, litorians, and faen would throw their lives away on such a fool's errand—dying for one imprisoned giant? I know you are no lord, nor do you have wealth enough to reward an army. Besides, what good is gold when you're dead?"

"It is not for gold they come, nor for hope of material reward."

"Then what?" The mojh hissed in frustration.

The question surprised Na-Devaon. Why indeed?

"I suppose," considered the giant, "it is because they have compassion. Compassion moved them to come for me."

"Compassion? Compassion is not enough. It is a pale emotion, and one easily quenched when faced with the reality of death."

Na-Devaon shook his head. He said, "Compassion brings us to a stop, and for a moment we rise above ourselves."

Dagath wrinkled its scaly brow, shook its head. "I doubt it. I have lived in this world a long time, you know. Before I was made mojh, I was human. I lived in many cities and knew many people. Few would have offered their lives for another out of compassion. Perhaps some may have been moved to take up arms against an injustice because they felt it was their duty, or because they were sworn to certain principles. But most creatures must see the possibility of profit before taking a risk."

The giant spread his mauled hands, winced slightly in pain, and said, "Then why are they here?"

The mojh pounded the iron bars with its staff, and yelled, "That is my question! Tell me!"

"I have already told you, yet you refuse to listen."

"The words you speak make no sense. They're dying out there! For no purpose!"

Na-Devaon said, "The army is not laying down its life for me alone, but for something larger."

The mojh waited.

The giant continued, "What diminishes one person diminishes everyone, because they are all connected by the land. Everyone comes from it. Whether you own up to it or not, you are part of the world. You just admitted to me that you lived in the world, and once you were human. No doubt you had parents, perhaps sisters and brothers? Can you remember what they were to you? What lengths would you have taken if harm had threatened them?"

The mojh mouthed a name, though the giant could not make it out. Dagath did not speak for a long time. Na-Devaon wondered what thoughts went through the mojh's mind. It almost seemed as if Dagath were concerned about the fate of the army . . . but, more likely, the clever mojh was merely trying to gull the

71

giant into disclosing some cache of gold or favors the Fleshrunes wanted for themselves.

As the giant considered what question he might pose to Dagath, the mojh huffed and spun away from the cell. As the magister moved off, it threw over its shoulder, "Compassion or not, they'll all soon be dead. It was a fool's errand."

Na-Devaon bowed his massive head.

It was a long night for Dagath. The words of the giant trickled and flowed through its thoughts, even as it descended into shallow dreams fraught with bloodshed and sacrifice. In one of these dreams, Dagath was a child again and had fallen into the crick behind his house. But his brother Jerem pulled him from the cold water, laughing away his tears.

The mojh woke with a start, dream fragments disintegrating.

A horn sounded again, the same sound that had awakened the magister. The citadel was under fresh attack!

Dagath grabbed up its staff and rushed from its chambers. Before it could reach the walls, a great explosion shocked through the stone, putting a stagger in the magister's gait, though it managed to keep to its feet. The rescuing army was bringing some sort of artillery to bear.

The mojh reached the walls. Dawn had yet to break, but there was light enough to see. Roiling balls of hellish flame leapt up from the plateau, casting a garish light upon the walls and the citadel and, indeed, all the valley. One after another, the balls arced high overhead, then came crashing down upon the walls. As each hit, it blossomed in a great blast of orange and white. A string of explosions promised to deafen the mojh, and the flashes stung its eyes. Mortar crumbled and stone cracked.

Enough!

Without thinking, Dagath grasped the power of the deep cyst at the citadel's core. Magical energy surged in the mojh's veins, crackled in its ears, and thrummed in its head. Light streamed from its eyes, its open mouth, and even from its fingertips.

The magister leapt into the air, carried aloft by the power of the cyst. *More!* Dagath needed more power. And so the mojh took it, siphoning more energy than ever before. It pried the conduit between its own spirit and the power cyst wider yet, and elán of elder days flooded through its body. Never had the mojh felt so filled with possibility.

Dagath had need of this strength.

Now high above the citadel and the arcing balls of flame, the mojh floated like a blazing star come down for a closer look at the tribulations of mortals.

The invaders had successfully hidden a power all their own. A strength sufficient, maybe, to truly threaten the Fleshrunes. The cascade of fire continued to pound the walls. *I must end this*, thought the mojh.

Dagath opened its arms as if to welcome a lover. In its right hand, its staff blazed as the mojh invoked the rune of ambient attraction.

The arcing, falling balls of flame wobbled in their trajectory. A few managed to hit their target, sending portions of the stone wall cascading to the valley floor. But the rest rose to meet Dagath.

As each globe enveloped Dagath, the mojh used the power of the cyst to contain its energy, compact it, and store it within the eldritch vessel that was its staff.

The flaming spheres continued to arc up from the plateau, each and every one intercepted by the mojh. Dagath's staff grew noticeably brighter with each absorption. There were so many! There was a limit to how many more the magister could capture, even with the augmentation of the power cyst.

Yet the spheres continued to arc upward.

Fools thrice cursed! They were trying to burn out the magister's endurance, Dagath guessed. Trying to overload the mojh with so much excess power that it would detonate overhead, a pretty firework for all to admire. But Dagath had more control than they knew.

Time to show those gathered in the valley what real power could accomplish.

I will blast them all to dust, turning their own spells against them. It was something that no Fleshrune had tried before as far as the mojh knew, but as Dagath conceived of the plan, it felt sure it would work. A magister of Dagath's training, armed with access to this particular power cyst, was a force that few could truly oppose. Dagath was unstoppable! The mojh gathered the full enormity of its strike, held it in check for a moment, glorying in the potency.

Carnage beckoned.

Even the Master of Claw would be awed by this bold act. The Master of Claw. Verthrax . . . the torturer. The killer. A sudden image of Jerem flashed through the mojh's mind. Jerem, whom Dagath had been unable to save when his brother had most needed saving. . . .

Dagath screamed, writhing in the air, one hand clawing at its temple while the other tried to retain its grasp on the bucking staff. With a supreme effort of will, the magister channeled the stolen energy from the staff straight into the deep power cyst. It was a charge so immense that the walls of castle began to glow.

The mojh had allowed the cyst to swallow the blast, sparing the lives of hundreds.

Why did I do that?

Dagath numbly noted that the cascade of fire from the plateau had ceased.

When the mental voice of the Master of Claw scratched through Dagath's head, demanding its immediate presence, the magister clenched its teeth and obeyed.

Verthrax was at the giant again. With the mojh were three lesser Fleshrune brethren, aiding their master in the questioning. A kobold carried a tray of sharp and slender instruments, some of which were red and damp with the giant's blood.

Dagath inadvertently allowed its eyes to find the giant's. Supplication was in that look. The mojh closed its eyes, looking away.

"I do not know whether to reward you or have you flayed, Dagath," said Verthrax, setting down a scalpel.

"Why is that, Master?"

"I was following your defense of the walls. I was particularly interested to see how you were able to tap the power cyst so fully. Not even I could have absorbed so much strength so rapidly without taking harm. But now, thanks to you, I perceive the proper technique. Because of you, the power of the Fleshrunes is about to become uncontestable. You've advanced the cause of the brethren by years, Dagath."

"It seems that is true," admitted Dagath. Verthrax was right—the magister's reckless usage of the deep cyst had revealed its potential to any of the brethren who had been tapped into it during the attack, especially those of exceptional skill. Such as the Master of Claw.

"But," continued Verthrax, "I cannot help wondering why you did not eradicate those vermin still encamped outside the citadel. I know what transpired. I saw the energy you held. I saw the devastating lance you fashioned."

Dagath wondered if that moment had frightened the vain cult leader. The Master of Claw did not like to be frightened. Verthrax tended to eradicate those who might pose a threat. And now, the Master knew how to suck in the elán of the deep power cyst without concern for burning up like a cinder.

"The attack would have been over. This giant would have been ours to question at our leisure. Yet you forbore. I want to know why. Answer carefully."

Dagath responded, "Perhaps you did not see as fully into my connection with the power cyst as you suppose. If you had, you would know that I had drained a quantity of power from it so great that I feared that the stabilization spells upon which this ancient citadel depends would weaken. While it would have been most satisfying to put an end to the invaders in one blazing strike, I realized it might be better to return the investment of power I culled from the cyst, with interest. Moreover, I did not want my brethren to pay for my rash act by having a castle come crumbling down around them."

A smile bloomed and grew on the Master of Claw's scaled face. Verthrax chuckled. "You are a sly one, Dagath. I've always said that. What you say smacks of something you might actually do, and for the reasons you submit. Perhaps I would have chosen to do the same."

Verthrax's oily smile argued against the statement. Dagath knew the Master of Claw would have blasted the army, damn all repercussions. It was Verthrax's way, a component of the ruthless personality that had advanced the Fleshrunes to their present status as a guild—or, as some would say, a cult—on the cusp of committing a great atrocity.

"And so the citadel is saved," said Verthrax. "The deep power cyst holds a charge larger than it has since the day we discovered it. But an enemy force—one that commands a great deal of aggressive magical power, if those spheres of hellfire are any indication—is encamped at our gate. What should we do, Dagath?"

"It is for me to obey, Master of Claw."

"I wonder. Well, let us worry about that later. For now, I must see to the army at the door."

Verthrax reached for its staff, which one of the other Fleshrune brethren held out. The Master of Claw grasped it in both hands and closed its eyes.

What's Verthrax doing? wondered Dagath. The magister reached out with its arcane senses. Then Dagath knew: The Master of Claw was tapping the deep power cyst. And it was using the arcane technique revealed by Dagath just minutes earlier. Already the Master of Claw was gleaming with excess energy. Sparks played across its scales and leapt between its teeth as Verthrax's smile turned into a gasp of laughter.

"It is intoxicating!" yelled the Master of Claw.

"What do you propose?" asked Dagath, moving to stand directly before Verthrax. All the excess charge Dagath had fed into the cyst was now being channeled into the Master of Claw's ebony staff.

"I'm going to end the threat of the invaders! As you should have done."

"But…"

"No, do not worry, I will not deplete the cyst. Why would I destroy something that can give me the power equal to that of a dragon scion of the elder age?"

The Master of Claw giggled. The peals of mirth thundered through the citadel, magnified by the connection to the ancient pool of energy. Verthrax's glow had become that of a blast furnace, glaring and nearly as warm. The other two brethren fled the cell, the mojh-born servitors close on their heels.

Only Dagath remained, protecting itself from the Master's emanation with cyst-enhanced magistry of its own, monitoring the Master's next move. Dagath's heart felt empty of all passion; it was as if the mojh's chest cavity were a void.

Dagath had felt the same thing once before. When Jerem had died at the hands of a simple bandit on the market road, Dagath had been too young to help the older boy. All he could do was hold his dying brother, watching his lifeblood spill out onto the dust. When Jerem finally died of his wounds, dead, too, it seemed, was Dagath's ability to feel.

Not all the power of the deep cyst could fill the hollows of his heart.

A frisson jolted Dagath. It was not that the mojh worried that Verthrax's next move would deplete the deep cyst. Truth be told, the magister worried just the opposite: that it would remain viable. Dagath could see the future in the Master's mind, thanks to its own connection to the primeval energy node.

It was to be an all-consuming slaughter. Nothing simple, no. Verthrax intended a very painful end for the hundreds of failed rescuers staged outside on the plateau. The dark glee that suffused the Master's thoughts was enough to sour Dagath's stomach.

Verthrax's blazing form blinked away, plunging the cell into darkness. But Dagath's shared connection with the Master allowed the mojh to track the location of the Fleshrune leader. Dagath could see it all in the mind's eye. The Master of Claw hovered over the plateau, over the cringing army assembled there, just as Dagath had done earlier.

What Dagath had only contemplated, Verthrax chose to do.

Time slowed. Verthrax spread its hands, the coiling, godlike energy within ready to rush out and slowly ignite the blood of every living creature below.

Back in the dark cell, Dagath raised its staff and said, "No. I choose differently."

The flow of power up from the deep cyst into Verthrax was a river of liquid effulgence to Dagath's arcane eye. With negligible effort, Dagath stabbed its own staff into the river, disrupting the current and sending out coils of uncontained energy in all directions.

The Master of Claw's demise preceded the rising sun that day, the mojh outshining the dawn with the ferocity of its passing. When the awful glare faded, only dust swirled away in the wind. Below, the plateau remained unscathed.

Echoes of reflected light penetrated even the roots of the citadel. Na-Devaon walked from his untended cell, keeping his feet despite the rocking floor. Masonry crashed around him, and he heard the distant screams of the mojh-born.

The shaking had started when the second mojh, Dagath, collapsed, only seconds after Verthrax had departed, and at about the same time as the reflected flash briefly painted the walls of his cell in tones of sepia. Were his rescuers all dead, baked in one mighty thaumatergic strike?

He knew it wasn't true. Something had intervened. Something had saved the rescuing army.

On the floor, Dagath moaned.

The giant bent and helped the groaning mojh to stand. Dagath's once white staff was now a black cinder, trailing filaments of smoke.

"Are we safe in here?" the giant asked.

Dagath looked around and said, "Probably not."

Na-Devaon prodded, "You did something. I can tell." Color was returning to the giant's pain-etched face, and a hint of emotion played at the corners of Na-Devaon's lips. Perhaps it was hope.

The mojh said simply, "I ended the Master of Claw."

"Why?"

"I had a change of heart."

──────○──────

ED GREENWOOD
THE FALLEN STAR

Yondren smiled lazily—and in a single catlike bound, he
vanished back into the shadows, leaving Ambrae to face
the frowning guard alone.

As he always did.

Ambrae smiled serenely at the sentinel to buy herself time.
She'd been perhaps the best mage blade in Khorl and had spells
enough to blast this man to ashes.

She did not, however, command enough spells to waste such
a death on one guard when there was a castle full of such
guardians all around her.

She'd long since ceased to be angered at Yondren's habit of so
often and suddenly being "not there." He was the best unfettered
Ambrae had ever met, a whirling wind one moment and a
patient schemer the next. Those sudden shifts of mood and
location were just his way. Along with his easy smile and his
deft, ardent, never-gentle hands, they were . . . Yondren.

And Yondren loved sudden vanishings almost as much as startling arrivals. Unreliable, yes, but one might just as well rail against the storm winds . . . and with about as much effect.

"Lady," the guard said sternly, stepping forward to bar her way. "This is not a place where you should be. How came you here, beyond the curtains?"

Ambrae let her smile broaden. Just now, despite this stern guard, Ambrae felt very far from railing against anyone.

She'd been awed and awed again by the city of Sormere—riches, courtesies, music, fashion, pride, and history; everything that had been just empty words in Khorl—until she had moved somewhere beyond awe to float along in an almost numbed, carefree state of wonderment.

And she stood now in the heart of Sormere, in the castle of Taireveltowers, one of the grandest houses in the city. Home of the Tairevel family, the House of the Fallen Star. Even Sormere-ans spoke of the Tairevels with awe . . . particularly a senior Tairevel known as the Lord Shield.

Yet this grandeur was only a small part of Sormere. Every-where outside the vast castle she stood in, towers soared above broad-curving streets, bristling with balconies, ornamental spires, and crenelated walls. Folk—almost all humans like herself—bustled about in those streets, exchanging elaborate courtesies and bedecked in splendid garments.

Like the gown Ambrae was wearing. Something far more colorful and impractical than she'd have ever dared wear in her many-shadowed, dangerous home of Khorl, to be sure.

Sometimes she'd worn masks in that dying, sinister port—but never a gilded and fancifully upswept adornment of feath-ers and metal dangle-tassels like the one on her face right now.

Nor was the guard facing her the typical unwashed, hard-faced gutsword of Khorl, ready to thrust home a slaying blade almost before uttering a challenge, always expecting trouble and never bothering with such frills as civility.

This obviously suspicious sentinel wore a beautiful tabard aglow with the intricate trumpets-and-flames arms of the Tairevel. His similarly magnificent blade was still sheathed.

"Lady," he said, voice grave but firm, "I ask again: How came you here, beyond the curtains guests were asked to respect? And who was that with you, who fled at my approach?"

"My . . . companion," Ambrae replied calmly, not trying to hide her harsh Khorl accent, "conducted me here, by ways no doubt familiar to him. This is, after all, *his* castle."

The guard stiffened, drawing breath sharply in what was almost a gasp.

Ah, so Tairevel men do go rutting, but they either hide it well or have made such deeds a matter to keep silent about.

Ambrae took care not to smile at that thought, and just as carefully said no more.

Long moments passed. Then, reluctantly, the guard drew back and bowed to her. Touching the intricate hilt of his blade and then the badge on his breast in what was obviously some sort of formal ritual or signal, he announced, "My duty is satisfied. I apologize for my challenge and now withdraw."

Not knowing what the proper reply might be, Ambrae nodded gravely and slowly turned away.

When she turned back, gloved hands carefully clasped together on one hip as she'd seen some of the older matrons at this revel doing, the guard had dwindled to a distant figure. Still facing her, he was stiffly retreating, stride by long formal stride, down the arrow-straight passage into a distant pillared hall.

Ambrae let out a long, silent breath of relief and stayed where she was, marveling once more at just how huge Tairevel-towers was. Even the most cavernous warehouses of her home city were smaller than the vast, lofty-domed halls she'd looked down upon as she and Yondren had made their casually-strolling way through the passages and balconies to this spot.

The crumbling and deserted once-grand mansions of her distant home were mere miniature echoes of this great castle, flickering candles to a bright hearthfire.

A fire that blazed warm and glittering all around her, riches upon finery upon more riches. Great wealth casually wasted, spilled forth on scented tapers and garlands of fresh blossoms adorning the wall lanterns lining this passage—to say nothing of all the wine and great-platters, the musicians and the . . .

Ambrae shook her head, lip curling in momentary scorn, and then found herself wishing—for just one glittering moment—that she belonged here, had grown up in this . . . even with all of its mind-dizzying rules and niceties, and feuds no doubt every whit as venomous as the familiar back alley struggles of Khorl.

These folk of Sormere were more than just wealthy. Their families, homes, and doings were solid and long-founded and . . . secure. They stood not alone. They knew what tomorrow and the days ahead would bring, and they understood their places in this well-ordered city.

A city where she and Yondren shared the rank of rats. Sneak-thieves but newly arrived in splendid Sormere, they wore stolen finery and hoped to seize much this night, before their true natures became known: a mage blade and an unfettered whose darings had finally made tarrying longer in Khorl deadly.

For years Yondren had been listening to visiting traders with an ear toward where next to go plundering, and had heard that the decadent nobility of the Old City wallowed in far more gems and coins than anyone needed. Ambrae had heard such tales, too, but dismissed them as the wild tongue-wavings of merchants desiring to impress.

Yet for once, it seemed, the merchants had spoken truth. Oh, there were scampering servants and dirty carters in ragged smocks to be seen in plenty in the cobbled streets, and modest dwellings crowded the shadows between spires of soaring gothic splendor, but . . . people were happy here. Happy and settled and proud, well fed and wearing the bright faces of folk who never need wonder where their next meal was coming from or grow used to dead bodies sprawled in the streets.

A weight had lifted from Ambrae's heart even in the handful of days that had passed between the docking of the battered, creaking coaster that had brought them from Khorl and this night of revelry. She and Yondren were pretending to be guests of the haughty Tairevel family during the annual Honorance of the Guardians of the Tairevel.

Amid all the bright finery and pretensions, there was hope. She could feel it. Hope grounded in permanence. Something she might dare to believe in. She needed something besides swindling to look forward to in life—because this couldn't go on forever. Someday, whenever it might come, they'd be caught and slain—and Ambrae of Khorl would drift up to face Great Niashra having done nothing, nothing, worthwhile to win herself favor. Only mortals who made a difference in the world were worthy of the favor of the goddess, and—

"What did you do, promise him some fun later?" Yondren's voice was a light, mocking whisper from directly overhead.

"Intimated that the elder Lord Tairevel and I were being . . . intimate. And that you—fleeing rabbit that was all he saw of you—were he," Ambrae murmured calmly.

"That old totterer?" Yondren hooted. "Did you see him, Brae?"

"Just about as well as yon guard is seeing you now," she replied, a trifle more tartly. "And shuffling white-hair or not, he must enjoy a certain reputation—or I daresay I'd be in chains right now, and you scampering for your life with hand-crossbow quarrels bristling in your behind!"

Yondren chuckled softly. "You sound about ready to skin me alive—something the authorities may do to both of us unless—"

A rustling arose beyond a nearby archway, and he was gone again. Up once more into the carved and curlicued cross-vaultings of the passage overhead, with their painted panels of past Tairevel heroics and victories.

Quelling a sigh, Ambrae chose to pace toward the rustling with slow dignity, secure in one thing, at least: The hiding-sleeve beneath her rigid girdle so far held no stolen gems . . . though Yondren must be fairly rattling with them by now. Why, he'd plucked a hairpin from that last matron while standing nose-to-nose talking with her, by Niashra!

On the other hand, if guards chose to search the unfamiliar lady who wandered where she wasn't supposed to be, they could hardly fail to find her athame, the trusted blade sheathed in the very prow of her girdle . . .

The rustling grew louder and became laced with giggling—and then Ambrae suddenly found herself facing the elder Lord Tairevel himself. He lurched forward with one arm around an overpainted lady in a coppery gown, her hair fairly sparkling with an ornate upthrust tiara adorned with a great arc of gems.

"M-my lord," the mage blade said swiftly, ducking her head and making the elaborate hand-flourishes she'd seen other ladies perform upon meeting their host.

Old eyes brightened, and ruddy cheeks grew even redder. "Fair lady," Lord Tairevel growled in delight, "I've not seen *you* before! Pray join us, and unfold to me your name and lineage!"

The lady gave Ambrae a look that had daggers in it, but the old lord almost shook her off his arm as he lurched forward to kiss Ambrae full on the mouth.

The strong, searing taste of berry wine stung the mage blade's lips, and then a heavy weight came down on her bare shoulder. Tairevel had lost his balance and flung out a hand as swiftly as Yondren might.

Ambrae staggered for a moment under his bulk, then managed to right him, mouthing frantically across his back to the lady of the gems, "I'll leave you both alone!"

That earned her a fierce smile from the lady—for just a moment. Then Ambrae's skillful steering of the chuckling lord brought Tairevel's face right into the woman's bosom and drove her back against the passage wall.

A nearby statuette on a pedestal rocked with the force of their combined arrival, as the copper-gowned lady lost her breath with an undignified "whoof!" Her face twisted in momentary pain as she thrust her hands urgently at Tairevel's chest to bear him upright—so it was hardly surprising that Yondren's deft plucking of the gem-adorned tiara from above passed unnoticed.

And then Yondren was gone again, and Ambrae was whirling past Tairevel and away, casting one glance back over her shoulder and seeing—as she'd expected—the guard who'd retreated from her advancing again. Swiftly. The man couldn't have missed seeing Yondren's arms reaching down from above, so 'twould be best to get gone in a hurry, before—

Yondren's long arms thrust out of an opening she'd not noticed behind the green cascade of a potted fall of ferns, and gathered her in. "*Come,*" he murmured, before she could draw breath for even a squeak of alarm, and drew her firmly into the darkness.

They rushed down a narrow, unlit servant's stairway and out into another passage, this one dominated by the quavering voices of older noble ladies busily gossiping. The chatter was coming from archways to either side, whence came the flickering radiances of floating candle-lamps. The passage between and beyond those rooms was dimly lit and given over to softly-gliding servants bearing platters of tall fluted glasses and sugared confections. Yondren boldly seized drinks for them both and whirled Ambrae back against the doorway they'd emerged from, in an apparently amorous embrace.

"Yond," she hissed promptly, "we should *go*. That guard saw you—and the Lord Tairevel certainly got a good look at me!"

Yondren shrugged and grinned. "Your ever-heavier worries about being caught? Isn't this what we came for? And have you ever known me to be taken yet?"

Ambrae caught the watching eye of a passing servant. Thrusting herself hard against her partner, she lifted her lips to him in apparent yearning—and hissed through them, "Sormere is full of riches, yes, and seemingly revels in plenty, too, but we'll not last long if we try to dwell here on the proceeds of plundering these nobles! They've certainly got guards enough, and surely they talk, one house to another! And to whom will you sell the gems you've plucked? Surely—"

Yondren kissed her, making it a hard biting of rebuke, and spun away, dismissing her unease with an airy wave of his hand. And then, to her utter horror, he ducked under the arm of a servant and boldly snatched a sparkling pectoral of haelstones from the ample breast of a noblewoman whose elaborate makeup couldn't conceal the sagging wrinkles of many years.

The matron shrieked, and Yondren spun around and punched the servant hard in the gut, flinging the startled man along the passage, platter and glasses flying. Then he sprang past the woman he'd robbed and into the room beyond.

Would he—?

Yes. Shrieks arose in a swelling chorus. Her partner must be wading through the gossipers, snatching at gems right and left. *Great Niashra, be with me now!*

Scarcely knowing what to do, Ambrae rushed forward. Servants were pelting along the passage toward the cries, and in their wake, in that direction at least, were hastening guards, swords already drawn.

From balcony windows beyond, the sounds of the Honorance in full swing rose ever louder. At least noise born here wouldn't travel far enough to raise a general alarm . . . which wasn't to say that the guards didn't have gongs to ring, or the Tairevel lacked some magical means of rousing all of their loyal blades. *Oh, Yondren!*

And as if her thought had been a summons, the grinning unfettered was suddenly out in the passage with her again, hissing, "Enough of prowling! This night, we dare all!"

And he turned, drawing one of his daggers from its sheath in his sleeve, a bright cluster of gems still clutched in his left hand—and drove the blade into the throat of the foremost servant.

The man had been leaping at them, hands widespread to grab back the plunder, and he managed a dying gurgle as he fell right on past Yondren. Ambrae caught a fleeting glimpse of helpless terror wiping away fury in his staring eyes.

Then Yondren whirled back to clutch her by the waist—and thrust her forward, right into the arms of the next servant. As they crashed together, Ambrae screamed like any noble matron and went down, tangling the man's legs and throwing up her own limbs to make sure she tripped the next onrushing man.

Moments of bruising confusion followed, in which her mask was jarred away and her gown torn half off her left side . . . before everything came to a panting halt as she lay gasping on her back in the dim passage—with three glittering swordpoints menacing her throat.

"Who are you," growled a large and senior-looking guard down the length of his long, glittering-sharp blade, "and where's the man who came here with you? Speak, or die!"

Ambrae fought to find breath enough to reply. The tip of another sword urged her to do so more quickly, gliding in to kiss the mage blade beneath her chin ever so gently . . . and leave drops of blood welling from her throat. "Ambrae, I'm named," she managed to hiss, "and—"

"You and the other came to steal gems, yes?" another guard snapped. Ambrae nodded wearily, letting her head fall back to escape the peering eyes of many revelers now crowding around.

"We must keep him from the Round Chamber at all costs!" gasped one horrified matron—in the moment before a dark cloak fell like a cascade of water over the head of the senior guard, and a bright blade flashed through the throat of the one who'd cut Ambrae.

Deafening shouts and shrieks erupted as Yondren swung down from above, boots first, sending a third guard staggering away, choking through a crushed throat—and the fourth stumbling back with a scream onto the impaling blade of the blinded senior guard.

As that cursing guardian snatched the last cloak-fold away from his face, Yondren lunged with a grand flourish to slide a stolen sword through the man's mouth, and then turned with a bright smile to the matron sobbing with fear to ask, "And why, fair lady, might that be?"

The matron promptly and unhelpfully fainted, but Yondren calmly turned and ran his blade through the helpless third guard and told the next nearest matron, "Fair one, I'd hate to have to spit *you* with this blade—still dirty with his blood, and all—so why don't you buy your life with an honest answer: Why should I be kept from the Round Chamber?"

"B-because that's where the Fallen Star is," the woman stammered.

"Ah, the famous Fallen Star is a *gem?*" Yondren almost crowed, eyes brightening to outshine the nearest wall-lanterns.

And almost before various voices gasped confirmation, he'd plucked Ambrae to her feet, her torn gown swirling, and was gone into the dark passages like a racing storm wind.

As they raced along, Yondren stuffing pouches of gems down her girdle, the breathless and bewildered mage blade found herself wondering why the last two guards, safe far beyond Yondren's reach, had greeted their departure with matching mirthless, unfriendly—and coldly knowing—smiles.

Just what awaited them in the Round Chamber?

The most formidable Guardians of the Tairevel were either off duty to be honored and feasted, or had partaken overmuch of fine Tairevel wine—for Yondren easily bested all three he crossed blades with, leaving them alive only long enough to gasp out the way to the Round Chamber.

Its doors were unguarded, and the passages leading to them empty and silent, in the farthest tower of the castle from the revelry. Yondren swarmed over them with the deft care of an unfettered who'd met with traps before, but he found no peril.

Whereupon he flung his usual reckless smile into Ambrae's apprehensive face and swung the doors wide.

The Round Chamber was the shape its name warranted, with a mirror-smooth floor of polished stone and a vaulted ceiling so lofty that its height was lost in dark shadows. Two tiers of stone benches lined its walls, pierced by aisles that led to two doorways besides the one that the two gem-thieves stood in.

The only radiance in the room came from a twinkling gemstone as large as a man's head. It floated in midair just within Yondren's tiptoe reach, in the very center of the circular chamber. The Fallen Star.

Flickering in the air around it were bright, moving scenes—images of the Honorance dancing and revelry they'd left behind.

A man was sitting watching those scenes. His back was to Ambrae and Yondren, and he filled a large and simple backless stone bowl chair. He was of massive build, helmless and bare-handed but clad in heavy, fluted-plate metal armor as grand and heavy as a suit once sold in Khorl as "torn from the body of a battle-fallen giant." His shoulders moved enough to show that he breathed and was apparently awake—but he gave no sign of having heard their arrival.

"A warmain," Ambrae whispered almost soundlessly, her uneasiness flaring into foreboding.

Yondren gave her the fierce grin that meant: "Aye, but what of it?" Drawing his best dagger from his right sleeve, he caused it to shimmer with its innate power to shield its bearer against fell magics. Then he raced forward, springing into the air in a great bound when he judged himself close enough to the seated man to leave the latter no time to turn and thrust up at him with a weapon. A large sword hung scabbarded at the warmain's hip, sharing his belt with at least two daggers.

The force of Yondren's pounce—and his enthusiastic stabbings—rocked the seated man, who rose like an exasperated mountain to pluck the unfettered from his shoulders. He hurled Yondren clear across the room to crash with a groan into the upper tier of benches. The warmain did not draw his sword.

As the armored man turned a hard but not unhandsome face to behold Ambrae, still frozen in the doorway, ghostly flames like green fire erupted from deep gashes in his neck, throat, and breast—and were matched by a glow of the same hue arising from a complex symbol on his cheek. A rune!

"Runechild!" Ambrae gasped.

"Correct both times, lady," the armored man said quietly. "Warmain and runechild both. I am the Lord Shield of the Tairevels, and I must bid you both begone from Taireveltowers. You are neither invited nor welcome here, but if you depart without further violence or thievery, you may keep the baubles you've stolen. Mere coins can replace them—but the Fallen Star must be left alone."

Yondren struggled to his feet, wincing, and stared at what was left of his dagger. Above the hilt he was clutching, naught remained of its blade but a drifting wisp of smoke. With a snarl, he flung it down and spat, "And what does a Lord Shield do— besides sitting alone spying on others through a gem?"

The warmain turned his head to meet Yondren's angry gaze. "I've dedicated myself to keeping Sormere strong and its ways unchanged. And for that cause, I do many things, both large and small. Among them, I warn you, I defend the Fallen Star to the death."

"A pretty speech," Yondren sneered, and sprang from the bench as swift and as agile as ever, snatching at the gem.

It flared into golden fire as his fingers closed around it—and remained right where it was, floating immobile. Yondren's fingers passed through it and vanished into smoke.

The unfettered landed with a shriek of pain, curls of smoke rising from the melted stumps of fingers—and then snarled and raced at the Lord Shield, plucking forth another dagger with his undamaged hand.

"No, Yondren!" Ambrae screamed, seeing the warmain's hand fall to the hilt of his massive sword. Before the words were even out of her mouth, the unfettered swarmed up the Tairevel lord, stabbing and slashing. The guardian's sword stayed in its scabbard, and green fire curled and billowed.

Pain creased the Lord Shield's face, and he gasped more than once as Yondren's fang bit into him. Sparks spat as he repeatedly batted the dagger away from his eyes, sending it skittering across his armor. With a growl Yondren swung himself around onto the warmain's shoulders and slit the Lord Shield's throat—yet the Tairevel noble kept his feet, swaying but not falling.

Green fire rained like spraying blood from that riven throat, but the armored man showed no signs of failing strength or breath as he bent to a side table. Yondren rode his back, stabbing him as tirelessly as an infuriated wasp, while the other man picked up a pair of gauntlets.

Calmly donning them, the noble reached around and caught hold of the unfettered's dagger. The two men strained for possession of it.

"*Smite* him, Brae!" Yondren snarled. "Magic protects him!"

Ambrae fought down her fear—the Tairevel lord should be dead already, but it seemed he could not die!—and drew her athame. A lance of slaying lightning . . .

Her strike crackled straight at the Lord Shield, who stood within easy reach, tall and calm. A handspan before the blue-white fury of her spell reached the cascading green fires of that armored breast, it veered aside and sprang across the room.

To vanish into the Fallen Star.

The floating gem flared into blue-white brightness, and by its light she saw that the Lord Shield seemed taller than before, and stronger. Yondren's dagger was savaging the man's neck and throat, often piercing right through it, yet the noble's head remained on his shoulders, and . . . yes, he was growing visibly larger with each wound he took!

Ambrae stepped back with a sob, not knowing what to do. Face set in a wolf's grin, Yondren dragged his blood-drenched dagger across the Tairevel lord's face, slicing open cheeks and nose.

The warmain sighed and cast a look at the Fallen Star. As if in reply, the floating gem flared up into a red flame, and the rune on his own cheek glowed with a matching hue. Yondren shrieked in pain.

Frozen in mid-gasp, Ambrae watched her longtime partner arch over backward in agony, as if trying to hurl himself away from the armored shoulders he perched on. What looked like racing red smoke was streaming from the warmain's wounds, cleaving the air in deadly arcs that pierced Yondren again and again.

The unfettered spasmed, his face twisting into a howl that died into silence . . . and his upper body fell apart, collapsing in a ruin of blood and shredded flesh, bouncing gems and tumbling bones. The sight left Ambrae too horrified to retch, or run, or do anything at all.

Frozen, she stared at the Lord Shield of the Tairevels as he strode slowly toward her. The rune on the nobleman's cheek was green again, shining as bright as a torch. His many wounds seemed to be fading away, as if Yondren had never made them.

As if Yondren had never been . . .

Rage and grief rose in Ambrae like a sudden choking flood of fire, and she shouted the most powerful battle-spell she had, hurling it at the calmly-advancing noble.

It turned just before reaching him and lashed the Fallen Star, which drank it with a few small winks and flashes. Ambrae was already hissing forth her next spell, a bolt of lightning that might be as deadly to her as to the warmain in such confines. She cared not, not when her Yondren—

The Fallen Star drank that spell, too.

And her next one.

Leaving her with only a last lone, paltry spell, and the runechild barely a pace away from her.

"*No!*" Ambrae sobbed, springing at him with her athame glittering like a mighty blade. "Nooooh!" Desperately she slashed at the glowing rune—and the warmain ducked, dodged, and then caught her wrist in a grip as unbreakable as mountain stone.

Ambrae beat vainly at the armored breast with her other hand, weeping and shrieking, until there was nothing left in her but grief. She fell against her foe, heedless of what he might do, and slid down the cold, hard metal armor to her knees.

Doors burst open then with booming sounds, and men shouted in alarm—but the voice of the Lord Shield rolled out over her head: "Depart, with my thanks, and leave us. Close the doors again. All is well . . . or will be."

The doors closed, one after another, as if the guards who'd flung them open were reluctant to obey. Ambrae cared not. She lay lost in a silent flood of tears, waiting to be slain.

Still keeping firm hold of her wrist, the warmain put an armored arm around her and murmured, "Let go your athame, mage blade, and try to find peace. Your companion is dead, but I'd rather not deal with you as he forced me to serve him."

Ambrae had no strength left to sob, let alone cling to her blade. She let it fall, knowing she was doomed anyway.

"S-slay me then," she gasped, as gentle hands rolled her over and that rune-marked face looked grimly down at her, "and have done."

"I would much rather not," the Lord Shield replied. "Killing is always . . . the easiest way. Easiest and most wasteful. It sunders rather than builds, lessens rather than strengthens. And I work to keep Sormere strong and unchanged, not to tirelessly collect new foes for it."

Ambrae stared up at him through glimmering tears. "What, then? Imprisonment? Slavery?"

"My ways are not those of Khorl," the Lord Shield replied gravely. "If you promise not to work against House Tairevel or the city of Sormere, nor lend your spells to those who do, I don't intend to visit any harm upon you at all. Would it pain you overmuch if your dead companion was interred with honor?"

The mage blade blinked up at him in utter astonishment. "I—what did you say?"

"Would you be pleased if House Tairevel gave your partner a dignified funeral?"

Ambrae swallowed tears and stared at him. Yond was gone. *Gone.*

He awaited her answer in patient silence.

Nothing would bring Yond back.

"Why?" she demanded at last, in a rough, forlorn whisper. "Why would you do this?"

The warmain shrugged. "In truth, lady, more for you than out of any high regard for him. I would have you as a friend—not an oathsworn foe."

"Why?" she managed to say.

"Sormere has need of those who know other lands and cities. If we seek to cling to what is good, and yet survive, we must know who may challenge us, and with what."

Ambrae frowned in bewilderment. "Do . . . do you rule here?"

"No, neither in Taireveltowers nor in the city around us. I have pledged myself to guard the Star—"

He inclined his head toward the floating gem, now glowing serenely again.

"—because it can guide us with its stored wisdom."

Ambrae turned her head to look at the huge gem. "'Stored wisdom'? It can think?"

The lord smiled thinly. "No, it leaves the thinking to us, which is perhaps great foolishness on its part. By means of magic, it holds the glorious past of Sormere as visions. And Sormere is perhaps the finest achievement of our kind, though it's not so great as its haughtiest citizens believe. Those of us who know how can call forth specific remembrances and learn by examining them. A mage blade should be able to do so."

Ambrae stared at him, clinging to the last tatters of her rage. "You—you slay my Yondren and smash me down and . . . and think to *recruit* me to your *service*?"

"Not to be a Tairevel servant, no, but rather to become a guardian of Sormere."

Not cast out to wander? Not . . . alone?

Ambrae waved a hand weakly to indicate the great castle around them, and asked disbelievingly, "And this city needs guarding by the likes of me?"

The Lord Shield smiled again. "Not its towers and gates and docks, no—but the dream of greatness and peaceful achievement and . . . sophistication it represents."

At the derisive disbelief widening across her face, he bent nearer and said, "Look at it thus: What life would you prefer to lead, from this day forth? More selfish theft and skulking and danger . . . or fed and provided for—as one of us, not a slave—while you strive in service and security to better the world?"

One of us. A place to belong. At last.

Now that it was too late to share it with Yondren. Now that she was alone . . .

Ambrae shook her head. "Fair words," she moaned, fighting not to weep. "Yond could always flourish fair words, too. I—I can't believe you'll not blast me the moment I—"

"This is no trickery," the Lord Shield said, almost fiercely. "By this rune I bear . . ."

As he spoke, it flamed forth green fire again, tongues that almost touched Ambrae's face as she flinched back. Their fire felt cool, not hot . . .

She locked eyes with the Tairevel runechild and whispered almost unwillingly, "I believe you."

"So we can now converse—and the burden of choice shifts once more to you. Will you consider my offer?"

Ambrae closed her eyes, shuddered, then shook her head slightly as Yondren's laughing face and the bright moments they'd shared—all too few of them—swirled around her. Gone forever, now. Gone, whatever hopes she might have cherished. Leaving her with . . . with what she'd dreamed of all these years. A place to belong. Friends to replace Yondren's bright laughter.

But only if she dared to say the right thing now. "I . . . I'm so tired of running and watching for foes . . . and of hurling words and spells and blades," she murmured, opening her eyes to meet the runechild's intent gaze. "I—yes. Yes."

The Lord Shield smiled and gently plucked her to her feet. "Come and look into the Star," he said, "and you'll find your choice much easier. Come see the glories of long striving in the arts, and stable governance, and proud lineage. Come and behold how bright your life can be, in years to come."

Ambrae found her sight flooding with tears again. Impatiently she wiped them away with her sleeve, a movement that dragged the hard points of stolen gems across her breasts. She'd forgotten them.

In a sudden flare of anger and grief she snatched forth the pouches Yondren had stuffed into her girdle, and flung them to the floor behind her. *Farewell, Yondren.*

"Of Khorl no longer," Ambrae whispered, and stepped forward, the gems forgotten in an instant.

The Fallen Star flared eagerly before her, and Ambrae strode toward its bright promise.

WILL MCDERMOTT
CHILD OF THE STREET

Nada Flesher crouched on the windowsill, balanced on her toes, and watched the children playing dancing bones and three's your uncle far below. Clad in black from head to foot, she was nearly invisible in the deep shadows that splayed across the back of the alley in the last hours before dusk.

Although she hadn't lived on the streets for many years, Nada still felt drawn to the alley, and to the rag-clad children who made it their home. She'd been lucky. Nada had found a way off the street that hadn't forced her to beg for scraps or sell her body an hour at a time.

No. It wasn't luck. Nada didn't believe in luck. That's why she'd always preferred the game of three's your uncle to dancing bones. Unless you were willing to cheat—and many of the older urchins won enough to live on that way—dancing bones was a random game of chance.

Nada was never willing to cheat her fellow street dwellers—or even those young apprentices who often tarried in the alleys between chores. So, she had relied on skill and cunning to make her way through De-Shamod's seamy underbelly. She'd honed her ability with the dagger, beating all comers at three's your uncle in these late afternoon tests of skill.

The knife-throwing game below her was getting interesting, so Nada grasped a drainpipe and leaned out to get a better look. An older boy well on his way to becoming a thug had finished his throws. All three blades had bitten deep into the stone wall and stuck fast. Nada knew this boy. His name was Kissel. He was big and muscular despite years on the street, and had a small gang that kept him well-fed while he kept them hungry for power.

A young slip of a girl stepped up to test the gang leader. Nada had never seen this girl before, but the filthy rags she wore and her dirt-streaked face showed she was no newcomer to the streets. That wasn't uncommon, though. There were so many lost children that Nada couldn't keep track of them all. They showed up and disappeared without warning. She used to try to find the ones who vanished, but there was never any trail to follow. Instead, she concentrated on helping those she could while they lived on the street.

Kissel laughed as he tossed another set of three knives in a slow, tumbling arc toward the scrawny newcomer. The girl plucked two of the blades out of the air and stepped back to let the third land between her bare feet.

Nada let out a low whistle just as Kissel's laugh died in his throat. She pulled back, worried that she might have been heard, but glanced down just in time to see the waif's first toss. The knife glanced off one of Kissel's blades, knocking it to the ground. The waif's blade stuck for an instant, but then fell next to the other knife on the ground.

It was a decent throw and far better than Kissel had expected. Nada had rarely seen any of his blades bumped loose.

Still, Kissel had two knives in the wall, and the newcomer had only two throws left. But the gang leader wasn't leaving anything to chance. As the waif bent to pick up the blade between her feet, Nada saw an almost imperceptible nod of Kissel's head toward one of his followers.

As the girl readied for her second throw, the second boy moved closer to the game. He pretended to trip when she pulled her arm back, and then tossed a handful of bobbers into her face as she loosed her throw. Even with the distraction, her blade nicked one of Kissel's remaining two blades, loosening it. Her misthrown blade fell to the ground in a clatter on top of the other knives.

The new girl now had just one knife left, while Kissel had two blades stuck in the wall. But Kissel still wasn't satisfied. Apparently he felt the need to humiliate the newcomer, because Nada saw him nod to his boy once again. Kissel's crony knelt down next to the waif to pick up his coins. The girl stood there patiently, balancing the tip of the knife on her finger as she waited.

Once the boy had cleared the coins away, the waif pulled her arm back and scanned the wall, concentrating on the throw. Nada could see a winning shot from her vantage point, but knew the girl had no chance to hit it, for Kissel's boy was moving in once again.

Time seemed to slow for Nada as she spurred her reflexes and senses into a heightened state. She had been trained to react quickly and deliberately, and now she decided to use that training to help the waif.

Nada slipped a dagger from her boot as she grasped the pipe with her free hand and leaned out as far as she could. Her own dagger ready to fly, Nada waited for the waif's shoulders to tighten for the throw.

The boy moved in, coins in hand.

The girl's muscles tightened.

Nada threw her dagger.

Kissel's boy tossed his coins.

The waif's arm whipped forward just as the bobbers pelted her in the back of the neck. She pitched forward slightly from the impact as the knife left her hand. But before the blade flew more than a foot, Nada's blade ricocheted off of it, sending the waif's blade into a pile of boxes in the corner of the alley.

Nada's dagger flew straight to the wall, looking for all the world as if it had come from the hand of the waif. It caromed off one of Kissel's blades, popping it out with such force that it landed five feet from the wall, and then imbedded itself right below the bully's last blade.

Nada's blade quivered after the impact, waving back and forth across the hilt of Kissel's last knife, which had been loosened from the previous throw and now hung at a precarious angle. Slap. Slap. Slap. The bully's last knife slipped out of the wall and clattered to the ground.

Kissel, who had been watching the wall the whole time, just stood there, unable to speak. His boy was busy picking up the coins again. But the girl—the dirty, rag-covered waif—looked right up at Nada, and then smiled.

Nada smiled back and then reached up to the roof and flipped her body onto the shingles in a single, fluid move.

"Remind you of someone?"

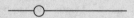

The voice had come from behind her. Nada tensed slightly, but she didn't jump. A good assassin doesn't surprise quite that easily. Besides, the voice had a familiar, gravelly quality to it, like someone speaking while trying to swallow small pebbles.

"Trying to sneak up on me again, Ranald?" asked Nada. She turned to face her mentor, but stayed low on the roof in case he had any other surprises for her.

Ranald the Sly stood there, nonchalantly leaning on his staff. A smirk played across his jackal-like face, traveling down one side of his long snout, across his long fangs, and then back up the other side. "And it was far too easy," he replied. The sibeccai's pointed ears curled slightly, indicating mild disapproval. "Especially for an apprentice who is late for her own Lifequest ceremony."

"I knew you were there," she lied, keeping her voice level and her shoulders relaxed to give the statement the appearance of truth. "You arrived just after the girl's second throw," she guessed. That was when she'd been most distracted by the game.

"A good guess, but off by one throw," said Ranald. "I'm glad to see that some of what I've taught you since pulling you from this very alley did sink in, though. I could barely tell you were lying. And I did arrive in time to see a shot worthy of one about to pass from apprentice to full assassin."

"Thank you, Master Ranald," said Nada. She bowed low in front of her master, but turned her head ever so slightly to keep her eyes on the sibeccai. Nada was ready when the black staff flashed out toward her feet. She rolled forward inside the arc of the weapon and came up with daggers in hand, their points stopping just inches from Ranald's fur-covered stomach.

A moment passed as Nada breathed heavily, yet silently. Then she was slammed in the side by the sibeccai's knee as Ranald twisted away from the blades and kicked at his apprentice. Nada fell to the roof on her back, helpless.

"You hesitated," said Ranald. His ears had almost curled over on themselves. "Never hesitate to take the kill when you have it in your grasp. That is my final lesson to you."

Ranald turned and walked across the roof, away from the alley. When he reached the edge, he merely stepped off, disappearing from sight. Nada picked herself up off the roof, secreted her daggers within the folds of her shirt, and followed her angry mentor home.

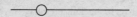

The Lifequest ceremony was a simple affair. Ranald, now wearing a shimmering black tunic and matching vest to complement his dark breeches, led Nada into a chamber she had only seen once before—on the day Ranald had brought her, shivering, caked in mud, and nearly naked, in from the cold. She'd been no bigger, and no better fed, on that day than the waif on the street today.

Today, Nada was still small and lithe, despite her burgeoning womanhood. She stood little more than five feet tall and carried only slightly more weight than the starving waif. But pearly skin rippled over well-toned muscles developed through years of training, and her short-cropped, black hair framed full, round cheeks earned in the dining hall.

Instead of the rags of her youth, Nada wore black pants, a tunic, and a vest, much like Ranald's, although her fabrics didn't shimmer in the firelight. The clothes were loose, with plenty of folds for daggers. But nobody brought weapons into this chamber, and Nada felt even more naked today without her weapons than she did in her rags years earlier.

A ring of tall candles illuminated the middle of the room. Ranald walked through the ring of light and bowed in front of a dais at the other end of the chamber. Nada couldn't see the chair on top of the dais, or its occupant, but she knew that it—and he—was there.

Ranald backed away from the dais and stood to the side to let Nada approach. The young apprentice walked through the light, which seemed almost blinding in the otherwise dark room, and came out on the other side before the dais. She bowed low, keeping her eyes on the floor this time. No one was allowed to look upon the face of the master.

"Present your hand, young apprentice."

Nada straightened, but kept her eyes on the floor. She stuck her hand, palm up, into the darkness in front of her. Even though she sensed what was coming, the muscles in Nada's shoulders and arm tensed right before she felt the flesh of her palm sliced open.

She fought the reflex to pull her hand back or to clench her fist to stop the bleeding. The voice boomed at her again. "Close your hand and state the pledge." The voice echoed off the walls, seeming to come from all around her.

Nada closed her hand around the blade, which still bit into her flesh. She and Ranald had practiced this part many times in the last two weeks, but he had said nothing about the dagger. She ignored the pain and intoned, "I, Nada Flesher, forswear any and all allegiances of the past and pledge my life to you, my prince, and to your element, and to the unending work of the Nightwalkers."

After she was finished, silence filled the room for a moment that seemed to stretch into an eternity. She hardly breathed, and dared not even glance to the right at Ranald. She knew that if the prince did not accept her, her sibeccai master would become her executioner.

The voice boomed again. "Take this gift, my child, as a token of your acceptance into the element."

Nada now felt the full weight of the blade in her hand, and just barely held it steady as it started to slip from her grasp. She pulled her hand back to see a jet black hilt dripping in blood sticking out from her fist.

She kept her composure long enough to bow once more and turn to the side as Ranald had instructed. Nada kept her gaze on the floor as she followed her mentor back through the candle circle and out of the room.

Once the door closed behind her, Nada finally took the blade from her injured hand. She examined it in the hallway as she followed her mentor, barely watching where he was leading her.

The blade hardly reflected the torches at all, almost drinking in the light. She tossed it into the air and let it flip several times before catching it again. It was heavier than her normal blades, but so perfectly balanced that she knew she could throw it farther and straighter than any other dagger she owned.

In her reverie, Nada almost bumped into Ranald as he stopped to open a door. "Put that blade away for now," said the sibeccai. "You can play with it later . . . on your mission."

"Mission?" asked Nada. She was astounded. She didn't think she would get her first mission so quickly. In her surprise, she forgot to catch the blade, which stuck hard in the stone floor next to her foot. She yanked it free and slipped it in her boot.

"Yes," said her mentor. "I've been saving this one just for you." Ranald walked into his office and rummaged through some scrolls on his desk. After a moment, he stopped and began scratching himself under the arms and across his chest. "Bitter suns!" he exclaimed as he ripped off his vest and shirt. "I hate tunics. Waste of fabric, if you ask me."

"Not everyone has fur to keep away the chill," said Nada as she entered. She loved her tunic, and not because of the warmth it provided, nor because she was self-conscious about her now-blossoming body. She had given up that luxury on the streets. And while her black clothes helped her hide in the shadows and gave her a place to secret her many daggers, they were more than mere convenience. She wore these clothes like a badge of honor. Like the Lifequest ceremony, receiving them had been a rite of passage from one life to another.

"True," grunted Ranald. "But I'll never understand why you humans insist on wearing tunics even on the hottest days of Eighthmonth."

"You said something about a mission?" prodded Nada.

"Yes," said the sibeccai as he continued to scratch at his arms and chest. "Call it a Lifequest present from me to you. I have the contract here somewhere." Ranald turned back to his desk and pushed the loose parchment around until he uncovered a brass scroll tube. "Ah, here it is."

As he handed the tube to Nada, Ranald glanced down at her bloody palm. "Get that bandaged before you go," he said in his gravelly voice, then turned back toward his desk.

"What do I do with this?" asked Nada waving the tube back and forth in front of her.

"Read the scroll and then destroy it," he replied. "The original contract is locked away, but everything you need to know about the target is right in there."

"Who's the target?" wondered Nada out loud as she turned to leave.

"I believe it's a runechild," said Nada's mentor as he closed the door behind her.

A runechild. Nada had always thought them to be a myth; fairy tales the children of the street told each other about wondrous people with magical powers who fought evil, righted wrongs, and protected the weak. The stories always ended with a runechild coming to save some lost child from a bully . . . or worse.

Nada returned to her room to collect her weapons and bandage her wound. It wasn't as deep as it had felt in the prince's dark chamber. In fact, the bleeding had stopped. She sat on her bed and read through the contract as she sorted out her many blades.

She had never really believed that runechildren existed. If they did, why was there still so much pain in the world? But there it was, named in the contract—a runechild who was interfering with the business of a Nightwalker client.

There was no mention of what business this client—a rather prominent merchant in De-Shamod—was conducting that had brought a runechild down upon him, but Nada didn't give that a second thought. If it were important to the completion of her job, the information would be in the contract, or Ranald would have told her.

It was best not to ask too many questions. "Don't get too close to your clients or your assignments." That was the first rule Ranald had ever taught her. Still, she wondered about the morality of eliminating such a force for good. It was one thing to intervene in merchant disputes. They were all scum who thought only of themselves and deserved what they got. But this . . .

Nada sheathed her daggers, placing her newest one—the dagger the Nightwalker prince had given to her—in a special sheath she had designed herself, slung hilt-down between her budding breasts. It was easily reachable through a small fold in her tunic, but virtually undetectable.

Her resolve returned as she finished her preparations. Even if runechildren were not a myth, she owed nothing to them. There had been no runechild around to protect her when her father practically kicked Nada out of the butcher shop, forcing her to find a life on the street. There had been no runechild in the alley to protect that little waif from Kissel this afternoon.

"If you want anything done in this life, you must do it yourself." That had been Nada's own first rule, ever since her days on the street. And so she had protected the children as best she could in between her duties and studies. And now, she would remove the myth that gave children false hope.

Nada climbed down a shaft beneath the Nightwalker lair, opened a secret panel, and dropped into the main sewer line under the grand city of the giants, pulling the panel closed behind her as she fell.

The effluent flowed toward the Ghostwash, the great river that cut through De-Shamod. Nada landed on a stone path that ran the length of the sewer and began jogging away from the river. Her eyes had grown accustomed to the darkness in the shaft, but she could run this route blindfolded if she had to.

After several turns and two long jogs through side tunnels, she came to a blank wall. Nada ran her fingers along the wall until she found a hidden catch. Pull, twist, twist, pull, and another panel opened up. Nada hauled her body through the small opening and clung to a vertical wall fifty feet above the plains surrounding the city.

The giants had built De-Shamod atop large mounds, presumably for defense. But the Diamond Throne's rulers were overly fond of decoration, so the sheer, paved walls of the mounds were carved with elaborate bas-relief scenes from the war with the dramojh.

Nada scrambled up the wall through a scene depicting the Battle of the Serpent's Heart. This was her favorite Nightwalker route. The writhing bodies of dying dramojh were striking, even in the moonlight, and the spines on their wings made for easy climbing.

The high walls erected at the top of the mound were tougher to climb, but with the aid of a couple daggers and a series of slits cut into the wall by the Nightwalkers, Nada reached the top with ease.

She crouched on the wall and scanned her surroundings. Her timing was perfect. She could see a sibeccai patrol moving away from her along the inner walkway. Nada dropped down onto the path and hid in the shadow made by the wall until the patrol was almost out of sight. She then followed them, matching her gait to theirs to mask her footfalls, and staying close to the wall to remain invisible in its shadow.

She trailed the patrol a short way around the walled city, then stopped and hid again until the guards moved out of sight. Nada checked to make sure the next patrol had not yet come into view and then leapt from the wall.

A conveniently placed flagpole jutted from a nearby building. Nada grabbed the pole as she fell past, twirled around twice to gain control, then used her momentum to fly up onto the roof. She landed on her toes and fingers, cushioning the blow and muffling the sound by flexing her arms and legs on impact.

She slipped around a chimney to hide from the approaching patrol. From there, Nada moved silently across the rooftop from shadow to shadow. She jumped across a narrow alley to the next roof and continued on.

The instructions that came with the contract said the runechild was meeting a contact in a park near the University of Se-Heton three hours past dusk. Nada was to eliminate the runechild and leave no witnesses. She would have to hurry to reach the park before the meeting.

The city was laid out in concentric circles, and she had no time to follow the buildings around to the Ghostwash, so at the edge of the next roof, Nada dropped down into an alley and crept out to the edge of the street. Several trees lined the cobblestones on either side, and a series of large statues separated the two halves of the boulevard.

Nada checked the street and then darted out of the alley to the shadow of a tree. She next made her way to a statue, hiding behind the massive legs of some long-forgotten giant hero. From there, a quick dash got her to the safety of the trees on the other side and then back into an alley. She grabbed the gutter and scampered like a rodent up to the roof.

Eventually, Nada found herself at the edge of Se-Heton Park. Bypassing the entrance, she jumped a low wall and made her way through the trees toward a small clearing that surrounded a fountain. Fire globes stood on poles around the fountain, casting light throughout the area.

Two figures stood together on the far side of the clearing, talking or arguing. Nada crept around to get a better look at her prey. The bubbling of the water in the fountain made it impossible to hear what they were saying, but it didn't really matter. She merely needed to determine whether one of the figures was indeed the runechild.

One of them was a human male with short, greying hair and a tangled shock of a beard covering his face and neck. He had wild, deep-set eyes that obviously had not seen enough sleep in a long time.

The tired, old human was talking to a large litorian male who appeared to be in the prime of his life. His mane was thick and had a lustrous, golden-brown color. The litorian was twice as broad as the human and stood at least a foot taller.

Neither of them wore armor. The human had on a simple white tunic and pants, while the litorian wore a braided vest and thick breeches that just reached the top of his leather boots. Nada had already decided which of these figures must be her target when the litorian turned slightly and she caught sight of some strange markings on his neck and cheek. They looked like tattoos burned right into the creature's brown fur, but they were in a script Nada didn't recognize. It seemed to move—just a little—independent of the litorian's own movements.

Runes! She'd found the runechild.

Nada pondered her next move. She should remove the old man first. He shouldn't take much effort. He looked to be halfway to the grave already. The runechild would be tougher. She saw no weapons, but litorians were formidable fighters even with their bare hands. Best not to let him get those huge claws on her at all.

Nada climbed the tree she'd been hiding behind, intending to eliminate both targets from the safety of its upper branches. As she crawled out onto a branch, the human turned, and she noticed a huge bloodstain on the front of his tunic.

She stopped and stared at the man closer. Could it be, she wondered? The wild beard covered his features, but the height and age were right. And the bloodstained tunic definitely looked like the butcher's shirts she remembered from her childhood.

She looked closer at the old man's eyes. Though sunken and rimmed by dark skin, they had a familiar slant, and there . . . Yes. There it was: the scar running from his left eye almost to the ear. The scar she'd given him by accident the day he tried to teach her how to trim meat from a bone. The runechild was speaking to her father!

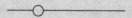

Emotions and thoughts coursed through Nada's body like poison as she looked at the man who had all but tossed her onto the street. Anger, hatred, sorrow . . . wonder. But through all the tumult, one thing was clear to her—Ranald had known. He must have. He'd told her he had been saving this mission for her. Ranald had sent her out to kill her own father along with the runechild. But why?

Nada had to find out. She now needed to know why the runechild had been targeted for assassination. She inched out onto one of the lower branches to get closer to the meeting and listen in on their conversation.

". . . but there is still no sign of her," said the litorian.

Her father began wringing his hands. The only other time she had seen him do that was while he sat next to her mother as she lay dying. "But you said the other children spoke of her."

"Not often," said the runechild, "and only cryptically." He grabbed her father's shoulders with his large pawlike hands. "The ones who would talk to me said they sometimes glimpse a young girl in the shadows, watching them. But when they look again, she's gone."

"Do you think she was taken, like the others?" her father asked.

"It is possible, but I do not think that is the case," replied the litorian. "The other children who have disappeared are never seen again."

Disappearing children? Did this have something to do with the contract? She thought about returning to ask Ranald, but knew that would only lead to trouble. No. Her answers were here. Her father was speaking again.

". . . can't find her, we can still do something about the others," he said. "We mustn't allow any more children to be lost."

"I have gathered some information about those responsible," said the runechild. "But it won't be easy to stop them."

"Just tell me what I can do to help," said her father.

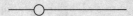

Nada heard a noise that could have been a small rodent, but she knew it wasn't.

"You broke the first rule," whispered a low voice from above Nada.

She looked up and saw Ranald sitting in the crotch of two limbs, his staff lying in front of him across the branches.

"You got too close," he continued, ". . . and you hesitated. I'm very disappointed."

"You knew," she hissed. "You knew my father would be here, and you sent me out anyway."

"It was a gift," said Ranald, that wicked sneer of a smirk running down his snout. "I thought you would want to kill him after what he put you through."

As Nada opened her mouth to reply, Ranald slipped through the branches. He caught himself for an instant by his staff, but then twisted the weapon and dropped silently to the ground.

"But now I see that he is nothing but a distraction." Her mentor grasped the staff in two clawed hands, said something under his breath, and then jammed the tip down onto the ground. A soft, red glow emanated from the staff as he moved around the tree.

As Ranald disappeared from view, Nada heard the runechild say, ". . . responsible for the kidnappings is a sibeccai named Ranald the Sl—"

"Butcher!" yelled Ranald as he sprinted toward the fountain. "I bring tidings from your daughter."

Nada gasped as she guessed at her mentor's intentions. She rolled off the branch, but landed hard on her ankle, which twisted, sending her to the ground in a heap. She could only watch as Ranald swung his staff into the back of her father's knees, breaking bones and knocking him off his feet.

The crippling blow barely slowed the magically enhanced staff, though. Ranald twisted slightly and whipped the weapon back up in an arc toward the runechild's head. The litorian sprang into the air and flipped over backward, away from the blow.

But the staff caught the runechild's foot, sending him tumbling to the ground back toward the trees. Nada pushed herself up to her hands and knees as Ranald turned and stood over her father.

He raised the glowing staff over his head, saying, "Your daughter wishes you were dead."

The moment froze in time in front of Nada, just as it had earlier that day in the alley. Questions, thoughts, and emotions flooded her mind as her mentor threatened to kill her father. Yes. She had wished him dead for years. But wishing it to happen and watching it happen differed from each other as much as dreams differed from nightmares.

In that instant, Nada made her decision. She pushed the distractions aside and concentrated on the moment. When she saw the muscles on the sibeccai's fur-covered shoulders tense, she didn't hesitate. Nada pulled the new dagger out from her breast sheath and whipped it at her mentor in one fluid movement.

The black dagger raced through the air as the staff arced over her mentor's head.

Ranald laughed.

The prince's dagger sliced into the sibeccai's flesh just below the snout, slashing open his neck.

Ranald's laugh turned into a gurgle. He dropped his staff and clutched at his throat as blood flowed over the quivering knife imbedded there.

Nada rushed toward the fountain as Ranald fell to his knees and toppled over her father's body. She grabbed two handfuls of fur between her mentor's shoulders and pulled his body to the side. She knelt next her father in the growing pool of sibeccai blood and grabbed his hand.

"Nada!" he gasped, his eyes widening in recognition and then narrowing into confusion. "Where? What are you doing here—" His question ended in a fit of coughing.

"I'm here," she said, wiping blood from his mouth with her sleeve. "That's all that matters now." The last few years melted away as Nada held her father's hand and looked into his blood-shot eyes. The arguments, the tears, the mindless insults thrown in fits of anger—all of the pain her adolescent mind had felt in the days and months after her mother's death—seemed so insignificant now.

Her father gave her a thin smile, but then his head lolled back and his eyes began to flutter closed. Nada clutched his head against her own and kissed his cheek. "Don't you die," she whispered. "I don't want you to die. Not anymore."

She felt his hand brush the hair back from her cheek. "I know," he said, and then cringed and squeezed her hand as another wave of pain wracked his body.

Nada looked down at his legs. A bone protruded from his right leg, while the left ankle had swollen to twice its normal size. "I'm sorry I walked out on you after Mom died, I—"

Her father shook his head. "I forced you out," he said. "It was my fault. I was so empty—"

"Your father has been looking for you for many years," said the runechild, who now stood over them. "He is a very brave man."

Nada looked up at the litorian, tears in her eyes. "Can you help him?"

The runechild nodded. He knelt down by her father's feet and held one large hand over both legs. He then touched the rune on his neck with his other hand and began chanting under his breath. The rune pulsed with a light from within. The light moved down the runechild's arm toward the hand on her father's broken legs.

"This will take some time," he said. "I am called Cheldorim."

"I am Nada."

"I have been looking for you."

"I was looking for you, too."

Cheldorim stared at Nada for a moment, and then looked back down at his patient. His hand glowed white as he massaged the swollen ankle. "I came to De-Shamod to stop a group of slavers," he said. "They kidnap orphans from the street and sell them across the lands of the Diamond Throne."

Nada thought back to the prominent merchant from her contract. *A slaver, preying on the children!* As the swelling in her father's ankle subsided, the runechild continued. "I found one such young slave who had been left for dead in the plains south of Navael. Sadly, I could not save him. But I vowed an oath to stop the slavers responsible for his death."

Nada's father fainted as Cheldorim pushed the exposed bone back through his skin. Nada gasped and began wringing her hands together. The runechild looked at Nada. "He will be all right," he said. "The pain will subside soon."

Nada reached out and stroked her father's hair. "How did you two meet?" she asked.

"I found your father on the streets of De-Shamod," replied Cheldorim. "He had been searching for you every night for two years. After his shop closed, he would spend the hours between dusk and midnight roaming the streets and alleys trying to find you."

Nada's shame threatened to overcome her, just as her anger had so many years earlier. She had never reached out to her father; never gone back to give—or to ask for—forgiveness. And yet, all this time, he had been searching for her, reaching out to her. If she had only known. She needed more time.

The bone slipped back inside her father's leg, and the jagged wound began to close around it. "When I told him of the slavers," continued the runechild, "your father despaired, thinking you had been sold and sent far away. But even in his grief, he vowed to help me fulfill my oath."

Her father's legs glowed for a moment longer as Cheldorim gently straightened them. After the glow faded, her father opened his eyes. Cheldorim and Nada pulled the butcher to his feet. Nada put her arm around her father to steady him on his newly repaired legs.

"With your father's help," continued the runechild, "I found out about this sibeccai here who works for the Nightwalkers—"

"I know," said Nada. She sighed. The only way to quell her shame was to confront it. "Ranald recruited me . . . and trained me . . . in the ways of the Nightwalkers."

Nada's father looked at her, shock and sorrow apparent in his eyes. "I'm so sorry," he said.

Nada shook her head. She had once blamed her father for her life on the streets and had felt beholden to Ranald for saving her—even though both of those feelings went against her own law of personal responsibility. Now, she finally faced the truth.

"We each choose our own path, Father," she said. "I blame no one but myself for the mistakes in my past. But now, it is time to set things right."

Nada hugged her father, and then turned to the runechild. She grasped his hand and said, "Your oath will be fulfilled tonight; this I swear, forswearing all other oaths. All I ask is that you swear a new oath."

"I cannot do so until I have completed the task already before me," said Cheldorim. "But I will gladly accept your help."

"I plan to help," said Nada, "in my own way."

Cheldorim glared at her, obviously not convinced that he needed that kind of help.

"There's only one way to stop the slaver," explained Nada, "and it has to be done tonight, before he knows that the contract on your life has failed. If you believe there is more work to do tomorrow, continue your oath. If not, then swear this new one to me."

Cheldorim stared at her for several seconds, but then bowed his head slightly. "What is it, my child?" he asked.

"Take care of my father for me, and watch over the children of the street."

"This I will do," he replied, bowing again.

She bowed in return and then turned to her father. The emotions she had held in check for the last few moments began to choke her voice now. She took a deep breath to hold back the tears. "I have to go now," she said. "I don't know if I will be able to return."

Nada's father grabbed her by the shoulders and shook his head. "No," he sobbed. "I just got you back! You can't leave again. Not so soon."

She hugged him again, and kissed him on the cheek as tears welled up in her eyes. "I must do this, Father," she said. "I have sworn an oath. This is my responsibility now. In a way, it always has been."

"I love you," he said. The tears running down his face mingled with her own. He hugged Nada tight against his body. "I won't let you leave."

"I love you, too," she said. "And that's why I must leave. After tonight, it won't be safe to be with me. Perhaps someday . . ." She sniffled, trying to control her tears. "Perhaps someday we can be together, but not tonight."

They hugged a while until Nada finally pushed her father away and walked toward the edge of the clearing.

She turned at the edge of the trees. The runechild held her father by the shoulders, keeping him from running after her. "Go," she said to her father. "Help Cheldorim protect the children of the street . . . even Kissel. I won't be able to watch over them anymore."

She glanced down at the body of Ranald, her new dagger sticking out of his neck. The reminder of her life among the Nightwalkers made her decision easier. She left the knife and her old life behind as she disappeared into the trees.

Nada jogged back toward the university. She stripped off her bloody clothes in an alley and stuffed them behind some crates. She then rummaged through the trash to find rags to wear before scampering up the drainpipe.

She made her way across the city, running and jumping from rooftop to rooftop and dashing through the streets. There was no time for stealth now. She had an appointment with a merchant. His slave trade would end tonight, and the children of the street would be safe again. She would make sure of that. But she needed to get to him before the Nightwalker prince heard of her betrayal—before *her* name appeared on the next contract.

MIRANDA HORNER

CLASH OF DUTY

Eloithe gathered herself for the attack, then sprang out of the trees at the mass of fur below her. The speed of the tiny spryte's aerial assault took her past two of the huge dire wolves before they even knew she was there, but the third one, the dark one the little girl had warned her about, saw her out of the corner of its eye and snapped at her wings with a deep growl that she felt in her bones.

Tumbling through the air, Eloithe kicked this wolf in the abdomen, her small legs a blur of motion. As it snapped again, she dipped down around its back and came up the other side, narrowly avoiding the sharp teeth of the lighter of the other two wolves.

Motion to her right caught her eye, and Eloithe climbed into the air to avoid the wolf as it threw itself at her. She glanced down at the three wolves, then swooped in for another flurry of attacks on the dark one, this time from her fists.

A whiff of fetid breath gave her a second's warning. With one last punch, which audibly cracked something in the dark wolf's abdomen, Eloithe tucked in her chin and dove down. Since the heads of the wolves were what she thought of as "human-tall," she had plenty of room to duck under the wolf's belly. She hovered briefly in front of the light wolf's snarling face, then darted left, to where the dark one stood. Before the light wolf could stop, it had stumbled into the dark one's wounded side. Momentary confusion among the wolves allowed Eloithe to land several more blows on all her foes. Then, as she took to the air again, the dark one pulled itself out of the tangle and, after nipping its companions out of the snarl, growled at her. The coldness and cunning in the wolf's eyes made Eloithe shiver.

You're the one who drove the others to the slaughter, she thought.

Eloithe dove back into the fray, showering her foes with kicks and punches. Two more blows landed on the side of the dark beast, causing it to whimper, but Eloithe was well and truly harried by the other two wolves. Weaving in and out of the fray once again caused some confusion among the two lesser creatures, though they all moved more cautiously now.

The dark one pulled out of the fight when Eloithe's multiple kicks caused more ribs to crack. Though she was tempted to follow it, the other wolves grabbed her attention by both jumping into the air after her.

Narrowly avoiding their snapping teeth and rancid breath, the spryte dove to the right. As she did so, she saw a large bush with inchlong thorns. Hearing her foes behind her, she hovered over the bush. Then, just as they sprang at her, she zipped straight up. The two wolves missed her narrowly, landing painfully in the thorns. Yipping and howling, they spent a few seconds disentangling themselves from that hazard, which allowed the spryte to get in a few more blows.

By the time the first wolf was free of the thorns, Eloithe had used the spikes tangled in its fur against it. She tumbled through the air, first kicking one thorn further into the light wolf's hide, then slapping another one. Concentrating as she was on this endeavor, the eruption of the third wolf from the thorn bush startled her momentarily. Seizing this edge, it sprang into the air and snagged one of Eloithe's legs with its fangs. Even as she felt herself being drawn into its mouth, she kicked her free leg against its nose and beat her wings madly. This maneuver freed her before she sustained anything more than a jagged leg wound.

Though pain arched through her leg, Eloithe took a deep breath to help maintain her focus and started in on the weaker wolf again. Avoiding further attacks from both wolves became easier, as the thorns in their paws put them off balance. Within a few minutes, Eloithe had brought down the light-furred wolf. The third one fled into the forest after its dark companion.

I've little time for these wounds to be slowing me down, she thought. *I can't let those murdering wolves harm anyone else. And that dark one is the worst of the lot.* Eloithe flew shakily to a nearby stream and rinsed her injured leg with cold, clear water. Then she bound the jagged wound tightly with a strip of cloth from her pack.

Wiping her hands on her rough cloth shirt, she headed off to follow her wounded prey.

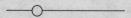

"So, elder, I'm not entirely sure the meeting went well. Your friend seemed to think I couldn't handle being out in the wilds all by myself." Phaeleana turned her head to look at her companion. She stumbled slightly as her bare foot found a root in the path. The quickling faen reluctantly put her foot down and continued walking despite the twinge in her toes.

"Careful, young runechild. Watch your path." The elder faen gestured to the forest around them. "Many obstacles abound, both in your journey through life and in your travels down forest paths."

Phaeleana smiled slightly. *My life has been one big path filled with tree roots—and I never seem to have any shoes.* "Yes, elder. But what do you think? Am I being oversensitive?"

The elder continued to walk, expression mild and eyes on the path. "You did prattle on: how much you enjoy walking through the forest, how you want to give every living thing a chance to provide meaning to itself and the lives around it. . . . Reeayean tends to be brief, as you might have noticed. She does get a bit impatient with those who repeat themselves."

"So, you're saying I talk too much for Reeayean's liking?" The runechild carefully picked her feet up and over the next gnarled root that crossed the path. The path continued to be wide enough to allow both faen to walk more or less side by side.

"Runechild, you talk too much for many beings' likings." Phaeleana looked up from the path ahead to catch the grin touching the eyes of her mentor and longtime family friend.

"Well, do you think she believes I'm earnest in my wish to learn more of the Harrowdeep and protect the lives within it?"

"Her thoughts are best left to her. That said, I'm sure you impressed her and everyone else nearby with your skills at creating those magical walls of yours."

The runechild grinned a bit at that. "Well, it's not the only trick I have, but thorny walls do seem rather handy. I just wasn't aware that she . . . ummm . . . well, I really did box her in good. You don't think she was too put out, was she, Elder Gareth?"

"Perhaps penning her up wasn't the wisest way to show your skills, Phaeleana. But I'm sure she's happy to have you here while she travels." The quickling girl's thoughts drifted to what Reeayean had said of her journey into the heart of the Harrowdeep: something about finding an "evil influence" on the wood . . .

She suddenly realized the older faen had stopped walking and fixed her with a serious stare. She brought her thoughts back to the present. "Now, remember that you're tending this area while she's gone, even if it's only for a week. Try to keep in mind that this is a continuation of your learning of the Harrowdeep, its life and balance. Reeayean chose to help this area reestablish its balance, and she did so at great cost to herself these past twenty years. I know it's not what you're used to, given your city upbringing, but you were born here, after all. It will come back to you. If you do well for this initial period, we can see about sending you deeper into the wood—if that's still what you truly feel drawn toward."

"Yes, elder. But couldn't I perhaps go sooner—"

"This is where I leave you, runechild. Remember all that I taught you of this area." The elder faen gestured to the expanse of trees surrounding them. "Much changes in the forest, yet much stays the same. It is up to you to uphold the balance in this area for your brief time here. Use your skills wisely."

Phaeleana nodded slightly.

"Oh, and one last thing. You won't have many people to talk to here, except for the stray traveler. Try not to talk anyone's ears off." He raised a bushy white eyebrow at her and waggled his gnarled fingers in something resembling a good-bye motion.

Biting her lip, the quickling nodded again. "I shall do so, Elder Gareth." She hiked up her robes a bit as she stepped over a large gnarled tree root. She had accounted for boots when she'd hemmed up her dark green robes. But her mentor had said it would be better for her to tread barefoot in the forest. She wasn't sure what to think of that yet. Her feet had no questions about the situation, however. They were objecting heartily.

The elder stared at her silently for a moment, then turned his back and walked away. Within seconds, his brown-robed form seemingly disappeared.

Nice trick, that. Lifting her robes again, she looked down at her aching feet. *All those years of Father working hard to keep me shod . . . and here I am wandering around a forest in bare feet by choice. I hope Elder Gareth isn't laughing at me.*

As she turned to take another step, a thought occurred to her. With a grin, she put her foot down and concentrated. Her limbs morphed and pushed her forward, causing her momentary dizziness. Fur sprouted from her skin, and her head elongated. Moments later, a large wolf with auburn highlights in its fur moved forward from her spot. It, too, had a wide grin on its face.

I'll get used to this forest living, she thought as she loped forward. *If I don't, I'll never get to go farther into the Harrowdeep.*

Eloithe alighted on a tree branch and looked down. The last two wolves had finally rejoined each other. She eyed them both, surveying their wounds. It had been a week since their last battle—her wounded leg had slowed down her pursuit more than she cared to think about. But her quarry had not recovered fully either. She'd hurt both of them badly in their last meeting, though they'd sustained a few injuries from her earlier frays with the pack as well. Over the past few weeks, she'd whittled their numbers down to these last two from a total of nineteen. Each fight had gotten easier, of course, given the decreasing numbers, but that did not prevent Eloithe from spending some time reconnoitering before joining battle. Caution had saved her more than once in past encounters, and that dark wolf had enough intelligence to avoid many of the tactics she employed in mass combat situations. *Malevolent intelligence,* she reflected. She'd seen more than enough to imagine how that wolf had acted as it tore Honeybriar's parents apart right in front of her hiding spot. *It kills just to kill, not for food. I don't know where that wolf came from, but it certainly begs to be destroyed—even were I not oathbound.*

Unlike the past clashes, which had taken place on the very edge of the Harrowdeep, the forest here, a bit farther in, consisted of larger, taller trees forming a canopy that prevented some of the light from penetrating. Where light fell, younger trees grew. As a result, the underbrush and foliage were very sparse. *No chance of thorn bushes this time around.* The ground was also flat, and no water source gurgled nearby. In her earlier battles, she'd used the advantages provided by terrain to great effect, causing wolves to fall to their deaths or drown.

Now, although she had only two foes, she enjoyed little in the way of terrain advantage. The tall trees had few low-lying branches, and even the younger trees provided little in the way of coverage. There was no underbrush to spring from. The dire wolves would probably hear her coming well before she was ready for them. But then, she'd faced worse odds earlier, and these wolves weren't the toughest foes she had fought recently. Perhaps she'd finish off these two, who were already wounded, then head back to the hamlet whose populace they had slaughtered just weeks before. The memory of that blood-soaked massacre of faen stilled her, and she dove down quickly to join battle.

As she'd expected, they heard her before they saw her.

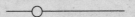

Gathering her haunches below her, wolf-Phaeleana leaped over the small brook that wound its way through the forest and loped onward. Over the last week of her stewardship of the wood, she had found traveling to be considerably easier in animal form. Wolves and bears were her favorites. She was on her way back to the cave where she'd been sleeping—a place that Elder Gareth had told her about—after a trip to gather some wild grasses, which she carried carefully in her mouth. While a cave wasn't exactly her favored type of abode, it was sufficient shelter while she lived in the area. Anyway, Reeayean hadn't offered up her own home—wherever that was.

These forest people, she thought, *they keep so many things close to their chests.* It was enough to make her stomp her paws in frustration. *But then, am I any better?* When it came to discussing her past or her sense of uncertainty about her path—well, then she wasn't her normal talkative self.

Her talk with the seer back in Erdaenos had finally convinced her to head back to the Harrowdeep. She hadn't been here since her father brought her to the city as a young child. "Find your path by seeking your roots," the seer had told her. "You know you've been resisting it."

And how long will it take to find my path? Here I am, in the Harrowdeep, but I don't feel any better. The restlessness is still there.

Although, to be completely honest with herself, during these past days in the woods, things had started coming back to her. Flashes of memory: sunlight slanting through dark trees, faen dancing amid the branches. . . . It didn't really make a lot of sense to Phaeleana, but she was hoping it would, in time.

Loping along the deer trail she had found, wolf-Phaeleana continued into the woods. She scared a rabbit at one point and wagged her great tail as she watched it flee to parts unknown. She passed beneath an odd archway formed by two intertwined trees. A flowering vine with tiny pale white flowers grew between the two trees, and a light scent drifted over to Phaeleana on the breeze. High above, the trees rustled in a stronger wind, and a few leaves drifted downward in the dim light. She made her way around the archway, not through it, and continued along the deer path. Soon after that, she noted two perfectly spherical marble rocks glittering with flecks of gold and headed southeast.

I'm so tired of not knowing where I belong, Phaeleana thought. When she reflected on her time in Erdaenos, she didn't even miss the city that had been her home. *They never understood me there, either.* She had tried to go about doing a runechild's work there, but people seemed to resist her every suggestion. *They didn't want me.*

An animal's whimpering stopped her mid-thought. Phaeleana's ears twitched, seeking the source of the sound. She located it off to her left and headed in that direction—somewhat warily, since she scented blood.

A large dire wolf whose fur was matted with blood both old and new rested nearby. When Phaeleana drew near, it whimpered more loudly.

Ah, now here's something that I can deal with. Poor thing.

Carefully and slowly, Phaeleana moved in to look over the dark-coated wolf. Despite its wounds, it attempted to get up and defend itself from this newcomer. She met its gaze and for a moment could not move. The creature glowered at her with hate-filled eyes—eyes that she was sure she'd seen before. But before she could dwell on it, the wolf lurched toward her. She sidestepped easily, and it fell over, its eyes rolling shut.

With a thought, Phaeleana morphed into a giant's form and examined the dire wolf. She—for the wolf was female—had numerous wounds, though most seemed to have come about by blows, not bites. Phaeleana gently ran her hands over the dark, blood-matted fur and pricked her finger on a thorn. She noted several more piercing the animal's skin.

Hmm . . . she's going to have a litter soon enough, Phaeleana noted. *Not right away, but she's starting to show.* The girl was pleased that her instincts seemed in tune with her new responsibilities. *Reeayean will be happy to see me protect her wolves, but what happened to this one? And why did it look at me that way?*

With a sigh, Phaeleana dealt with some of the immediate wounds while her patient remained unconscious. She had only about an hour before darkness would descend, and she had to get back to the cave. Having the wounded dire wolf, one of the few major predators in this part of the outer Harrowdeep, wake up before she could figure out what had happened wouldn't help her one bit. Elder Gareth and Reeayean had warned her that the dire wolves were important to the area, for more reasons than had been immediately obvious to her.

But then, in the city we always destroyed dire predators of any sort. Reeayean told her that when she first came to these woods most local predators had been killed, leaving the rabbit and deer numbers entirely too high. So she managed to train these dire wolves to stay away from settlements and keep the animal populations under control. She recalled her own sessions with Reeayean, pleased that the older runechild's training techniques had come easily to her. *Maybe I'm getting closer to my path after all,* she thought.

With one last look at the tracks in the mud and decaying leaves in the area, Eloithe drifted up into the air. Her nose ignored the slight coppery smell of blood and instead savored the clean scent of the trees around her. She hoped her reading of the situation was correct. It looked like the dark wolf had been found by another wolf and a barefoot giant. The giant had taken the wolf away somehow, though the smaller wolf's tracks had vanished entirely. The depth of the giant's prints had increased as they left the area, so Eloithe guessed it had lifted the heavy canine. She was dealing with one very strong potential foe. Dipping down every few feet to check the floor of the forest allowed the spryte to stay on track.

I can't let this one go, she thought, feeling the pull of her oath grow stronger, as always happened the nearer she came to fulfilling one. Eloithe remembered the agony in Honeybriar's eyes and the tears streaking down her face as the faen girl had haltingly told her what had happened in the village. Honeybriar had been the first child found among the carnage. There had been five other children among the living as well. Now Elvineth, a follower of Niashra and her former traveling companion, was seeing to it that these children got to a safe place. Meanwhile, it was up to Eloithe to fulfill the oath she had made that day on that bloodied spot: to hunt down and slay every last one of the dire wolf pack.

"I see no other choice but to destroy them, Eloithe," Elvineth had said. *"They have gone beyond redemption into bloodlust. I see no evidence that they struck from hunger. They will attack towns again. Their tracks head toward Morninglight."* And thus Eloithe had started her journey, following the pack and whittling its numbers.

As the tracks went farther into the forest and up a slight rise, Eloithe's luck stayed with her. The giant hadn't worried about leaving tracks. In fact, it looked very much as if they were seeking softer ground.

The landscape continued to make a gentle ascent as she turned due north. As Eloithe progressed, the forest grew somewhat shadier, and the undergrowth began to reappear, though it differed much from that found in the fringe of the forest. This ground-hugging vegetation preferred shade, and it looked as though no faen had thinned it out as they had closer to the tragedy-ridden hamlet where Eloithe had made her oath.

Because of the approaching night, the thickening undergrowth, and the need to keep a wary eye out for aggressive plants, Eloithe didn't notice the rocky outcropping ahead of her at first. She had dipped down closer to the ground, seeking out tracks, when she noticed that the forest floor had grown rockier than before. Unfortunately, that meant no easy tracks to follow. With a quick fluttering of her wings, Eloithe took to the higher air and saw that the approaching blackness was not merely more trees.

Hovering for a moment, she studied the area. A mixture of tree types grew densely here, and the undergrowth consisted of thorn bushes, climbing vines with dark violet blossoms that smelled both sweet and somewhat sulfurous, and a variety of fernlike plants in hues of dark green, brown-red, and flaming orange. The rocky outcropping started just feet away from

Eloithe, and she avoided the branches of nearby trees to get a closer look at where her giant had led her.

The stone of the outcropping was covered by patches of dark, mottled moss that glowed faintly crimson in the dusk. What little rock she could see was a strange silver-touched grey studded with what looked like little garnets. The faint footprints had led to her right before disappearing entirely, so Eloithe settled to the ground and walked along the rock wall. A musty smell grew stronger as she continued, and suddenly she saw the entrance to a cave.

Before moving into the cavern, she decided she'd better not take any chances. Using her innate magic, the spryte made herself invisible. Unfortunately, she had no magic to make herself silent as well. She moved slowly and carefully to avoid making even the slightest noise with her wings and feet.

Her caution paid off, though she wasn't entirely sure she understood what she saw. The cave entrance opened onto a small room. A lithe quickling faen sat in the middle of the chamber with her head bent forward. Her russet hair blocked her face from view, though it seemed to Eloithe that the quickling was braiding some grasses. A few hide blankets and a firepit suggested the cave was her home. Patches of moss on the ground and walls provided the room with a weak scarlet illumination. The spryte saw another exit from the room that led into deeper gloom. No dire wolf was in sight, however, so she assumed that it and the giant were in the area beyond her view.

Eloithe slipped into the cave, trusting to her invisibility and working hard to be as silent as possible. The patches of moss growing here and there inside the cave provided her with a spongy path. Unfortunately, the more she walked on the moss, the slipperier it seemed to get. She paused and looked more closely at the stuff she was standing on. Even her sleight weight had caused a slimy, phosphorescent liquid to ooze out of the moss. It now coated her feet, making them slick and, sadly, as visible to the eye as if she had coated them with dust or flour.

Should I take to the air? Eloithe wondered. *Perhaps the quickling is too distracted to hear the sound of my wings.* Eyeing her surroundings, she decided to trust in her balance and hope her feet weren't glowing quite as rosily as they looked.

Tense moments later, the spryte was peering into the exit that led deeper into the cave. A path led downward and around at a fairly steep angle, and the moss hadn't spread quite this far. Eloithe was about to start down when a loud yip erupted from a creature down below her. She heard the quickling behind her jump up. Eloithe backed into the wall and tried to make herself extremely small, but her glowing feet gave her position away. *I hate trying to be stealthy.* Eloithe refused to look down at her traitorous feet, instead trying to calm her mind enough to figure out what to do next.

"Hold!"

Eloithe decided enough was enough. She flitted into the air. But before she could zip down the tunnel to the source of the noise beyond, the quickling gestured, and a wall of thick and twisted thorns appeared in front of her.

"I said, 'hold!'" The quickling moved to stand before the wall.

Eloithe noted the rune marking the quickling's cheek. *Interesting, but not necessarily a good sign,* she thought.

"I mean you no harm, runechild."

"Really? What brings you here?"

"Well, ordinarily I'd say my wings, but I spent the last few minutes walking along this thrice-blasted moss."

The quickling's mouth quirked a bit, as if she wanted to giggle, then it grew studiously blank. "I saw that. I'm not sure how long the glow will last if you don't wash it off. You could have bright cherry-red feet for weeks to come. And your wings are tinted by it, too."

Eloithe shrugged minutely. "Stealth never has been my strongest quality." She gestured invisibly to the quickling's robes, which were also faintly red. "You're glowing yourself."

The quickling pulled her overlong robes around and peered down briefly. "Well, at least it doesn't smell bad. Not like some sewer slime I've gotten on me." Then she looked back at Eloithe's glowing feet and let her hem drop. "You mind showing yourself? Being invisible won't do you much good right now. And you still haven't told me why you're here."

Eloithe bristled at the complication. *You stand between me and the completion of my oath,* she thought. And the pull of her unfinished bond was getting worse with every passing moment. She clenched her jaw against the thought. *At this rate, I'll soon have no teeth left.*

Doing her best to ignore her driving need to push past the runechild, Eloithe let herself come into view. "Well, now, that's a story," she said. "You have a wounded dire wolf down there, right? I heard it yip just now."

The quickling's head moved slightly as if she wanted to look behind her. "You have . . . business with a dire wolf?"

Eloithe nodded. "Several weeks ago, a pack of dire wolves came down from farther in the Harrowdeep and slaughtered the hamlet of Silvernigh. All but a few small, well-hidden children died."

The quickling paled, and her hazel eyes widened. "Silvernigh? I know of it."

"Then you'll let me pass. I've sworn to destroy the pack, runechild. This is the last of them."

"Sworn . . . ?" Hazel eyes locked onto Eloithe. "No . . . no, I can't."

Eloithe continued to hover and stared steadily at the quickling. "You must have a reason, runechild."

Mild irritation passed over the quickling's face. "Call me Phaeleana. And, yes, I have a reason. Many reasons."

Eloithe waited, holding her jaw slightly open in her closed mouth to avoid grinding her teeth again. The silence grew as she watched Phaeleana pull back her riotous mass of russet hair with a quick motion and tie it back with the braided greenery she had been making. A pungent, yet pleasant scent drifted over to the spryte as the quickling's arms settled back down at her sides. The whole time, the quickling had watched Eloithe closely. "So, what's your name, spryte, or do you want to remain anonymous?"

"I'm Eloithe."

"I'd say that I'm happy to meet you, but you're hunting a creature that embodies what I'm supposed to protect."

"You protect violence, tragic death, and nasty surprises?"

"No! That dire wolf, if it's the last of the pack, is the only thing that'll keep local herbivores in balance with the rest of the forest." She gestured back toward the thorny wall. "If there's nothing to eat the deer and rabbits, they'll increase to the point where they'll start eating the crops of hamlets like Silvernigh. The dire wolves are part of the local . . . balancing factor."

"Then can you explain why these 'balancing factors' went all the way over to Silvernigh and ate the local nondeer and nonrabbit inhabitants?"

"No, I can't," Phaeleana said. "It shouldn't have happened. But, if you kill this last dire wolf, the consequences for other hamlets near Silvernigh will be, well, dire, too. Those settlements all grow a fair amount of their own food."

Sadly, this all makes sense, Eloithe thought. *But this is no ordinary wolf.* She recalled its hate-filled, intelligent gaze. *If I let it go, it will lead a new pack into Morninglight. And who knows where after that?*

Eloithe looked past the quickling to the wall between her and the wolf and remembered the giant tracks she had been following. "Are you and the dire wolf the only ones in this cave?"

"Well, yes, we are. Why?"

"I saw another set of wolf tracks, smaller in size than a dire wolf's, and a set of tracks that could belong to a giant." Eloithe looked back at the runechild in time to see confusion lead to understanding.

"Would you leave if I said they were here?"

Eloithe shook her head. "I'm sworn to finish this."

The girl looked agitated. "Oh, no . . . but I've explained. You don't know what killing her will do!"

"I know what she did, and I know what I've sworn." The spryte pushed away images of those who had died in Silvernigh and focused on the problem in front of her: how to get by the runechild and her thorn wall.

"You're really oathsworn?" Phaeleana gestured back behind her again. "You must kill her?"

"I'm sorry, Phaeleana, but my oath must be fulfilled." Eloithe fixed her eyes on the runechild. "I understand the dire wolves served to keep some sort of local balance in place, but they destroyed the balance by leaving their normal hunting grounds."

The runechild shook her head. "But, you can't just kill them all. Without them, things'll get worse!"

"You already said. The deer and bunny rabbits."

"Look, there are other . . . concerns within the Harrowdeep, should one tier of the food chain be eliminated," Phaeleana said. "These wolves also feed the predators above them." She shuddered. "Some of these predators are terrible. We don't want to anger those who live further in the Harrowdeep. You know, the darklings."

Eloithe had heard rumors of the darklings. The psychotic wild quicklings, denizens of the deepest wood, were said to be dangerous and unpredictable. "I see." She kept her eyes on the runechild. "And you are here to uphold that balance? Sent by the darklings?"

"Me? I have my reasons." Her expression furrowed at some thought. "And I've avoided the darklings so far. I came 'at an opportune moment,' or so said an old family friend. This is my task for now."

"I see," Eloithe said again.

"You should probably also know that the wolf you seek is going to give birth soon. I can train her pups to stay away from hamlets. Truly! I've learned how to train wild animals recently. Please reconsider!"

Eloithe hovered higher in the cave, which made the quickling have to look up. "Really?"

Hazel fire leaped in Phaeleana's eyes. "Could you not delay your oath just for a little while—"

"The whole pack must be destroyed, including young ones." Eloithe felt the strength of her oath surge through her, along with the memory of the aftermath of the bloodbath she and Elvineth had come across. She closed her eyes briefly, wondering if Phaeleana's need to protect the wolf was as strong as her need to destroy it.

"Listen to me now as I have listened to you, Phaeleana. I understand that you must do what you can for this wolf. Truly, I do. I know runechildren have their own path, their own calling, to follow. However, you were not there where the dead lay sprawled in their last defense of their hamlet and of their young. You did not see the throats and bellies of the young torn out. You did not smell the stench of blood and worse. A child watched this very wolf, the darkest of the lot, tear apart her parents. They killed for the blood . . . for the sport. This female you protect, though heavy with young, is beyond redemption. I do not care to think what its young will turn out like; I can't afford to. It is very intelligent, and it has a malevolence I must destroy now before more evil is done."

Eloithe cocked her head a bit, listening. "Speaking of the wolf, it's calmed down remarkably well. I'm surprised it isn't up here trying to get through the wall. It should know my scent quite well by now. I'm sure that's why it yipped earlier." She clamped her teeth, containing her oath-energy for another moment.

The quickling turned around, as though to look through the wall. "Yes, I —"

Eloithe darted past Phaeleana and brought her wings in tight against her body as she threw herself into the thorns of the wall. Pain ripped through her as the thorns stabbed her flesh, but Eloithe wriggled her way around and through them. She thought she had nearly pulled herself through when the wall disappeared.

"Don't! Think of the babies!" the quickling cried out.

Eloithe dashed ahead, ignoring the runechild and her own pain. The power of her oath thrummed in time with the blood pulsing in her ears. The wolf slumbered on a pile of leaves and evergreen branches at the end of the passage.

Abruptly, a gigantic bear stood in her path, crouching in the low-ceilinged tunnel. The spryte's forward momentum served her both well and ill, for it added force to the blow she struck at the animal's abdomen, but it also caused her to wrench her ankle in the process. Her vision exploded into light and pain as the bear swung at her, throwing her hard against the wall. Falling to the ground, she barely tucked herself into a roll and sought a weak spot to deal another blow.

This is going to take some doing, she thought. *More than I have. Best to focus on the true target.*

"Please, don't!" called out the bear in Phaeleana's voice.

Eloithe avoided another swing by the bear, then, with great concentration, dashed past it while ignoring the pain that even her slight weight placed on her wounded ankle. The bear was at a disadvantage due to its cramped quarters, but even so, the spryte only barely found her way past its huge legs and into the area where the wolf slept without taking another blow. Using her forward momentum from her dash past the bear, she dealt the wolf a mighty blow to its head and sent it to its final sleep.

"No!" she heard the runechild shriek.

Eloithe turned to keep her eye on the bear, but not fast enough. She felt its paws slam onto either side of her, crunching her wings and bones, and she blacked out.

"You don't know what you've done," she heard the runechild say. "Now it'll be worse. More deaths as the darker things come out of the deep forest looking for food."

Eloithe opened her eyes slowly and found herself back in the outer part of the cave. She was lying on some leaves. With care, she moved first one limb, then another, and found herself whole and free of pain. Not only that, the soft glow of an oath fulfilled suffused her tiny body.

"I understand," Eloithe said. "And I thank you for your healing despite our differences."

You feel the pain of seeing your balance ruined, runechild, Eloithe thought, *but this evil wolf had already ruined it before we met.* She did not regret her actions, but she did regret hurting this young runechild.

Phaeleana shrugged. "The pack had left its hunting grounds and killed an entire village. I understand what drove you to your actions, too." She sighed. "I just worry about what will happen now."

"What must you do to prevent worse things happening, runechild?"

"I don't know if there's an easy solution. I suppose I could find something to replace these wolves in the food chain. But I can't do that until I figure out what set them against the settlement. I just can't understand why they did what they did."

"There may be more here than either of us sees right now," Eloithe said, "This dark wolf was granted an evil intellect, and she led the others in the attack. Someone must have done this. But who?"

"I just don't know," Phaeleana said. "I'm pretty new to this. Who would want to harm the faen who live on the outskirts of the forest? I really wish I could talk to Elder Gareth. He gave me these woods to protect, and I allowed the balance to be destroyed! Now he will never take me farther into the Harrowdeep. And I had been so sure I was on the right path." She let her head drop forward, her hair hiding her expression. "This is almost as bad as I was when I tried to work in the city."

"You aren't sure of your path?" Eloithe asked. "I thought a runechild would know instinctively about such things."

"No, not really." A pause. "I just know that something still isn't right."

"Then maybe you aren't supposed to be here."

The runechild sighed. "I can't see for certain where I'm supposed to be. I must be an awful runechild." She looked up. "Look, I don't really know you, but I've been among those who hold their oaths dear before. Your oaths define who you are and what you do—though, I must say, they make you the most stubborn folk I've ever dealt with in my life. It doesn't seem to be that easy with me."

"The oaths we swear are indeed very important to us. We gain much while seeking to fulfill them, and we lose much should we become foresworn." The spryte began to pace. "As for your situation, you wish to re-establish the balance, for you were given the task of protecting it. But you're not sure your path ends here. Which obligation do you hold more dear: to your duty or to yourself? Or can they both exist within each other?"

A stunned look crossed Phaeleana's face. "I've felt . . . drawn to the deeper parts of this forest, but I tried to bury that feeling, telling myself I needed to take things slowly, like my mentor told me. But maybe you're right—maybe they are the same." She paused and looked thoughtfully at Eloithe. "We've both heard stories of the Harrowdeep while growing up. I need to get closer to it. I know that Elder Gareth means well, but I think I need to see the forest, and its deeper balance, with my own eyes and listen to it with my own ears now."

She looked over at the passage that led to the dead wolf. "You told me you felt this wolf's malevolence. I get the sense that something twisted—or tempted—these wolves from their original purpose. And where there's one, there may be more. I believe their original caretaker sensed this was happening and went into the darker reaches of the wood to look into it. She mentioned something about an evil influence she had to find, but I thought she meant hunters from the outer forest."

"If you must go, then you will need someone to go with you and provide protection for your journey, will you not?" Eloithe felt a sense of purpose forming in her heart and mind. *Perhaps this is where my own path will take me next,* she thought.

"Well, it can't hurt. Why? Do you think I should take Elder Gareth with me? I assumed he'd stay here—he's got his own duties and other students. Of course, he is much more learned in these things than I am right now. . . ."

"I have another thought in mind." Eloithe said.

"What?" Comprehension set in. "*You'd* come with me? You won't make it an oath, will you? I think I tend to . . . clash with those who stick to their oaths."

"Do you not, in your own way, have oaths to fulfill, rune-child? Isn't that what we dealt with here?" Eloithe gestured to the passage that led to the dead wolf. "While we have clashed today, I think we have both reached a greater understanding, and I dislike leaving you alone to deal with the consequences of my actions. I should help you rectify the balance."

Phaeleana nodded slightly. "Very well. You know, I feel much better now." And she did look as though her spirit had eased. "But now, I need to take care of the wolf. There are things out there that will find a use for her in this state, though maybe I should check her over more thoroughly in case she had a malevolent intelligent parasite. Elder Gareth says there are things like that in the deep, deep forest."

Eloithe raised her eyebrows. "I think you'll want someone at your back on your journey, Phaeleana. Sometimes spells aren't enough."

Phaeleana moved down the passage. "Perhaps you're right." Moments later, she returned. "Now I know you're right," she said. "Come look at this."

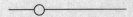

As Eloithe made her way down the passage, Phaeleana silently pointed. The dire wolf's body was gone. The runechild thought back to her first sight of the creature, its compelling gaze so strangely familiar. Again, a vision of small bodies dancing in treetops flashed through her mind. These people—they were faen, she was sure of it—had the wolf's hateful eyes.

In the wolf's place was a bundle of what looked like dried vines and a bone, held together with sinew. The spryte, shooting Phaeleana a surprised look, moved past her to inspect the bundle.

"I see a bone with some sort of rune on it," she said.

When Phaeleana didn't respond, Eloithe looked up. "What's wrong, runechild?"

The quickling took a breath and answered slowly. "That's not just 'some sort of rune.' That's *my* rune."

Eloithe sucked in her breath as her gaze flitted to Phaeleana's cheek. Her eyes registered her shock. "But why—"

"And it's not just a bone. It's a darkling fetish." She could see them again, in her mind's eye, dangling from the low-hanging branches, each bundle a component of the wild ceremony of the hunt.

A shadow behind the spryte moved. Lifting her gaze, Phaeleana beheld an elderly quickling male.

"Elder Gareth!" she shouted.

"Reeayean has returned," the old man stated. "I came to tell you that she's found evidence that the darklings are encroaching on the faen towns. But I see you have discovered the same thing for yourself."

"The darklings sent the wolves that destroyed Silvernigh," Phaeleana said. "And they know I'm back in the Harrowdeep." She pointed to the strange bundle.

The elder moved into the room to kneel down before his pupil. She kept her expression even, despite the warring emotions inside her. Eloithe hovered protectively nearby.

"Why do the darklings know my rune, Elder Gareth? Why do I *remember* them?"

"I was sure you were too young to recall any of it." His voice grew gentle. "Phaeleana, your father is quickling, but the woman you know as your mother is not your blood-mother. Your real mother was a darkling."

Phaeleana nodded, not surprised after all to hear the words.

"You were barely walking when your father ventured out of the Harrowdeep with you in his arms," Gareth continued. "He wanted to protect you from them, to take you as far from them as he could."

"That is why the seer told me to return here . . . to my roots." She stared down at the fetish. "My roots go deeper into the Harrowdeep than I thought."

Gareth sighed. "You have much ahead of you, child. Yes, your blood calls you farther into the Harrowdeep. Whatever the danger, it would be wrong for me to deny you that any longer. That time is over."

Phaeleana pressed her lips together and nodded. "I must find out why they call me. Why they seek to kill."

Eloithe landed and furled her wings. "Would you accept my help in this task?" she asked formally.

Phaeleana stared at her for a second, thinking of all they'd been through this day. *Well, this ought to be interesting*, she thought, then smiled. "You are welcome to accompany me, Eloithe," she said aloud. "I know I'll need your help to get to the bottom of this."

"We all have work to do." Gareth agreed. "We protect these woods. That is what we are." He picked up the bundle and placed it in the quickling girl's hands. "Just be mindful of *all* that you are, Phaeleana."

He motioned to Eloithe, and the two walked together toward the front cave. The runechild could hear her mentor's voice echoing back to her. "Now, who exactly did you say you were, my dear . . . ?" Phaeleana started to follow them, then paused to look again at the bit of bone and sinew in her hands.

This is my path, after all this time, she thought. *And lucky I am that I don't have to walk it alone.*

MIKE MEARLS

THE PEBBLE
BEFORE THE
AVALANCHE

I t was the twelfth day of Eighthmonth when Fralleg the Long-Minded first laid eyes on the small town of Vesper. Had it been the sixth day of that same month, or even the ninth, or almost any day of Seventhmonth, he would have noted the poorly tended fields, the abandoned homesteads at the edge of town, and the sullen, downtrodden buildings that drooped with sagging roofs, boarded windows, and cracked, dirtied whitewash.

But this was neither the sixth nor the ninth day, but instead the twelfth, the second day after Ka-Thordek—the giant standing next to him in heavy scale armor—had punched a litorian mercenary and incited a brawl. The fight had left Fralleg with a long bruise along his side, a still-aching lump on his head, and a burning desire for a cool bath, warm meal, and soft bed. The road can do many things to a traveler, even one as wise as a runechild. Dulling the senses or blinding the eyes to signs of trouble was perhaps the least of the dangers Fralleg had faced in the past months.

Despite the heat, the two pressed on at a faster pace. Fralleg's ancestors were feral, jackal-like beasts of the desert before the giants crafted them into the sibeccai: humanoid aides and allies—though none of his wild ancestors bore the mystic rune that marked his dark fur in a white, perfectly shaped patch upon his forehead. Ka-Thordek had the strength of three sibeccai, the product of endless hours of training and sparring in the fellowships of battle, but the heat sapped even his stamina.

Hastened with a renewed sense of purpose, the companions strode down Vesper's main road. Sullen-eyed humans peered at them from windows facing the street, their eyes tracking the pair with nervous expectancy. Fralleg stopped short just outside the lone inn, the one place in town that showed any signs of prosperity. He stopped himself in mid-stride, like an actor caught out of place on stage just as the curtain unexpectedly rises. He glanced over the run-down buildings, the expectant eyes peering back at him. Well, not at him, he noted, but at the towering Ka-Thordek and the twin steel axes that hung from his belt. The giant reached down to place a hand on his shoulder.

"Is there anything wrong, Fralleg?" he said in his deep baritone, resting his hands on his axes. "This doesn't look like the liveliest stop we've seen, but it should do well enough."

Fralleg stopped and closed his eyes, casting his mind into the akashic memory, the collected pool of all knowledge that his years of careful training and study allowed him to access. He saw in his mind's eye a bustling town in the midst of a harvest celebration. Garlands and wreaths hung from the balconies that jutted over the streets from the wood and stone dwellings. Something was wrong. Vesper had long been known as a prosperous, though backwater, town.

The sibeccai's eyes snapped to attention, his ears tense. "I believe that the town has dispatched a welcoming committee, or perhaps two, to greet us," Fralleg said as he turned to look up, down, and then again up Vesper's main road. The sibeccai's keen ears, a talent amplified and strengthened with his rebirth as a runechild, detected the sound of heavy, military-quality boots trying, and failing, to move quietly along the alleys nearby. Metal armor jangled and sang, while low, angry voices barked orders. Not one group, but two small ones, no more than three men each. In an instant, the town's decaying state, the mixture of fear and hope in the eyes of the folk who even now watched them from the windows, the news of bandit kings and skirmishes in this region in the wake of the great fires—all these pieces came together in Fralleg's road-weary mind like a jigsaw puzzle.

"I hear two parties approaching, one from each end of the street. They are armed with clubs, and perhaps have murderous intent on their minds. Since they are only a total of six, I thought perhaps I would leave you out here to welcome them alone," Fralleg said, turning to the inn that, mere moments before, had beckoned like a welcoming beacon. "I'll handle our rooms."

The giant crossed his arms and squinted his eyes in puzzlement at the sibeccai. "Are you sure? You're usually better suited to welcomes than I. And you do remember the litorian?"

Fralleg rubbed his side gingerly, the bruise still a sharp reminder of that episode. "Of course. The litorian. Maybe that's why I'll ask about a room while you stay out here."

Ka-Thordek shrugged, smiled, and took a spot in the middle of the street. He stretched his arms and legs like an athlete preparing for a race. Two groups of humans swaggered from alleys both up and down the street from him. They glared at each other and readied their cudgels, giving the giant the distinct feeling that he was an outsider caught in someone else's fight. He didn't have to be a champion of war, a herald of battle, to see that both groups struggled to figure out whether they were here to fight him or each other. Ka-Thordek smiled. If they couldn't make up their minds, perhaps he would have to do it for them.

Fralleg ducked into the inn, eager to escape the carnage about to break out in the street. For once, he was happy that Ka-Thordek never questioned the opportunity to practice his fighting skills. If the giant had stopped to wonder why Fralleg had, for the first time since their strange partnership began, set him up for a fight, the thugs may have heard too much.

The inn was cool and dark compared to the blistering heat outside. A lone human sat at the bar, his long, lanky legs propped atop it as he leaned far back in his chair, a narrow scabbard dangling from his belt. Judging from the rickety, broken furniture in the common room, this place had seen rough use lately. Fralleg looked for any sign of a barkeep.

"Greetings. I was wondering if the innkeep was about?" he asked the man seated at the bar.

"He hid out back as soon as he saw you and your friend outside his window. It isn't every day that a runechild and a herald of battle walk into Vesper. Not that I'm complaining. I can serve myself well enough," he said as he leaned over to pour a fresh mug of ale. "The current regime doesn't take kindly to strangers," said the man. "I'm Toren Longstrider."

Toren, his mug now full to the brim, swung his legs to the floor and sprang to his feet in one smooth motion, the crest of foam in his cup remaining perfectly still. Even Fralleg could see that he was a trained swordsman. Ka-Thordek undoubtedly could have named Toren's fighting school and perhaps even the swordmaster he studied under.

"What brings you to Vesper? You don't seem like a local," Fralleg said.

"Well, the current regime isn't into civic improvement. With the giants busy dealing with the fires, the gangs have decided to take a more active role in running things here. Once thieves had the decency to stay in the gutter where they belong," Toren said, pausing to take a long draw from his mug. "There's been a gang war here for as long as anyone can remember, and without the giants to oversee things, the crime bosses have decided to play at being generals. All the fighting in the streets has folks scared."

"And where do you fit in?"

"I don't. I'm here to slip a blade into Xu-Harzad's side," Toren said as his hand strayed to his sword's pommel. "He deals in slaves, and I don't like slave traders. Haskar is the other crime boss in town, and he's not much better. I've tried to see about raising the local folk against them, but they're like a pack of whipped dogs, no fight in them," Toren said. He paused for a moment and laughed. "That must be one of the drawbacks to being a runechild. Wherever you go, people throw their troubles at you."

"I'm used to it. Besides, I believe my friend is about to involve me in Vesper's troubles, whether I want to be or not."

The two studied each other for a long moment before their concentration was broken, along with the inn's front window, as Ka-Thordek tossed aside one of the men attacking him. The six thugs were no match for Ka-Thordek. As a champion of war, he could defeat twice their number, though not without risk. Luckily for Ka-Thordek, they let their mistrust get the better of them. The first group charged in while the second stood back, giving the giant enough time to dispatch the men piecemeal. The giant strode through the inn's front door, stooped to pick up the man and toss him back through the window like a sack of refuse, and smiled at Toren.

"You studied at the Darting Swallow school. I can tell from the way you're standing," he said as he approached the bar. "Let me have a drink, and we can have a practice duel in the street. It's been six weeks since I've laid eyes on a real warrior," the giant said as he reached over to pour himself some ale.

"I think you're going to have more pressing concerns in a few minutes," Toren replied. He gestured with his mug toward the shattered window. Outside, one of the badly beaten thugs pulled himself from the ground, staggered across the street, leaned against a building, then broke into a ragged jog back in the direction he'd come. "That's Luka, one of Xu-Harzad's men. Knowing Xu-Harzad, he'll send a dozen armed and armored men to deal with you. And knowing Haskar, he'll do the same just to keep an eye on what Xu-Harzad's up to."

The giant shot a puzzled look at Fralleg.

"The town's under the control of two competing crime bosses. We have much work to do here," Fralleg said.

Ka-Thordek smiled and patted his axes. It'd been a while since he had a chance to use them. "And again you have led me to a glorious battle, as was foretold."

"Let's not get ahead of ourselves. Both bosses have spies everywhere, and they probably had more men on the way already," Toren said, discarding his mug as he finished his drink. "We may want to run out the back door, and I think . . ."

Toren's voice trailed off as something outside the inn captured his attention. Fralleg and Ka-Thordek both followed his gaze to see a small crowd gathered outside. Humans, sibeccai, and even a few faen clustered in the street. An elderly man moved through them, the others parting before him in a sign of deference.

The old man stopped in front of the inn's door, his hand shielding his eyes from the noonday sun as he looked within. "Whoever you are, you've bought yourself a lot of trouble. There are more men on their way, and they don't mean to keep their blades sheathed this time. You might do best to leave."

"If there's trouble, it would be best if you stayed out of the way," said Fralleg. "I can't have innocent blood on our hands."

"Innocent? These folk can fight well enough. If they tire of the bandits who run this town, let them join us in battle against them," said Ka-Thordek as he stood to survey the crowd. "The spirits of war will guide them to a glorious death or a mighty victory. What shame do they face in either result?" said Ka-Thordek as he turned to Fralleg. He pointed to the tables and chairs in the inn. "They can scrounge enough weapons to defeat both sides with the three of us fighting alongside them. The men I fought were barely trained rabble."

Ka-Thordek's speech rippled through the crowd, sparking a low murmur of agreement, argument, and discussion. The old man stood a little taller, as if Ka-Thordek's speech had awakened a fire long dormant within him. "I'm Jurek. Once I was mayor here, but crime lords run things now." The man pinned Fralleg with his gaze. "Do you really think we have a chance?"

Fralleg saw the hope rising in the crowd, but at the same time he could not ignore their ragged clothes and the farm tools or crude clubs they carried. Against armed mercenaries, they would stand little chance. Ka-Thordek had fought on a dozen battlefields. In his eyes, anyone who felt uncomfortable taking on three men at once was a rank amateur. The villagers were perhaps ready to make a stand, but were they prepared for the possibility of the glorious death that Ka-Thordek's course of action offered?

"No. It's best if you hid. We can't afford an open battle now, not while we are unprepared. The warriors are almost upon us, and time is too short," said Fralleg, his ears twitching.

"But we can help you. Let us end this now," pleaded Jurek. Something about the man's tone called Fralleg back into the seas of the akashic memory. He saw Vesper in the old days, during the giants' wars against the dramojh. He saw an approaching army of liberation, an armory looted, townsfolk armed and ready for combat, the oppressors marching through the streets to battle, their flanks exposed, their generals caught unaware.

"The time is not yet right. The giants are still over the horizon, but perhaps tomorrow you'll see their banners," Fralleg said.

Jurek gave Fralleg a long, hard look. "The giants are distracted. We've received no news of their return. Do not speak of false hopes."

"I do not speak of hopes. I speak of history. Those who remember the past can learn to repeat it. But not until tomorrow."

Understanding broke over Jurek's face like the dawn. The creases of fear and worry melted away as a smile broke over his face. "Yes, history. We know it well here, though perhaps lately we have forgotten."

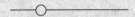

Fralleg kept watch out the inn's small, second story window while Toren and Ka-Thordek struggled to maneuver the ladder into place beneath the trapdoor. He could see warriors in mail moving down the street toward the inn. He cast a glance down to the main room. From the stairs, he could see both the front door and the second floor hallway where Ka-Thordek finished positioning the ladder. If they could make it to the roof, they could leap from building to building and escape. Toren had proposed an alliance and, for good or ill, Fralleg accepted. They needed all the friends they could find, and they seemed to be stuck in this situation together.

With a loud, groaning snap, the ladder gave way beneath Ka-Thordek's weight. The three froze, indecision locking them in place for a brief, critical moment.

"Toren, downstairs, quickly. Distract them while I think of something. Perhaps we can talk our way out of this," said Fralleg.

Toren sprinted for the stairs, leaping over the banister to sail into the common room just as the front door shattered open. Three men clad in boiled leather and carrying crossbows surged through it into the room. Two men leaped through the broken front window. They swung their weapons to bear on Toren as splintered timbers from the crumpled door clattered to the floor. Another dozen men rushed toward the inn from the street, swords, axes, and crossbows at the ready. Fralleg loosed his mace in his belt while Ka-Thordek reached for his axes. As Toren hit the floor, he stood straight up, his hands above his head.

"Don't shoot!" he yelled.

The crossbowmen hesitated, the weapons trained on Toren's chest. Several more men rushed up the stairs, their bows trained on Fralleg and Ka-Thordek.

"Look, I'm here with a runechild, for Niashra's sake." Toren paused for a long moment pregnant with impending violence. After a single moment of an eternity, he spoke. ""We're here for the head of Thrull Haskar, foe of your lord Xu-Harzad. That bastard has it coming!"

The grim-faced bandit peered at Fralleg, Ka-Thordek, and Toren from across the table. He sneered and scratched his stubble, thrilled to not have to deal with Ka-Thordek's axes but perplexed as to how his master was going to take this most unexpected development. Still, he had the relaxed air of a man whose enemies sat ten feet away from him, and who had a dozen men behind him, crossbows ready to fire at the first sign of trouble.

"So let me get this straight," he repeated. "You claim that these two are your servants. They've sworn fealty to you, and you're here to deal with that scum Haskar. You want to work for Xu-Harzad?"

"That's right. I've heard of this Thrull Haskar, and the world would be better off without him," answered Fralleg. "With the town under Xu-Harzad's control, the people will be safe."

The bandit's second-in-command choked back a laugh. "You've heard of Thrull Haskar but you don't know nothing about Xu-Harzad?" The commander answered his second's question with a quick, hard elbow to his mid-section.

"Obviously this Fralleg here has heard of him. Why else would he be so willing to leave Vesper in his hands? Our boss is interested only in fixing things as fast as possible. With Thrull Haskar out of the way, things can finally get back to normal," the leader said. His eyes narrowed as he leaned forward toward Fralleg. "You haven't been talking to folks around here, have you?"

Fralleg smiled and shook his head. "I'm afraid we were jumped by Haskar's men before we could, but there's no reason to doubt you. As Toren explained, Ka-Thordek didn't realize that your men were there to help him. I'm sure that if Xu-Harzad was poorly suited to run the town, I would've heard about it."

Fralleg never felt comfortable lying, but at this point he didn't have much of a choice. That damnable fool Toren had put him in this position. Fralleg saw that his stratagem, though obviously the product of an addled mind, was cunning on two counts. First, it forced Xu-Harzad's men to consider a viable alternative to fighting Ka-Thordek. They saw the carnage outside the inn, and it didn't take much imagination to connect it to the giant. Second, and perhaps more importantly, his announcement had rendered Fralleg speechless with surprise long enough for him to embellish the lie with a few details, information that Fralleg would need to carry off his end of the deception.

The bandit smiled, revealing a gaping row of darkness punctuated by a single tooth jutting from his lower gums. "Well then, why don't we take you to the boss? You gents can follow ahead of us. Horth," he said, looking to his second, "take two of the more expendable boys and put 'em up front with these three. Everyone else marches with crossbows ready." He turned back to the trio. "Any funny business, and we shoot. I don't care how well you handle those weapons, a dozen bolts'll slow you down."

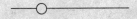

The bandit king's hall was a simple affair in a mansion near Vesper's small, riverside docks. Only the reinforced, heavily guarded stone wall surrounding the place set it apart. After traveling with Ka-Thordek for so long, Fralleg had to remind himself that not every giant was a muscled warrior who had fought his way from one end of the continent to the other. Xu-Harzad's gut bulged over his belt like an overripe watermelon ready to burst. His sallow skin had the unhealthy pallor that marked one given to drunken debauchery. His lank, oily hair was plastered to his skin, while sweat gave his face an oily sheen. Listening to the giant was a trial in patience, as he paused between sentences to stuff his face with mushrooms and seared meat piled high on a platter next to his makeshift throne. Fralleg could feel the tension rising within Ka-Thordek. The giant warrior's disgust and anger simmered like a kettle on the edge of boiling. If not for the dozen guards around them, Fralleg would have used a few choice words to unleash Ka-Thordek's anger and end the bandit's reign with a couple short axe strokes.

"My lord, this audience is an honor. We have traveled far to put that scum Thrull Haskar to death, and the presence of a sagacious, farsighted giant such as yourself is truly a blessing," Fralleg said as he bowed low. "I couldn't have hoped for such a ready, willing, and able successor to be on hand." Fralleg sometimes surprised himself at his ability to speak words that so utterly opposed the feelings in his heart.

"Of course, of course" said Xu-Harzad, pausing to wipe his mouth with the sleeve of his long robes. "I am glad to see that one with such foresight, skill, and," he paused for a moment as a he searched for the right word, "useful allies," he finished, waving at Ka-Thordek, "has arrived to help restore order. In fact, it is my intention to launch a full frontal attack on Haskar's headquarters tomorrow afternoon. After all, we must strike quickly, before any unforeseen complications could arise to ruin our plans."

Fralleg felt the giant's eyes bore into him and take on a particularly sharp cast as he spoke of complications. At that moment, he understood that Xu-Harzad was no corpulent, fat, lazy crime lord. He had a cunning mind, and already he doubted that a runechild would so eagerly support him.

Xu-Harzad continued, "I will, of course, offer you the honor of leading the attack. My men will fight beside you, and many more shall cover your advance with crossbows."

Toren smiled, "And an honor it is, to rid this town of such swine. Through victory or death, the lords of battle shall be pleased."

"Oh yes, they shall, my newfound ally. They shall."

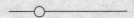

It wasn't until shortly after midnight that the three found themselves alone. True, there were guards just outside their door and a full squad below their chamber's window, but Xu-Harzad had assured them they were there to repel any assassins sent by Haskar.

"My friend Fralleg, we have been through many dangers in our time together since the ritual of joining. You know that I have never questioned your wisdom, and I've never said a bad word of you."

"I know, Ka-Thordek."

"Good. Then I want you to keep that in mind when I ask if you've lost your bloody mind." Veins bulged in Ka-Thordek's temples and neck as he struggled to keep his voice from rising to a shout. "You do realize he means to kill us in the melee? Dying in the service of a bloated toad is hardly honorable."

"We have bought time, my friends, something that we didn't have this afternoon at the inn," said Toren. "Haskar is a coward. You've seen how his men fight. The only reason that Xu-Harzad has not yet purged him is that he knows he'll lose too many men in the fight to keep a grip on the town. With the three of us fighting for him, we can soften the blow. And if we don't fight, we'll end up with crossbow bolts in our backs."

"If Xu-Harzad would push back the attack, we could at least sabotage his gang from within," said Fralleg. All through the night, the three had never been allowed near Xu-Harzad's men. Instead, they had been sequestered away under the watchful eye of the gang lord's most trusted lieutenants. Even with weapons at hand, the trio had never gotten a chance to make a break for freedom without facing certain death at the hands of a dozen swordsmen. "If we could only delay the attack."

Fralleg broke into a smile. "Xu-Harzad's plan has a fatal flaw. He wants Haskar to kill us for him. What if he doesn't want to?"

Toren's eyes furrowed in confusion. "What exactly do you mean? If Haskar runs, Xu-Harzad kills us anyway. We're too dangerous to keep around."

"Not if we somehow get to Haskar first. If he knows the attack is coming, he can strike at Xu-Harzad's reserves. And if Xu-Harzad's reserves go down, we only need to fight our way through the rabble that accompanies us in the first attack. Knowing how Xu-Harzad's men operate, they'll put the most expendable, least skilled warriors in front with us," Fralleg said. "That leaves us only with Haskar, and from what I've seen, he's a coward."

"I like this plan. It leaves us our own masters and, should death find me, at least I won't die in service to a spineless, fat villain," said Ka-Thordek.

Fralleg frowned, "But this still leaves us the problem of contacting Haskar. I couldn't hope to escape this place, and Ka-Thordek's strength is in fighting his enemies, not avoiding them."

"Leave that to me," said Toren. "I've slipped out of tighter spots than this." He moved to the window and opened it with a quick yank that sent the loud, creak of wood sliding along wood echoing through the night.

The guards in the courtyard below looked up at the window. "Just getting some fresh air, boys, before our fun tomorrow," Toren said to them. He looked down at them for a few long minutes before they finally grew bored enough to look away. Fralleg drew close to him. "What do you intend to do, Toren?"

"This," the man whispered as he reached out, grasped the eave above the window, and hoisted himself up to the roof in utter silence. Fralleg darted his head out the window in surprise, forgetting the guards below. He saw Toren's foot disappear above the roof, though not before it caught on a clay shingle just on the roof's edge with enough force to send it tumbling toward the courtyard below.

Fralleg's hand shot out, snatching the chunk before it could clatter to the ground. The guards looked back just as he slipped the shingle out of their sight.

"Just getting some fresh air, boys, before our fun tomorrow," he called down.

That he managed to hold his tongue from loosing a torrent of oaths and curses on the heads of all impulsive, foolhardy men was a testament to the patience and serenity of all runechildren.

Fralleg could not sleep that night, but Ka-Thordek slipped into a deep slumber with ease. *He's been in so many battles,* Fralleg mused, *he must be used to this.* Worry tore at his mind, leaving him barely able to focus on anything other than the multitude of questions that gnawed on his nerves. Would Toren succeed? Even if he did warn Haskar, what would that accomplish?

The runechild sat at the window, so lost in thought and worry of the coming day, that he almost caught Toren's booted foot full in the face as the human slipped back through with nary a sound.

"It's done," Toren said. "Haskar has been warned, though I'm lucky I managed to escape with my life. Xu-Harzad's men are everywhere, and Haskar hasn't been sitting on his hands. His men are in full armor. It looks like he hit one of Xu-Harzad's armories and grabbed everything in sight. I think we timed this just right."

"Let's hope so. If Haskar is too confident, he might try to take us down along with Xu-Harzad tomorrow."

"Better to face an uncertain death than a certain doom," answered Toren.

"I'd rather not face either."

"Well, we can always escape in the fighting and come up with a better plan. While Haskar and Xu-Harzad do battle, that should give us the opportunity to get away."

The day dawned bright and clear. The heat had abated, a welcome respite from the searing temperatures of the previous days. Toren, Ka-Thordek, and Fralleg walked abreast down a cobblestone road that led to Haskar's estate at the edge of town. A dozen ruffians armed with swords and clubs and clad in boiled leather jacks flanked them. Fralleg never turned around to look at the few dozen men that moved along the streets behind them. He knew they were there—he could hear the faint jangle of mail and the muffled grunts of the servants who bore Xu-Harzad on his wooden litter. The giant wanted to witness for himself the destruction of his bitter rival. He carried a long-handled steel axe across his lap, a weapon intended to deliver the final blow to Thrull Haskar.

The companions and their impromptu honor guard rounded a corner to one of the squares in town, and there before them stood Haskar's men. Nearly two dozen warriors in leather armor with long, sharp pikes stood across the open space from them. Only a tall obelisk scribed with some testament to a better time stood between the two groups. The ruffians around the companions came to a sudden, surprised halt. They gaped for a moment or two before hustling back around the corner. The three companions stood for a moment. The massed soldiers blocked any escape through the square.

"There's Haskar," said Toren, pointing to a slight, lanky, bald man wearing steel armor and carrying a bow. A half-dozen burly litorian mercenaries surrounded him. "Haskar!" Toren shouted and waved.

The bandit chief responded by drawing an arrow and letting fly at the swashbuckler. Toren leapt to the side, the arrow clattering on the cobblestones where he had stood a split second before.

"Back around the corner!" yelled Fralleg. Toren scrambled down the street, but Fralleg had to grasp Ka-Thordek by the shoulder and give him a strong tug before he followed. They wheeled around the corner and into a chaotic battlefield. Haskar's men leapt from alleys and buildings to attack Xu-Harzad's main body, a few firing arrows from the relative safety of the many balconies that extended over the streets. Though not as well trained as the giant's warriors, their greater numbers and the advantage of surprise gave them a critical edge. Already, many warriors from both sides were slumped still and dead on the cobblestones. Fralleg gripped his mace, desperately looking for an escape route, but finding none. Haskar's men swarmed from every avenue and lane, while the main body of both their nemeses stood before and behind them. The sound of two dozen booted feet marching from the plaza drove home their dire circumstances.

"Fight through them!" yelled Fralleg.

Ka-Thordek launched himself into the fray. His first few foes, warriors of both warlords, fell before his onslaught. His axes were a single, well-orchestrated blur of carnage. A warrior would rush in, only to find the giant's superior reach knocking aside his weapon, in some cases shattering it with the savage fury of his strength, leaving him open to a single, deadly blow from Ka-Thordek's second weapon.

Toren and Fralleg kept close to the giant's back. The human's rapier danced through the air, deftly parrying his foes' attacks, sending wild strikes just wide enough to leave an opponent's gut and chest wide open to a quick stab. Fralleg sent his mind back through the akashic memory, recalling the great victories of the ages. He used the hero-king's parry, Lord Etherton's counter, and the dancing, confusing fighting stance of the ancient Pharthan warriors to batter a path through his foes.

The three had fought their way close to an open alley when Haskar's men finally rounded the corner. True to form, the human bandit chief had little stomach for the fight, but he committed himself nonetheless. In contrast, Xu-Harzad threw himself into the fray with a vicious delight. He left a trail of broken bodies in his wake, sometimes leaving one of his own men in a broken heap as his anger carried him through the fray. Whatever hopes Fralleg had of escape disappeared with his arrival.

"You are doomed, Xu-Harzad! Your allies have betrayed you to me. Your death is at hand," Haskar yelled, his face contorted into a grim mask of terror mixed with exultant victory.

The giant howled in rage. Fralleg's eyes involuntarily journeyed from the bearded, mail-clad warrior who had carefully circled Ka-Thordek in a bid to strike the giant from behind, to the gore-covered Xu-Harzad, who towered above the men around him. His axe had been busy in the battle, feasting on the flesh of Haskar's men. The mad giant's eyes locked with his own.

"You! Before I'm done with you, you'll want to crawl back into whatever misbegotten whore spawned you," Xu-Harzad shouted, hefting his axe high. "And when I'm done with them, you're next," he finished, pointing at Haskar with such fury that the human bandit stumbled back as if the giant had poked him in the chest.

Xu-Harzad attacked the mob of warriors in front of him, swinging his axe in a wide arc that forced both his men and his foes to part before him or fall to the ground, split in twain by his bloodied axe. Fralleg saw now that beneath the giant's flabby body he had the strength and skill of a hardened warrior. He made a direct line for Ka-Thordek, who turned to him and bellowed a feral war cry.

Fralleg leaped at the mailed warrior, battering his shield and forcing him to give up any hope of striking Ka-Thordek from the rear. In the corner of his eye, he could see Toren struggle to hold four men at bay. His rapier sang, dancing from foe to foe in a desperate bid to turn their weapons aside. Fralleg's mind cleared as he delved into the collective memories of his people. When the mailed warrior chopped at him, he caught the blade on his mace just as Tharra the Hellhammer had done against the dramojh war captain at the Battle of Cleft Peak. The memory came to him so perfectly that he almost expected the mailed warrior to hiss like a dragon-kin as the mace crushed his neck. He threw his foe back and blocked counterblows from two more, his arms moving to the speed and rhythm of a duel fought centuries past.

Ka-Thordek had fought giants before, and he knew that his kinsmen were among the deadliest foes he'd faced. The spirits of battle awakened within him, quickening his pulse, firing his blood. His heart sang, his spirit soared. As a champion of war here, in the midst of blood, agony, and death, he felt most alive. Xu-Harzad swung his axe in a wide arc, forcing Ka-Thordek to parry lest he step back and collide into Fralleg, who was barely holding off more of the giant's skilled mercenaries. Xu-Harzad swung again, forcing Ka-Thordek to duck and roll forward. He sprang to his feet, too close to use his axes, but not so close that he couldn't smash Xu-Harzad's considerable gut with his right fist. Xu-Harzad stumbled back, crashing into a column that held aloft a short balcony that jutted from the building to his right.

Ka-Thordek leaped forward to press his advantage, raising his axes high. The crime lord rolled back, springing to his feet as he slipped a hand into his belt. He pulled forth a throwing knife and let fly with a flick of his wrist. Ka-Thordek, his forward momentum preventing him from putting up any guard, ducked back and to the side. Rather than plunging into his eye socket, the blade left a deep cut in his forehead. Blood spurted from the wound, washing down into his eyes and partially blinding him. Ka-Thordek stumbled backward to the opposite column, one of his axes clattering to the ground as he struggled to clear his eyes.

Fralleg was too busy with his own foes to notice the giant's predicament. He heard a crash of stone, a deep-throated howl of pain. He knew he was doomed. After all, Tharra the Hell-hammer had fallen at the Battle of Cleft Peak. Again and again, the mail-clad warriors advanced. Each time, Fralleg barely held them off. For each one he sent to the ground with a crushed helm or a shattered limb, another stood to take his place. His mace had several deep notches along its haft, and his arms felt as though they were cast from the same heavy iron as his weapon's head. Toren continued to hold his enemies back. Several of them had retreated with cuts on their arms and hands, but fresh, eager warriors took their place each time.

Ka-Thordek could see the dark, shadowy form of his foe through the blood that coursed over his eyes. "Now you die," Xu-Harzad growled as his shadow blended into the dark stone of the ledge above him.

Ka-Thordek reached back and grabbed the stone of the column behind him. He stood, ready for one last stratagem. He could almost imagine Xu-Harzad's porcine smile spread across his face as he swung his axe back sideways. Ka-Thordek caught the motion as the axe head slipped from the shadow beneath the balcony to the light beyond. That was all the herald of battle needed to duck and roll beneath the blow. Xu-Harzad's axe splintered into the column, sending shards of stone flying. In a single, fluid motion, Ka-Thordek rolled into a fighting position and leveled a single punch at the battered support. His fingers broke with an audible crunch, but not before blasting through stone and mortar. With a loud crack, the ledge snapped free from the building and crushed Xu-Harzad beneath it.

Overwhelmed with pain, blood loss, and fatigue, Ka-Thordek crumpled to the ground.

Fralleg readied himself for the last push. He and Toren stood back to back. Foes from both gangs pressed in for the kill.

"It's been good fighting beside you, friend. We've only known each other for a day, but I've already seen more adventure in that time than in the two months before I met you," Toren grunted between parries.

"I have that effect on people," Fralleg laughed. *If this is how it would end, then let me die in a way that would make Ka-Thordek proud,* he thought, as his aching arms held his mace up high for one final blow against his enemy.

Fralleg never had the chance to deliver it. A sharp twang sounded from the building above him, followed by another, and another. The warrior before him collapsed, a crossbow bolt in his back. Another warrior fell, then another. Fralleg could see Haskar, panic in his face. He yelled to his warriors, but whatever command he wanted to deliver was lost to the world, silenced by a dozen bolts to his chest.

The townsfolk were on the roof around them, brandishing the weapons stolen from Xu-Harzad's armory. The surviving warriors from both sides panicked, fleeing toward the nearest streets and alleys. The folk awaited them there with knives, clubs, and more stolen weapons. The fight was short and bloody, and at its end, the followers of Xu-Harzad and Thrull Haskar were no more.

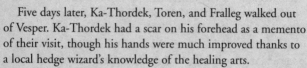

Five days later, Ka-Thordek, Toren, and Fralleg walked out of Vesper. Ka-Thordek had a scar on his forehead as a memento of their visit, though his hands were much improved thanks to a local hedge wizard's knowledge of the healing arts.

"Tell me, Fralleg," said Toren, "is this what it means to be a runechild?"

Ka-Thordek laughed. "You will learn that things tend to work out well whenever Fralleg is involved, but not before they get interesting. Why else do you think I follow him? The spirits of battle favor his every step and speed to meet him wherever he goes."

"The rune marks my past," the sibeccai said, "but the akashic memory guides my actions. I saw the simmering anger of rebellion in the townsfolk's faces, especially their leader. They were on the verge of taking back their town. We merely supplied the spark with our presence."

"And reaped the benefits! I've never met so many innkeepers willing to pour me a free drink, or so many young women eager to hang on my every word," said Toren as he turned a longing stare back to Vesper. "With the spirits of battle at your heels, is every week of your lives like this?"

Ka-Thordek smiled. "I can only hope so, Toren. I can only hope so."

WOLFGANG BAUR

NAME DAY

Pantomel's gold coins were long gone, fallen from his fingers like the leaves from the trees of the Harrowdeep. He still had his story, the one he told with a wink to the quickling maidens who every year visited the Seven Oaks. Under the spreading branches of the inn's oaks, by the warmth of its three fireplaces, faen young and old settled down to learn what went on in the great wide world beyond the forest. Pantomel was there to tell them. He took a deep breath and began the tale for the thousandth time. His stories hadn't been going over well lately.

"I was minding my own business, like, addressing Kortimea, goddess of spoiled breakfasts, and picking through the ruins of good eggs and bacon, when Janrick, the bearded lord of the runepriests, sat down at my table. He's twice as tall as I am, and ten times as fat, and when he sat, the bench creaked." Pantomel stood on the smooth storyteller's bench, his back to the bar, the better to project his voice and take the measure of his audience.

His listeners were almost all quicklings like him, though none had ears quite as pointed as his, or hair as purely, lustrously silver. It was important to watch their reactions—talespinners who loved only the sounds of their own voices rarely lasted more than a season at the Seven Oaks, or any other inn in the Harrowdeep. Pantomel had been telling his tales at the Seven Oaks for twenty years.

Pantomel had a taste for wine and an eye for lissome quickling lasses, dancing fast as hummingbirds, too quick for lesser eyes to follow. He bought them fine silks, danced the courtship dances, dangled them from his arm like ornaments, and dazzled them with baubles.

Tonight, the regulars ignored him, as they had heard every variation he had to tell. Of the new listeners, Marissae, a pretty loresong girl who had cast glances his way for a week, squirmed by the fireplace. Perhaps the story was getting a bit stale after all. He'd already failed to impress Marissae with the story of the bandit squirrel, the lost forester, and the outfoxed dog. The "breakfast story" really described how Pantomel kidnapped a human child years ago.

"I stood in the audience room of the runepriest laboratorium, on a floor tiled in gold-trimmed marble. The runepriest told me that he was looking for the spirit children of the Rune Messiah, children marked with a rune. Well, I'd seen a child like that—a human child of three years, probably barely walking. His parents had half a dozen others, and ignored this one. I often played with him while I was staying at the inn there. His parents kept losing him and I kept returning him, until the day when the runepriest told me he'd pay true gold queens and a charm to the one who brought him the child."

The real problem wasn't in the story of the kidnapping and fostering of the human child. The real problem was that, after ten years in the Harrowdeep, Pantomel thought that perhaps he'd made a mistake. The runepriests had been such nice people, so persuasive, so eager to give him their money. At the time he was sure of what he did, taking the human infant from a small hovel north of Navael and giving him—snot-nosed and squalling—into the runepriests' care.

Pantomel turned and gestured as he described an invented bit of heroism—"and I stole the sword from the bandit's scabbard in an eyeblink, and ran him through!" The story rattled on, Pantomel carrying the audience along on its flow as smoothly as a gentle current to the end. "And so I brought the boy safely to the runepriests' stony fortress, where they saluted me with trumpets and a feast. The scar-faced Janrick rewarded me with his own hands, giving me a bag of gold coin—for it's bad luck to break an oath, and twice as bad to break an oath sworn to a quickling."

The gold didn't last. It never did. Pantomel had spent every gold queen in the Harrowdeep but had never spent the other half of his reward, the part he never showed the audience. Janrick had said it was a magic acorn, a detonation containing a spell bound and ready. Pantomel kept the small lump of the acorn in a secret purse, tucked inside a boot. The quickling feared the acorn was a trick, a fraud, so he could never quite bring himself to explode or sell the detonation. At times, he thought he could smell the magic in the small nut, waiting for a chance to unravel, coil, and strike. Pantomel had considered using the acorn's charm against angry creditors more than once.

Now came the most important moment of any performance: the end. "And so, my friends, that's how I saved a child from hunger and neglect, and left the priests poor but happy." Pantomel finished with a bow and a flourish that ended with his hat of Organdian velvet on the floor, inviting any stray pennies, clips, or oak-minted faery gold to jump in. Pantomel held the bow for another heartbeat, hoping. The hat's fine velvet remained unmarred by the touch of metal, and Pantomel withdrew to a corner of the Seven Oaks near the kitchens.

Pantomel gestured to the barmaid for two goblets of honey mead. He was always paid in drink and a small portion of walnut loaf. It was all he'd have to eat until he found a patron willing to buy better. Pantomel waved to Marissae and smiled. She had drunk half his pay last night. Tonight, she ignored him and snuggled closer to a loutish human merchant wearing a woolen vest set with silver buttons. Pantomel muttered a small curse to Igraemir, god of lost lovers: "May she never trouble my sleep again. Please." It was always a good idea to speak respectfully to the Ten Thousand Gods, even when cursing, since you could never know when they might answer. Pantomel's stare did not discomfit Marissae in the least, though the merchant turned away.

Nodberry, the innkeeper's wife, stopped by his table; she'd often given him an encouraging word after a rough evening. "You know, Pantomel," said Nodberry, "I'm not so sure I believe your fostering story. I mean, have you heard anything from the child? Has it grown up?"

"Well," said Pantomel, "I'm sure he's a prince among the runepriests, or at least a valued scholar." Actually, he was sure of no such thing.

Nodberry seemed not to notice his hesitation. "A fellow came through here a week ago, said that runepriests are all butchers, cutting up the rune-marked. I'd believe you more if you ever visited the lad."

Pantomel thanked Nodberry for her thoughts, and ground his teeth as quietly as he could. She had a point. His stories were played out here; he needed new material. He'd been repeating the same tale for years, and everyone in the Harrow-deep knew his story. Maybe he had missed something important about the priests, those years ago.

Pantomel was not overly prone to reflection but, looking back on it, perhaps there were a few things that should have told him that everything was not entirely as it seemed. The child had been marked not just with any pattern, but with a silvery rune shaped like the oak leaves of the Harrowdeep. Pantomel was fairly sure that most human children were not tattooed. Though perhaps they were, and the tattoos faded with the onset of adulthood. Pantomel promised himself to pay closer attention to their markings next time he saw a child.

Pantomel jingled the coins in his purse, to appease the god of small change. The Harrowdeep no longer seemed such an idyll. Marissae would have to wait a long time before he bought her mead again. He would go find a new story, or at least a new ending to the one he had.

The road south was gentle with spring winds. Crocus and honeydrop blossomed white, gold, and purple all along the way. Pantomel ate acorn flour, gathered moldering chestnuts from the previous year, burglarized a squirrel's cache of nuts, and liberated a plate of meat dumplings from a neglectful farmwife. He slept in barns and shepherds' huts, caught a cold, and sniffled the last two days' march.

The city gate was crowded with farmer's carts, pilgrims, and herds of wet humans, goats, and sheep. Pantomel walked under one of the carts, slightly stooped, and the harried guards never noticed him. Why pay a toll to someone else's king? It was especially unwise, thought Pantomel, to try to pay a toll that one did not possess. His purse was as bare as the city was full.

The city of Navael stank of slaughter, dye, smoke, unwashed humans, and wet sibeccai. Pantomel muttered a quick prayer to Ygritte, goddess of flatulence and ill winds, and his nose thankfully stayed clogged. He left the town gate and headed directly for the leather quarter, down by Tanner's Creek.

The runepriests' laboratorium was as he had left it, a small half-timbered house with a grey thatched roof in need of repair. Together with an apothecary's dispensary, a stable and servant's hall, and a separate set of kitchens, the laboratorium created a small courtyard hidden from the city streets. Pantomel remembered it almost as the fortress he had described in his stories for years; it was a disappointment to him to see it come down in the world, reduced to its former self. It stank, and the place needed a new coat of plaster.

A man in a dirty leather jerkin sat by the door, an empty mug dangling from one hand. Pantomel slipped quietly past him, moving only when the man's eyes turned away, then ducking through the door as quick as a gust of wind. Why disturb a guard's serene contemplation? Better to leave others alone.

The front room was painted with the rune gospel that he remembered from his last visit, crude images of human faces marked with signs. He wasn't sure whether they were icons or warnings or simply previous members of the order. They were ugly things, lacking all quickling grace.

Two runepriests were drinking in the front room, where a red-haired serving girl was sweeping and a potboy was placing fresh reeds on the floor. Pantomel cleared his throat. Humans sometimes had trouble noticing his arrival.

"You're early."

"Yes, I am." Why argue with promptness? Pantomel was rarely on time for anything, so he savored this particular moment. He felt so virtuous, to be early.

"Who are you?" said the larger runepriest. He stood twice Pantomel's height, with hairy arms like a bear's. "Are you here for the Name Day, then?"

Pantomel was confused. Name day? He'd been given his own truename years ago, and the potboy looked a little young. "I brought you a child some years ago, and—"

The second runepriest interrupted, "And now you're here to celebrate Andrec's Name Day. Good of you to remember. Hope you brought a gift." He smirked and waved his mug drunkenly over Pantomel's head.

Pantomel stepped back, out of arm's reach. "Yes, I suppose." The best answer to human questions was invariably "Yes." The truth was something else, too precious to waste on scruffy cultists.

"Andrec, come here," said the bearish runepriest, gesturing to the tow-headed potboy.

The boy stopped his work and came forward to be introduced. Andrec was much bigger than Pantomel, a full head taller, and twice his weight. Andrec's right arm was bruised from a beating or from a tight hold, the pale skin smeared with yellow-black. He gripped his broom tightly, and his stance showed he trusted no one. "Yes, Dornateo?" he mumbled.

The bearish priest pushed him forward. "Listen to me, boy. Look at your guest, come for your Name Day," said Dornateo. "He's the one as brought you here."

Andrec the potboy brushed aside his lanky hair, and the face staring down at Pantomel was covered in a silvery tattoo with veins like those of an oak of the Harrowdeep.

If there was a small mercy in the reunion, it was that Andrec seemed to bear no grudge against the quickling who had brought him to the runepriests. Pantomel was ashamed to admit he couldn't understand much of the boy's mumbling. When he recovered from his surprise at finding the boy was little more than a servant, he wished Andrec a fine Name Day and watched him shuffle toward the kitchen.

The lad was polite, but not much else. Where was the learned young man Janrick had almost promised him in story after story at the Seven Oaks, night after night? Why didn't these people live up to Pantomel's fine-spun tales? Perhaps Janrick had never promised to turn the boy into a young gentlemen. Pantomel felt that he should have; it was a generous gesture from a leader. And it made a better story.

"Runepriest, I need to speak with Janrick," he said. Pantomel had expected that the boy would be well treated and gently raised; he needed to set things right.

"He doesn't need to speak with you, quickling," said Dornateo. "He's getting ready for the ceremony tonight. Come back later, after sunset. Maybe you can speak to him then."

"I'll wait around for a little while," said Pantomel. Dornateo shrugged and turned back to his beer. Pantomel took a seat far from the windows, watching the cultists and waiting for them to forget he was there. Eventually they did, and then they spoke of things best not mentioned to strangers. His sharp ears picked up every word.

"The boy is getting sulky. He needs to be put to use, or at least kept in his place," said Dornateo. "He's almost old enough to breed with that hag Korina, and speed the return of the Rune Messiah, blessed be her name."

"What if it doesn't work?" said another cultist.

"Don't dwell on that; think about what if it does work, you idiot. The child will be a runepriest, or even the Messiah, and the blasphemers shall be cast down." He smacked his lips and cracked his knuckles, savoring the inevitable triumph of the righteous.

Pantomel wasn't surprised; of course the runepriests were delighted to have a rune-marked adult, and all their fancies took a similar vein of indignation and reprisal. They didn't care about Andrec so much as what Andrec might do for their cult. If he left the child with them any longer, the lad would certainly become one of them, rather than a true child of the land. At eleven years of age, he was surely almost an adult human. Pantomel had waited too long already. It was time to shape the boy into the young prince he had always imagined. He was already planning how to talk Janrick into a reasonable deal: Perhaps he would become the boy's tutor. He wasn't sure what he would teach, exactly, but he could surely talk Janrick into this arrangement with a few carefully chosen words.

Pantomel slipped out the window and walked back into the laboratorium through the front door. "Sorry to step out, but I really must talk to Janrick. Can he see me yet?" he asked. "I'm sure I can be of service." Just a few words would set everything right.

The priest stared down his snout with small bearish eyes, hawked phlegm, and spat. "I'm sure we don't need you. Why don't you go somewhere else for a while?"

"Why don't I stay right here?" said Pantomel. He calmly rested his hand on his rapier, a fine blade of Sormerean steel sharp enough to cut a raindrop in two without a splash. The guard fingered his cudgel and loomed over Pantomel, leaning forward and scowling. Pantomel had the feeling that the lug wanted to pick him up by the scruff of the neck and toss him into the street, so he moved first, pulling his dagger from the scabbard at the small of his back, reversing it, and striking the lug's fingers with the pommel. The man dropped his cudgel and put his fingers in his mouth. Pantomel drew his rapier and held its point motionless, resting on the guard's gut.

The guard was too dumb to see his peril. "That wasn't very smart, quickling. Get you gone before I call my brothers. We'll carve you up to see what's inside a faen." His eyes blazed, and Pantomel asked himself how he had been blind enough eight years ago not to see the runepriests for what they were: fanatical cultists. Cold-hearted butchers. Bullies who would cut anyone apart if they thought it would make them into the next Rune Messiah. Why had he ever helped them? He swore an oath never to work for fanatics again.

Pantomel was tempted, but there was little to gain from thumping this particular halfwit. He was furious with the runepriests for treating the boy so badly, but really more angry with himself, and liable to kill this hairy nosepicker in his anger. Pantomel turned on his heel and strode down the street.

Having sold Andrec to runepriests wasn't a story he cared to tell any more.

Nothing was as Pantomel had expected. The runepriests were supposed to have taken care of the child—wasn't *he* one of their chosen? Something had gone terribly wrong; Pantomel had seen the beaten look in Andrec's eyes and the bruises on his arm. It was clear that the runepriests were not to be trusted, and he swore an oath to steal back the child. Two oaths in a day—he was slipping into very bad habits. A quickling who swore an oath might be expected to uphold it, and Pantomel rarely enjoyed explaining why this or that oath might not apply in a given situation. This oath was different. It burned in his guts; the cultists were taking entirely too many liberties with his tale of the boy prince.

Pantomel walked down the street, thinking. When he had first arrived, the runepriests had asked him if he had come for Andrec's Name Day, and he had agreed. Looked at in the proper light, that seemed as good as a gilded invitation to Pantomel. It didn't do to quibble over details when paying social calls. He would wait until after sunset before returning.

On his return, the party was just as loud as Pantomel had expected; he heard their toast—"To the Messiah!"—from down the street. It would have been nice to take Andrec away before the runepriests began their celebration, but walking off with the guest of honor tended to generate suspicion. As he approached the runepriest laboratorium, Pantomel ducked under his own shadow, snuck inside, and found a quiet spot under a corner table where he could see everything. Few humans could see through a quickling hidden under his shadow, and he'd long ago learned to navigate under furniture and recognize humans by their legs and shoes.

Pantomel would wait for everyone to finish their toasting and revelry, then walk out with Andrec in tow. He had barely gotten comfortable under the table when three cultists pulled out the chairs and sat down, leaving him almost no room. Their shoes smelled foul, and blood spattered their leggings up to the ankle. Pantomel recalled Nodberry's warning and swallowed nervously.

The cultists called for food, and their mugs landed on the table with a thud. Pantomel guessed these weren't their first drinks of the night. The sounds of quiet drinking, and the click of the mugs on the tabletop continued for some minutes. Finally, the three cultists spoke, slurring only a little.

"Has Janrick started the naming?"

"Maybe soon. He went to the stables."

"Where's the potboy?"

"He's the nameboy, and he's not joining us. Janrick's cautious."

"Not much of a party without the nameboy."

"Have another ale, and remember why the little wretch is worth a party."

"Mark me, he'll be a disappointment like the others."

"Have a little faith."

Pantomel avoided the first speaker's legs when he stretched, but almost gagged when he slipped his feet out of his half-boots. It was time to move on.

The room was more crowded than ever; staying out of everyone's way took most of Pantomel's attention. He grabbed a serving tray, held it over his head to obscure his face, and headed for the kitchen. The servants were far too busy tapping a new cask of ale to pay him the slightest attention.

He zipped past the kitchen to the servants' quarters above the stable. The boy's room was nearby, in a loft built in the rafters. A narrow set of stairs led up to a landing outside the room. The cultists were coming down the stairs—Pantomel recognized the runepriest Janrick leading the way. His heart froze in his chest; the man was even larger and more scarred than Pantomel remembered, and his stringy grey hair had grown even more ragged. Worse, he seemed sober, compared to the revelers below. He moved to the stall at the base of the stairs and let the runepriests pass.

Pantomel climbed the stairs under the cover of the stable's shadows. His shadow stayed intact, and he slipped inside the room. Pantomel waited a moment to hear Janrick's tread on the floor below, going back to the celebration, then looked around. The room was small but clean; the slope of the eaves made half the chamber little more than storage space. Andrec wore a blue robe over his breeches, and a crown of oak leaves that matched the rune on his cheek. Pantomel stepped over his shadow, and bowed, but Andrec barely noticed his arrival; his reaction seemed sluggish, or perhaps merely drugged.

"What are you doing here?" he mumbled. Pantomel wasn't offended; he was used to catching humans by surprise.

"I'm here to rescue you." He made a small bow, but when he looked up again, Andrec was frowning.

"Rescue me from what?" he said. The boy spoke clearly now, without slurring or hesitation.

"From the runepriests. They want you to help them breed their new messiah, and if you can't help with that, they'll drain your blood and dissect you. The gossip is unanimous about this."

"You're crazy. They only cut up unbelievers, and some day I'll be holding the knife. I'm not going anywhere." The thought that Andrec might not want to be rescued had not previously occurred to Pantomel. Things like this were always destroying his clever and heroic plans. It was most irksome. The boy would have to be made to understand his position in the scheme of things.

"Trust me," said Pantomel.

"Why should I trust you? You brought me here!" Pantomel silently cursed Dornateo, the runepriest who had let that detail slip.

"You have a good point." This was Pantomel's favorite response when a conversation wasn't going as planned. It gave him time, without making him seem like an idiot. "That rune of yours, it looks familiar."

"It should, you faen love the forests. Haven't you ever been to the Harrowdeep?"

"Of course I have. And the rune makes me think that you should go there as well."

Something in Andrec seemed to wake up, and a bright glint shone in his eyes. "Pretend for a moment that I believe you. Why should I leave the people who raised me?"

The boy was showing more brains than Pantomel had expected. "Three reasons. First, I don't believe you really want to ever hold the knife, even to cut up unbelievers. Second, because once they give you a truename, you'll be tied to them. You won't have a choice when they ask you to serve them. And last, because you are marked for greater things than a bloodstained laboratorium and reciting dogma. Do you really want to stay here and turn into one of them?"

A knock came at the door, followed by a man's voice. Pantomel hadn't heard the man come up the stairs. "Andrec, are you ready? Janrick and your guests are waiting."

"I'll be there in a minute."

"I'll wait," came the reply. "But I won't wait long."

Andrec put a hand on Pantomel's shoulder, stared directly in his eyes, and spoke very quietly. "The priests told me I was abandoned, that they took me in. Did you really steal me and bring me here, or was Dornateo just saying that?"

"I brought you here. They told me you'd be raised a gentleman and a scholar. And I believed them." Pantomel looked away.

Andrec pushed him back. "I think you'd best leave." He turned to the door.

Pantomel couldn't believe it; the boy really didn't want to go. "I will leave if you ask it. I'll plant myself in the Harrowdeep and dream the forest's dreams, and listen to the loresong sing about the spring nests, and forget the boy too dumb to know when he's being rescued."

"You're just one of Janrick's tests of my loyalty to the order. Get out of here." Andrec straightened his robe and ran a hand through his hair, and moved toward the door.

"I'm no trick—the runepriests hate quicklings!" said Pantomel. All his clever words deserted him. "Come with me to the Harrowdeep!" But Andrec's hand was on the latch, and Pantomel scrambled to find a spot flat against the wall by the door. He would slip out behind any runepriest who entered the room.

Janrick's deep voice rumbled outside the door. "Boy, if you are talking to a pet rat in there, it's time to stop." The latch rattled.

Andrec opened the door, squared his shoulders, and stepped out into the hall. Janrick stood there with Dornateo, the doorman from the afternoon, his hand still bruised. Janrick looked down at Andrec and said, "Time to show yourself to the others and take a new name, boy. I'm sure you'll father the new Messiah. This way." Pantomel heard them making their way down the stairs.

It was hopeless; the boy was an idiot, already twisted by the cultists' teachings. Pantomel stayed in the room, waiting for Andrec to leave the stairs and stables. Better to go out the back alley, now; the front room was crowded and the main door was surely guarded. The cultists suspected nothing; Pantomel decided to leave before that changed. He moved away from the wall to the open door.

As Pantomel stepped out of Andrec's room, a nail-studded club almost took his head off. Dornateo had stayed behind the others, and Pantomel's quickling reflexes weren't quite fast enough to save his skull. The man's cudgel connected glancingly with the left side of his head, delivering a crunch strong enough to spin Pantomel round and knock him to the floor.

"Got you," said Dornateo.

The world came unmoored. The wooden boards under his cheek rolled like waves. Pantomel heard footsteps at the stable door, steps that seemed very close. For a moment, he thought he could see a small host of gods—one or two unknown, others clearly the gods of dueling, of treachery, of courage, of flesh wounds, the goddess of silence—perched on the rafters. They were watching him and commenting on his skill. Strictly speaking, the goddess of silence wasn't commenting, but she gave him a very meaningful look. It made Pantomel's shoulder blades itch; he hated being watched.

Pantomel shook his head. He had more pressing problems than his standing among the gods, or the noise down in the stables. Dornateo was swaying, drunk, and couldn't resist gloating. "I knew you were up to something, you forest rat!" The cultist sneered, but he also backed up out of arm's reach, toward the stairs. "Admit it, you're a thief, you're here to make trouble. What were you doing in that room? Surrender yourself to me, and you'll live." Pantomel said nothing, stalling for time. The world stopped spinning.

"No surrender?" said Dornateo. "Good." Dornateo stepped forward again, club held high. Pantomel drew his rapier and cut at the man's legs weakly. He pushed himself up to his shoulders, and tried to stand, but couldn't. If Dornateo had the courage to rush him, it was over.

The drunken priest was a coward, or perhaps he just remembered how quickly Pantomel had rapped his knuckles with the dagger earlier. He hesitated, and in that moment Pantomel reached into his boot and flung the detonation acorn at the cultist with a quick prayer to Jigshoot, god of saplings: "Please, let it be as potent as I was told." The acorn split with a flash of green light, and branches covered with oak leaves filled the small space. The boards of the rafters bent to hold the priest in mid-stride, rustling the branches that now bound his arms and legs. Pantomel was impressed; the acorn was every bit as powerful as he'd been told.

Staring at the newly-born forest, Pantomel almost didn't see the second runepriest in time—he had come up the stairs at a silent run and almost caught the quickling still prone on the floorboards. Pantomel heard the whoosh of his body and his staff cutting through the air, and he rolled to his left just in time. He couldn't stand up fast enough to counter. The second runepriest was Janrick, and he was both more sober and more skilled than the drunken guard. He drove Pantomel down the hall, keeping him dodging.

Janrick struck quickly again with his staff and roared, "You aren't getting away, little one!" Pantomel finally rolled out onto one of the rafters, giving himself enough space to stand up and dance away from Janrick, bringing his rapier up into a guarding line, and forcing his opponent to come out onto the narrow beam if he wanted to give chase. Janrick was a little too canny for that, but said, "You are trying to stop our grand experiment, but it won't work. Andrec is ours to mold or destroy. He's paid for—you have no claim on him."

Pantomel said nothing. Other cultists would arrive in a moment. He leaped off the rafter, swung from a small bit of harness into the stables near the base of the steps, and turned to run.

Janrick thundered down the stairs in pursuit, loud as an avalanche and with the same unstoppable momentum. Pantomel saw a broomstick flash out from the stall beside the stairs, entangling Janrick's legs. The runepriest's face turned from triumph to dismay as he tried to catch himself, but the big man was too slow. He struck the dirt floor at full speed, and his staff spun away from his open hand. Janrick's eyes rolled back into his head, then closed, and he lay still, sprawled awkwardly in the straw and dung of the stable. The tow-headed Andrec stepped out of the stall and grinned from ear to ear.

"Thanks, Andrec. You've been wanting to do that for years, haven't you?"

"I owe him a few bruises," said the runechild.

"But why deliver them now?" said Pantomel.

"He said you have no claim on me. But you found me first, and if you think it's time to go someplace new, I'm ready to go." It seemed a very convenient way—or, rather, a quickling way—of looking at the situation.

Pantomel nodded. "Time to go, then." Andrec pulled a leather cloak around his shoulders, Pantomel cut the rune-priest's purse, and the two of them left the stables at a run.

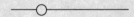

Pantomel and Andrec slipped out the city gate after dark, thanks to a small bribe paid out of the runepriest's purse, and they left their pursuit behind. By the next morning, though, the boy had lost his courage. He looked nervously at the road leading north from the city into the dusty plains. Pantomel more than half suspected the child hadn't been outside the city walls for years.

"Where are we going?" asked Andrec. He had been sniffling quietly all morning, a condition that Pantomel had studiously ignored.

"Home. To find you a proper set of parents instead of drunken fanatics."

"How did you know I dreamed about the forest?"

"What? I didn't." Pantomel felt the whisper of the gods in his mind, but ignored it.

"Yes, you did. Back at the stable." Pantomel counted his blessings; if it hadn't been for the boy's broom handle, he'd surely be some runepriest's experiment by now. "Will you give me a truename?" The child's questions were wearing.

"We'll find someone. Don't worry yourself."

"Who will help me find my real parents?" said Andrec. His tears had stopped, but the boy's quivering lip threatened to bring back the waterfall at any moment.

Pantomel was never sure where the words came from. He wasn't really prone to jokes about religion, but the name just jumped from his lips. "I'm the high priest of Unshelas, the goddess of lost children and lost parents. We'll look for them together." And as he said it, he knew it was true. For years he had paid close attention to the ten thousand faces of the faen gods, demigods, saints, and semi-gods. He was as sure of the goodwill of Unshelas, her rituals and rites, as he was of the three copper bits remaining in his purse.

With the knowledge came a burden the quickling couldn't evade: the responsibility to look after the child, and others like him. He'd seen others who'd discovered new gods in the quickling pantheon; they were remembered, celebrated, but much was expected of them. They taught the proper forms and rituals of the god or goddess, their preferred sacrifices and prayers. Most of all, the discoverers all became talespinners, telling the stories of the god, writing down the sacred texts, and explaining how the god's words translated into deed. Pantomel resigned himself to being a teacher; somehow, without a word from Unshelas, he knew the boy's real parents had died of plague years ago. Quickling nobles sometimes fostered children, but Pantomel would raise the boy himself if he had to. He would teach the word of Unshelas through example. Why annoy any goddess who cared about him enough to make him a priest? In fact, why annoy any goddess, ever? There was no advantage in it.

"Come on, Andrec. Let's go find you some new friends. The forest is full of gods, and runes. Your sort of place. I'll look after you," said Pantomel. The boy smiled, a wide and goofy grin entirely at odds with all Pantomel's notions of comportment. And yet the quickling found it appealing, in a slipshod, human sort of way.

The road turned north, and Pantomel could already feel the coolness of crossing into the first shadow of the Harrowdeep. He could hardly wait to tell his new story at the Seven Oaks.

Pantomel walked over the horizon to the deepest heart of the Harrowdeep, where the priests would never follow, where Andrec's rune could grow from an acorn to an oak. But there was something he needed to hear first, and so he turned to the boy and said, "So, Andrec, we have a long walk ahead of us. Tell me your story."

JEFF GRUBB

SINGER
FOR THE DEAD

The last shades of an ochre sunset had leached from the western sky by the time Na-Tethian reached the stockade. The giant had slept rough for the past two days since leaving Jerad, and there were to be many such future nights on the trek to Zalavat. The chance of a warm hearth and some hot stew promised by the lights at the head of the valley appealed to him. Still, the distance deceived him, and by the time he made it up the vale, night had fallen fully. A chill wind swirled around him now, and seemed to carry on it ragged, soft music.

The stockade gate was secured but unmanned, and he had to bang on its timbers three times before a small, human-sized head popped over the edge of the wall. Na-Tethian heard excited, muffled voices on the other side, then the bar scraped back and the gate swung outward to admit him.

Na-Tethian was footsore but relieved to see the smooth-shaven face lit by lantern light as the gate opened. These humans looked very much like giant children, but thinner and more delicate, and that always made him smile. Na-Tethian bowed slightly and said, "Do you have quarters for a traveler? An inn, perhaps?"

The human (Was he twenty years old? Forty? It was so hard to tell with their short lives.) bowed deeply and half-walked, half-ran toward the largest building in the village. Na-Tethian followed, his armor rattling in his knapsack.

The sign above the door showed a child astride a raptor, the pudgy human baby marked with an arcane rune above one eye. The inn was human built, of course, meaning that it had high ceilings, but Na-Tethian still had to duck going through the doorway.

He was apparently the only guest this evening, not a surprise given the valley's fairly remote location. As he entered, the inn-keep was just throwing on his vest. Outside, the youth who had opened the gate continued up the street, pausing only to knock on doors. Lamplights flickered on in the windows in his wake.

The innkeeper possessed the heaviness that Na-Tethian always equated with middle age among humans, with a bright smile and fervent, excited eyes. Surely the inn was not so far off the beaten track that he was the only visitor in weeks? But here was the innkeeper bowing low, as if Na-Tethian were the first guest in a fortnight, pumping the giant's hand and bellowing for the chair.

The innkeeper's children (grandchildren?) were already pulling a Giant's Chair out of storage. The chair was heavy, comfortable, and dusty, and small hands stirred off the bulk of the grit as Na-Tethian slipped off his pack. The giant appreci-ated the effort but, given his own trail dust, he worried that he would just dirty it again.

There were no other travelers, the innkeep confirmed, and Na-Tethian could have the pick of the beds in the sleeping quarters upstairs, or he could move them together if that was his desire. The innkeeper's wife appeared briefly to say that they still had some good stew from dinner, and she would fry up some red potatoes, but she wanted to make sure that Na-Tethian had no objections to the herbs she used. Na-Tethian had never heard of several of the ingredients before but assured her it would be no problem.

The innkeep pressed a heavy tankard of mulled wine into the giant's hand and motioned for him to sit next to the hearth, where the fire had been re-stirred and built up to a hearty blaze. Na-Tethian felt good to not be moving, but thought that these people were making too much of his arrival. He started to protest, but the smiling innkeep only said, "Nothing is ever too good for the guest," and bundled off for more red wine and cinnamon.

More villagers were now drifting into the inn, awakened by the gatekeeper. They poured in, in ones and twos and threes. A few ordered ale, and others some dried meat. Several youths working the inn relayed the orders, but Na-Tethian saw no silver change hands. In fact, one local man reached for his belt and was stopped by the smiling innkeep, who said a few un-heard words. The local nodded, looked at the giant, and raised his mug in a toast.

A young woman, perhaps the innkeep's daughter or grand-daughter, appeared at his left side with a ewer and refilled his mug. She stared at him as if she had never seen a giant before. He smiled at her in thanks, and she blushed furiously.

"Is something wrong?" he said.

"Nothing," said the young woman. "I thought you'd be a . . ." and here she made a motion on her forehead, sketching a sigil with her finger in her pale flesh. Na-Tethian was puzzled for a moment, then realized that it matched the symbol above the child's eye on the sign outside.

"What, a runechild?" Despite himself, Na-Tethian brushed his own forehead in response. "I have heard much good of such people. But, no. Why would I be one of the runechildren?"

"We're glad you're here, regardless," she blurted suddenly, blushing even more furiously. "We're glad they finally sent someone."

Na-Tethian started to say, "No one sent me—I am just looking for a place to stay," but she was gone to get more wine, and then dinner arrived, and everyone watched as the giant ate.

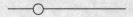

It was disconcerting to have people watch one eat. The meal itself was good, giantish food—baked squash, new greens, and tart ruddy greatberries. The stew had just enough meat for flavor, but not the huge lumps that humans seemed to prefer. The innkeep's wife skillet-fried the red potatoes before putting them into the stew, their succulence sealed in. The ingredients were fresh and the carrot-bread soft, baked that day.

But it was obvious to Na-Tethian that the humans were watching his every bite. When he looked up, they would look away suddenly. And if he caught them staring, they would manage a weak, embarrassed smile and offer yet another raised mug of a toast, which Na-Tethian felt bound to return.

The giant shook his head—he'd met sibeccai who were less worshipful than these humans. Still, there were all manner of isolated human communities with their own customs, evolved over the centuries of the dramojh occupation. While it pleased him, the hairs on the back of his neck prickled with concern. Surely they were not as accommodating to all their travelers. Why him? Why would anyone expect a runechild, of all things? And why were they awaiting his arrival, especially since he had not known he would be here himself?

Two courses later, and Na-Tethian had to demure on a third. His mug of wine was always refreshed, and soon he realized he would have to stop returning the villagers' toasts, if he was going to avoid getting drunk. These people had not met many giants before, and obviously they assumed giantish constitutions were mightier than they truly were.

As he mopped up the last of his gravy, they presented a singer, a young man whose eyes seemed to drive into his soul. Considering the friendliness around him, Na-Tethian found the lad's gaze even more disconcerting. What was the youth looking for? Some telltale runechild mark? If the young man was looking for some special sign, he would be sorely disappointed.

Na-Tethian managed a smile, and started to say, "So, why do *you* think I'm here?" but the innkeep tapped the lad on the shoulder and said, "Sing for us, young Tammath,"

The young man blinked, nodded, and began to sing.

The youth sang well, that lovely tenor that humans have. It was a battle tale, though not one he had heard before. Most of the battle tales were of the giants and their allies fighting the dramojh to free the land centuries ago. This one was older. It spoke of humans fighting humans, each seeking to control a great flat-topped mountain, which was said to be a gateway to the heavens, the first rung of a great ladder. The two mighty forces, driven by pride and power, destroyed each other utterly, and the last to die were the army's two generals, who breathed their last while clutching each other's throats.

It was a lament in a minor key, a tale of sadness and death, with no victors, no survivors, and no moral, other than the futility of the conflict. The giant cast a glance around the room and saw the smiling faces turn stony as the humans listened. A young woman shuddered and clung tightly to her husband. Were these people the descendants of the warriors who fought here? No, there were no survivors, the refrain kept underscoring. Then why was this song so important to them?

Tammath finished the last refrain, and there was a silence, then a weighty sigh moved through the crowd. The innkeep looked expectantly at the giant.

"A good song," said Na-Tethian, and the innkeeper nodded.

Na-Tethian repeated. "A very good song. And well sung."
Again came the nod.

"Let me return the favor," said the giant, and as a single
body, the crowd leaned forward, expectant. The giant cleared
his throat and began his oldest song, the song his mother had
taught him about his grandmother.

His grandmother had been one of the great warriors of the
Hu-Charad and had fought at the Battle of the Serpent's Heart.
She was carrying his mother as well—to conceal her condition,
she kept letting out her armor, a bolt at a time.

Despite the subject matter, it was a light, riotous tune, better
suited to a gathering at an inn than the human's mournful tale.
And, Na-Tethian's own voice, in his humble opinion, was more
than suitable, a low bass that his father always called a "glass-
rattler." And indeed, the humans seemed to appreciate it; several were smiling and nodding in time as he got to the part
where his grandmother's water broke at the same time that she
killed the last dramojh. His mother was born on the battlefield
immediately afterward, life out of the death.

He finished the song, and the humans let out a chorus of ap-
plause. Na-Tethian blushed despite himself—it was the spirit of
his grandmother that, in part, had set him on his current path
south, on half-a-promise from a group of adventurers intent on
exploring the Naveradel jungles. It was a path that might give
him a song or two of his own to sing.

Still, he was proud of his heritage, and it showed in his
singing. The innkeep stepped forward and said, "They sent a
good one. Fire and battle run in your veins!"

Na-Tethian furrowed his brow and opened his mouth—he
was bound for Zalavat, not for here. They obviously thought he
was someone else. Who were they expecting?

Then he looked at the crowd. Their faces were expectant and
hopeful. The giant felt his face darken further with embarrass-
ment, and he changed the question he was going to ask.

"So, are there any, um, facilities nearby? All the wine." He patted his belly.

The innkeep blinked—it was obviously not what the human had been waiting for. "Oh. Oh! Yes, we have an outdoor, but it might be a bit cramped. There's a midden behind the main building. Here, I'll show you."

"Be back in a nonce," said Na-Tethian to the crowd, hoping they would take the hint and not follow him. There were worse things than having a group of humans watch you eat.

"I am afraid you have me at a disadvantage, good sir," said the giant, as gently as possible. He and the innkeep both stood on the edge of the midden, urinating.

"I'm sorry?" said the human.

"Your hospitality is excellent," said Na-Tethian, "but it's clear that you are expecting something of me beyond mere payment in exchange for all this hospitality. And until I know what it is, I'm afraid I cannot rest comfortably."

There was a quiet moment between the two of them, and the wind piped up. Then the human spoke, and his voice sounded unsteady. "So, they didn't send you?"

"I've been wanting to ask this," said the giant, "but I didn't want to embarrass myself. Who are *they*?"

"De-Shamod," said the human, and his voice cracked as he spoke the name. "The giant government. We sent for help two years ago, and when nothing happened last year, we thought they'd forgotten us. But now that you've shown up on the first night, we thought they'd just been delayed."

"Delayed," said Na-Tethian, thinking of how a request from a remote hamlet would likely be handled in the bureaucracy. "Yes, that does happen. Things do get delayed. There are so many matters to deal with. But why do you need De-Shamod's help?"

"Why, with the haunting," said the human. "Listen. You can hear it. It's just the first night."

Na-Tethian cocked his head and listened. The wind surged and spun around them, and now he could catch a sound riding on the breeze. It was the ghost of a tune, high and mournful and sour, carried down from the tor above the village. A shiver that had nothing to do with the night's cold ran up his spine.

"Aye, that's it," said the innkeep. "Every year for three days before Moon's Eve, we hear it. Evil things haunt the tor, where the two armies fought. And every year, someone is up there, trying to raise the dead, bring back the armies. It grows stronger each night. We've seen figures moving up there in the moonlight, and we hear the song, so we know that they're back. That's why we sent to De-Shamod. And we just thought . . ." His voice trailed off.

For his part, the giant grunted and laced himself up. He wanted to be honest, to say that it was a mistake, that he was just a traveler, and that their request to De-Shamod had been at best lost, or worse, ignored—or worse still, had never reached the capital in the first place.

He wanted to say that all this wasn't his problem. But he looked at the innkeep. The human appeared as crushed as if the giant had struck him. Na-Tethian considered himself fortunate he had not tried to explain the village's mistake to the entire common room.

Instead he said to the human, "We should get back."

The innkeep was silent now, his chin lowered to his chest, as the two walked back to the inn. Yes, Na-Tethian could still hear a song on the breeze. Faint, but growing, and sung in a language he had never heard before.

When the pair re-entered the common room, the conversation stopped as suddenly as if a lid had been dropped on it. All eyes looked at the giant as he crossed the room and sat down in the great Giant's Chair by the hearth. The innkeep retreated back behind the others, frowning and knuckling something at the corner of his eye.

Na-Tethian looked at the gathered humans, shook his head, and smiled gently, as he would smile at an insistent niece or nephew.

"So, I understand that you folks need help with a haunting," the giant said.

And the humans all began talking at once.

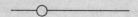

Na-Tethian arose late, having spent half the night listening to the humans' descriptions, stories, and theories, and the other half alone in the common sleeping room, lying diagonally across three human-sized beds, listening to the growing power of the haunt on the tor.

If the voice had a color, it would be pale silver. If it had a flavor, it would be cold metal. If it had an edge, it would be that of a finely crafted blade. It wound around the village, creeping in every crack and through every window joint, snaking in and dragging its sharp edge down one's back. No wonder the villagers were relieved—no, desperate—to see "official help" from De-Shamod finally arrive.

The words of the song were unknown and unguessable. They had the rhythm of ritual, but they fit no ceremony, human or giant, that Na-Tethian had ever heard. It wasn't spell-casting, not quite. He knew enough mage blades and magisters to know a good spell, and this didn't sound like one. Maybe it was an old language, spoken by one or both of the original human armies. Maybe the dead soldiers responded only to commands in their native tongue.

And there were dead up there, of that the villagers had no doubt. Humanish forms moved across the flattened hilltop on the three days before Moon's Eve, accompanied by the singing. Some say the forms shuffled, some say they danced, and some say they fought among themselves at the commands of the ghostly singer. None of the villagers showed any desire to determine the particulars on those three nights.

What the dead had *not* done was come down into the valley— yet. But each year, the song grew stronger and the villagers cowered behind the palisade. Each year they dreaded that the next anniversary of the battle would be the one when the dark forces finally gathered their troops and spilled out to slay the living.

So Na-Tethian awoke late, ate a cold lunch of leftovers, and set out. The humans wrapped up the remains of the previous meal for him, and the giant left his large pack at the inn, taking only his armor, blade, and a smaller bundle with the meal and other sundries. He could easily have brought the entire pack up, but leaving things behind would reassure the humans that he would return.

The valley wall rose quickly behind the inn, and a narrow goatpath wove its way to the top of the flattened tor. It was mid-afternoon by the time Na-Tethian crested the ridge, and to some degree he was glad—he could feel the eyes of every human in the village on his back, pushing him uphill.

The flattened hill looked as if a mighty axe blade had cleaved off the hilltop, leaving a broad plateau. The blade had been heated to do the work, it seemed, for the entire plateau was littered with shattered black volcanic glass, a choppy sea of obsidian chips. Larger, grey-white boulders punctuated the area in twos and threes, their stone unlike the rest of the hilltop. Monuments, perhaps? Menhirs left as memorials?

Or perhaps altars, Na-Tethian thought grimly.

According to the youth's song (and underscored by the villagers in the discussions that went on till well after midnight), the hilltop was once smooth as glass, the first rung of the

Ladder of Heaven. Which heaven it led to was not recorded, but two factions sought to control it. One army was led by a darkbond seeking to wrest from it the ultimate secrets of life, the other by a warmain who wanted to unleash the fury of heaven's armies on the world. They met and fought here, and in the process shattered the obsidian surface and presumably any other rungs of the heavenly ladder. This happened over a thousand years ago, before the dramojh incursions.

There was no sign of the dead—either they were buried, or incorporeal, or imaginary. Na-Tethian doubted the last, for if the song was real (and he had heard it himself), then likely the reason for the song was real as well.

The obsidian chips crunched beneath Na-Tethian's heavy boots. When he stopped, there was silence—nothing else lived on the tor, and he heard neither birdcall nor any sound of other creatures moving among the rubble. He reached one of the grey boulders and ran a hand over it. Yes, etched lines cut deep across the surface, but he couldn't say for sure if they were runes or just natural weathering.

On the far side of the boulder, someone had made a clearing of sorts—most of the flinty shards were cleared away, and a firepit dug in the center. Na-Tethian crouched by the boulder and watched. After nothing happened for five minutes, he moved to the side of the pit.

The ashes in the pit were warm but not hot, and next to it lay a bundle of fresh wood tied with a loose rope. It would seem that at least one particular ghost was planning to return and wanted heat and light when it arrived.

Na-Tethian nodded absently and scanned the area. No one seemed to be watching, either living or dead. A cluster of three slender monuments reared up about a hundred feet toward the lee side of the hill. A good place to hole up during the day, he thought. He moved toward them carefully, in case his "ghostly singer" had had similar thoughts.

No one was there. The ground had settled between the three monuments, such that they now tipped together to form a rough stone lean-to with a good view of the firepit. There was ample space for a giant, but would seem too open and exposed for a smaller individual. He pulled himself beneath the outcropping, bringing his knees up to his chin and resting his scabbard on the ground between his heels and his seat. He laid his hand on the hilt, pulled his cloak around him, and tried to look as boulderlike as possible as he waited for night to fall.

Na-Tethian awoke in darkness, his hand automatically grabbing the hilt of his blade as his brain came to groggy awareness. He had not shifted in the hours he had slept, and, indeed, was unaware of when he had dozed off. He was stiff and sore, but he did not move. Above him, the moon floated on a sea of rippled clouds, casting bands of shadow across the flattened hilltop.

A woman's song drifted over the tor, and flames danced in the firepit.

From his vantage point, Na-Tethian turned his head slowly toward the fire. A small blaze burned there, yellow with bits of green and blue at the tips of the flames. Kneeling next to it, profile to the giant, was a figure in a hooded white robe. Human-sized and female, he decided, her face lost in the shadows of her cloak. She would only see the flames before her, blinded by the firelight and the blinders formed by her deep hood.

She was singing. The tune was high and sweet and mournful, the words coherent but in a language strange to the giant. If he had felt a knife-edge running up his spine before, at this range the song bit deep, flensing the flesh from his form. Na-Tethian shivered.

The pale figure leaned forward and threw dust into the fire. The dust was golden as it left her hand and the flames responded with a burst of green, blue, and copper snaking skyward. Her voice changed timbre, and the tongues of fire wrapped around themselves and answered her with a crackling counterpoint to her song. A ceremony, but unlike any with which the giant was familiar.

Na-Tethian moved slightly, but froze at the sound of stone scraping on stone just outside his hiding place. He waited, and another humanish form shambled into view. It was slumped forward and missing an arm, and one shoulder seemed higher than the other. It was bedecked in the tattered remains of armor: bits of chain hanging loosely from a torc, a dented helmet, open-faced in the ancient styles, still on its head.

The shambling figure stopped in front of Na-Tethian's lair, facing the pale woman and her flames.

Na-Tethian held his breath but could not hold his heart, which thundered in his chest. The shambler might have heard it, or might have smelled the fresh blood surging through the giant's veins or may simply have felt Na-Tethian's living gaze fall upon it. For whatever reason, the one-armed figure turned.

The face within the dented helmet had once been human but now was a travesty of the race—its eyes greenish pinpoints in ruined sockets, its teeth elongated and sharpened. It was a ghoul, whose form was wracked and twisted by the grave hunger, and whose claws paralyzed its prey and spread its curse.

The ghoul let out a hissing rasp and sprang toward him. Na-Tethian's blade was faster, pulled from its scabbard and brought up and around in a smooth, deadly action. The blade caught the charging ghoul beneath its ribs and smashed it against the boulder. Its head slammed against the stone, and it slumped there, leaving a dark stain on the white rock.

The chanting continued without interruption. The pale woman seemed not to even have noticed the altercation, so intent was she on the flames. Na-Tethian uncoiled and rose. He saw that other forms were also rising from among the shards of obsidian. They pulled themselves from shallow graves in the hilltop, the sharp stones dripping from their ill-formed bodies like shattered gems in the moonlight. They were once soldiers, dressed in the tatters of their deadly craft—the moldering remains of a uniform, fragments of armor, the bashed remnants of a helmet. Some still bore notched swords and dented shields, but most loped slowly forward, knuckle-walking on clawed hands. Na-Tethian could not tell whether they were from one army or the other, or both.

They moved slowly in long, leisurely strides, making their way toward the firepit. Na-Tethian moved slowly toward the ceremony as well, wondering whether their fascination with the ritual would protect him from their notice.

He overtook a ghoul in a high, ornate helm. The undead mockery stiffened slightly, its head jerking toward the giant as he passed it, its eyes burning green with remembered hunger. It opened a cadaverous mouth as if to shout, but instead only a sibilant sigh emerged from its rotted lungs. Na-Tethian thrust his blade into the creature's chest, which caved in under the impact in a cloud of moist, powdery gravedust.

The beast did not fall. Instead it gave another silent shout and tried to force itself up the blade, scrabbling with its taloned hands to reach him. Na-Tethian pulled the blade out and hacked at the creature with a downward, angled stroke. The blow caught the cadaver where helm met neck, and its head bounced off into the darkness. The body flailed for a moment and collapsed.

The protection provided by their fascination was apparently limited. Draw too close, and the ghoul's basic instincts overwhelmed the command of the ceremony.

Na-Tethian moved more quickly and carefully, dancing over the piles of obsidian shards that now bulged upward to disgorge more ghoulish warriors, trying to keep himself apart from the growing, shambling mob now slouching toward the firepit.

None had closed with the pale woman herself, and the giant wanted to get there first.

The most direct route was through a large, brutish ghoul, more rhodin than human, its ramlike horns sprouting from its scalp. It mattered not—by the time it caught wind of Na-Tethian's scent, his blade had pierced the ribs of its back and come out its chest, sending it sprawling forward. With a clear path to the pale woman, Na-Tethian jumped over its twitching body and entered the firelit circle.

Throughout this episode, the white enchantress neither missed a beat nor marred a note. Her song seemed a living, serpentine thing now, roiling around the hilltop, expanding out from the firepit to summon the dead. Na-Tethian could imagine the ghouls pulling themselves from their famished sleep all across the tor, and he thought of the innfolk huddled behind their stockade, their palisade useless against the inevitable attack.

He was upon the pale woman now, and she finally noticed him, her voice wavering as he raised his blade, her tone marred by a half-flat pitch as he reversed his grip and smashed the heavy hilt into her. She sprawled backward from the blow, away from the multicolored flames, which dimmed and yellowed and turned eerily normal at once.

Na-Tethian spun the blade again, and thrust the tip against the pale woman's collarbone. Her song died in her throat.

"Not another note," started Na-Tethian, but the words died in his throat as well.

The pale woman's hood had fallen back to reveal a dark mantle of hair, cropped short at the neck, and a human face, fair but aged in the human fashion. But what caught Na-Tethian's attention was the sigil inscribed above her right eye: an ornate rune, dark against her pale flesh, which seemed to surge and writhe of its own volition.

"Runechild," said Na-Tethian.

"Giant idiot," spat the woman, "Why do you spoil the ceremony?" She tried to rise.

Na-Tethian pressed the tip of the blade forward again. "What runechild seeks to raise and command the hungry dead?"

The pale woman let out a dismissive snort. "Raise? Command? Twice the fool! The ceremony is not to raise the dead, but to keep them resting in their gnawing sleep on these nights, the anniversary of the battle. Look around you, and see what you have done."

Na-Tethian allowed himself a glance away from the pale woman, and indeed, the nearest ghouls seemed to be pulling themselves fully upright, shaking off the effects of the ceremony like a guard shaking off the temptations of sleep.

The nearest ones were already sniffing the air, and their eyes glowed a brighter green.

"I am an idiot," breathed Na-Tethian to himself.

"I already said that," said the woman, pushing his blade aside and sitting up. He did not stop her.

"We need to get out of here," said Na-Tethian, knowing his voice sounded tight and worried.

"No," said the pale woman, who rose and looked around. "The ceremony is interrupted, not broken, its enchantment delayed, not shattered. Where is my bag?"

Na-Tethian looked around, but the nearest ghoul was on top of them. He brought his blade up sharply, cleaving the front of the creature open. Two others were behind it, and more shapes shambled at the edge of the fire.

"Here," said the pale woman. "Let me regather the spell. Let me weave over your mistake."

"Soon, please," said Na-Tethian. The next pair launched themselves, claws extended, jaws agape. The giant brought his blade around, catching one in the midsection and slamming its dying corpse into the next one. Both tumbled into a heap.

"Don't push them into the fire!" snapped the pale woman, "Do you seek to make matters worse?"

Na-Tethian stepped onto the back of the two toppled ghouls and, with a single stroke, decapitated the pair. He stared at the woman and said, "Whenever you want to fix my mistake, you are welcome to start."

But the pale woman had already closed her eyes and reached into her bag, the first notes of her serpentine song on her lips.

And behind her rose the rhodin ghoul, black bile streaming from its chest and dripping from its maw. Its eyes were the green of death and hate, and it was upon her before Na-Tethian could shout a warning.

The pale runechild's eyes flew open as the clawed hands closed on her throat. Instead of sweet notes, she managed only a strangled gasp. She pitched forward again, and the giant leaped at the brutish ghoul, stabbing it again in the chest. This blow apparently took where the earlier one had failed, for the beast toppled backward into the darkness.

Na-Tethian dropped to one knee over the runechild. She looked unharmed save for red scratches along her pale throat. She clutched the half-opened bag in one tight fist. Her eyes were locked open, her jaw set in a terrible rictus.

She shot him a look with wide, frozen eyes, and with a rattling voice whispered, "Paralysis." Her lips did not move, and she breathed the words more than spoke them.

The giant swore, for the touch of the hungry dead froze their prey. He looked up. More shadows moved toward them, as the ghouls roused fully from their induced somnambulism and reverted to their unnatural instincts.

Na-Tethian turned and pulled the woman's arms up over his own shoulders, gripping her pale wrists in front of her with one hand, holding his blade in the other.

"We will fight our way out," he said. In the moonlight, it seemed that the entire tor now buckled and heaved with the bodies of the undead, and he was unsure of the path back down. He shook his head and said, "I am sorry."

"You cannot kill them all," hissed the woman in his ear. "And you cannot let them leave their graves for the world outside."

"Then I swear I will protect you as best I can. I will die fighting," said the giant.

"Another way," said the runechild. "Drop your sword."

Na-Tethian froze for a moment as if struck by a ghoul himself.

"Drop your weapon," hissed the woman. "Reach into the bag and gather the grave dust."

Na-Tethian looked around for any immediate attack, then carefully bent down and planted his blade in the loose stones, its hilt resting against his knee. He reached into the bag and took a bit of the dust.

"Into the fire," whispered the woman softly, "and repeat after me." And she hissed out a line of the song.

The shapes were moving into the firelight now, their ivory fangs gleaming and their deathlight eyes glimmering in the flames. Too many to fight, not when a scratch could mean death. Na-Tethian stammered out the line, and tossed the grave dust onto the flames. They leaped up, copper and green and blue, but the ghouls continued to shamble forward.

"Again," hissed the pale rune child. "This time match the tone as well," She repeated the words. Na-Tethian nodded and sang, taking another pinch of dust and casting it into the flames. The ghouls wavered for a moment.

"Better," said the woman. "Now sing only what I tell you to, and say nothing else, until morning." She hissed another line of the ceremony.

Na-Tethian obeyed, his bass rumbling matching her soft whispers. The ghouls were at the fireside now, but already the greenish light was dimming from their eyes. A third line, carefully matched, and another bit of dust cast into the flames. Slowly the ghouls lowered themselves to the ground, sitting by the flames, entranced by the song.

Na-Tethian felt the sweat drip from his brow, from the warmth of the fire and the fear of the ghouls and the power of the song that the runechild poured into his ears. The first attempt sounded ragged and worn and off-key, and more than once the ghouls stirred as he hit a wrong note. He would repeat it, sweetening a line here, cutting a grace note there, matching the accent of a particular word. When he looked up, all he could see were ghouls across the hilltop, dead warriors who now doted on his performance. The second try was better, and the third time through the verses was better still. And by the tenth time he was saying the words in time with the pale woman, and by the twentieth he remembered when to cast the dust and when to add more wood without her prompting.

And after an eternity, the eastern sky finally reddened, and the ghoulish armies began to retreat, pulling themselves back under loose piles of obsidian to slumber for another day. Na-Tethian slumped by the dying embers of the fire, his voice raw and ragged.

"You did well," whispered the rune-scarred woman, "Perhaps you are not such an idiot after all." She moved a little, but stiffly—the ghoul's touch still ran strong in her blood.

"Your voice," said the giant. "Will it not heal?"

"With time," said the woman. "This is a powerful place, holding back powerful dead. The strength of their evil, their flesh-freezing touch, is great. One more night. We must do this one more night. Then you can carry me to a magister."

Na-Tethian said, "I should take you down to the inn. We must tell them what you're doing up here, so they won't be afraid."

The woman managed a hacking chuckle.

"Do you think they will be less afraid to know of the numbers of hungry dead that remain above their town? Eh?" She hacked again. "Will they be less afraid to know that their survival rests on a single song, sung three nights a year? And will they realize that the safest place for themselves, regardless of the outcome, is in the safety of their homes, or would they be encouraged to come up and watch?"

Na-Tethian thought about what he knew of humans and grimaced.

"I thought so," said the woman. "As I said, one more night, then you can carry me to a magister. Afterward, we must gather more grave dust for next year."

Na-Tethian frowned. "I am merely passing through, on the way to Zalavat." For half-a-promise, he thought, and his voice wavered.

"You swore to protect me," said the woman softly, and Na-Tethian could almost hear a smile in that voice.

"I . . . that was spoken in a dire moment," said the giant.

"But I accept your oath," said the woman. "And I swear to you in turn that you will not die fighting. Not if I have anything to say about it."

Na-Tethian scowled.

"And *should* something ever happen to me, it would make sense to have someone else who knows the ritual. And when I'm gone, you'll find someone on your own to carry on. Someone with a good voice, a sense of obligation, and no fear of the dead."

Na-Tethian thought of Tammath, the young singer at the inn, whose eyes seemed to drive into his soul. At last, the giant nodded in agreement.

A soft chuckle came from the runechild's unmoving lips. "Now pay attention. In the third canto, your pacing is horribly weak . . ."

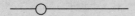

Beneath the battle tor, below the cropped mountain where dire forces fought and died long ago and live again for three nights a year, there is a village behind a stockade wall. The residents of that village gather at the inn and listen to a young man sing songs about the ancient battle on the plateau above them.

And the villagers also tell tales of a demonic necromancer who sought to raise the dead, and the giant hero who set off for the tor to battle her. And they will show you the gear the giant left behind at the inn when he went, armed only with his sword and armor, to fight the fell wizard of the mountain.

And they will tell you that, ever since, for three nights a year, you can hear the dead singing on the mountain top, joined by the deep, bass voice that rumbles through the valley, a voice deep and damned and rumbling.

And the natives of the inn cower in their beds on those evenings, for they know that voice. They think they know who won the battle on the tor. And they don't send to De-Shamod for any more help.

PRECIOUS THINGS

The sun was still hovering just above the horizon to the east, a pale and fiery disk fighting against the smoky pall of the overcast day, when Bailthor crested a rise and spotted the cart on the side of the road. He paused, studying it for signs of danger. The vehicle had tumbled into a ditch and rested sideways; the horse was dead. A body lay sprawled near the cart, a human man in a leather jerkin, undoubtedly a soldier. The man was bloody and rent, leaving no doubt that he, too, was dead. A halfspear rested in the mud near one outstretched hand, a crossbow near his other hip.

The litorian could sense the rhodin even before he got close enough to see their tracks in the dust, and he realized the tumbled cart was no mere accident. The bestial smell of the raiders hung thick in the morning air, mixed with the metallic odor of blood and mud. Their kill was fresh; they were not far away.

Painful images of Bailthor's slain mother blossomed in his mind's eye, made sharp by the rhodin's unmistakable scent. Those memories were suddenly so clear and distinct that for a brief moment he was a child again, watching as she was battered and broken by deadly horns. The anguish made the fur of Bailthor's mane rise. He issued a low growl from deep in his chest, feeling the full power of all his old oaths surging from within.

Make them pay. Avenge her death.

Bailthor blinked, returning to the present, and shook his head.

Oaths made in haste, that inner voice reprimanded. *Fools' errands. You have other responsibilities.*

Reminded of his present oath, Bailthor glanced back and winced slightly at the sight of the man following him. His bearded face was haggard and drawn, the flesh pale and sunken around his eyes and mouth.

Too much at stake, that inner voice insisted, making the litorian feel agitated and eager to be on his way.

Regaining his composure, Bailthor scanned the wreck for any signs of danger and spied a leg protruding from beneath the cart. It was draped by the fine silk of a torn and bloody dress but was missing any sort of boot or shoe.

The passenger was someone of means, he realized. The litorian sighed, saddened, but he would not let such misfortune detour him from his course. She shouldn't have been traveling with such a light escort through the hills during the dark of night, he insisted silently, reassuring himself that it was all right to keep moving.

The leonine creature returned his focus to the surrounding hills, sniffing the air cautiously as he padded along the road, passing the site of the wreck and its victims. He did not really expect another rhodin attack, especially not in the light of dawn, but he was not foolish enough to let down his guard.

"Wait," the man said from behind the litorian, his voice raspy in his throat. "She might still live."

Bailthor let out a soft sigh of exasperation, expecting resistance from Elvar, but he did not slow his pace. "No," he said, "It's not safe to stop. And we can't spare the time."

"*You* can't spare it, you mean," Elvar snapped, but the sharp words made him wheeze, and he broke into a coughing spell. The force of it doubled the man over, clutching at his ribs with both arms. When he finally regained his breath and stood upright again, the litorian could see a bit of blood flecking Elvar's greying whiskers.

Bailthor shook his head gently in consternation as he turned back to face his counterpart. "You can't spare it, either," he said softly, studying the man's exhausted face. "You don't have much time."

Elvar eyed the litorian as he wiped his hand across his mouth. "Depends on how you look at it," he replied, chuckling, but there was no smile on his wan face. "To a condemned man, a few moments' delay before the impending execution is a blessed thing. Even if he is dying of lung-rot." Then he turned his attention back toward the wreckage. "We must see if she lives," he said, taking several steps in the direction of the cart.

Growling softly, Bailthor moved to block Elvar's path, feeling his own unease grow as he halted the man's progress. "I said no."

The litorian could see Elvar's hands trembling as the two travelers eyed one another, though whether it was from rage or the lung-rot causing his strength to fail, the litorian wasn't sure. The rune that had been on the back of the man's hand for so long was almost completely faded. It seemed that the healer's power was almost spent.

Elvar clenched his fists, and Bailthor wondered if the man would try to strike him. He did not fear the blow, for he doubted the ill human could deliver it with much force, but the exertion might hasten his deterioration, might weaken him enough to keep him from continuing on his own.

The litorian's own muscles quivered in anger—anger and nervousness, for those old doubts were rising up inside him again. If they stopped, if Elvar succumbed to his coughing sickness, Bailthor might not be able to deliver the man to Trisic in time. The thought of failure—again—made his heart beat rapidly and his breath shorten in fear.

"Will you strike me, now?" Bailthor asked Elvar, hoping to calm the man before he made his condition worse. "Are you going to let your temper get the better of you again?"

Elvar swallowed suddenly, his eyes flicking away, unable to hold Bailthor's gaze. The litorian could see the guilt and the anguish in the man's face, could see the struggle as Elvar tried to bring his rage under control.

"No," Elvar said, his voice and gaze distant, as though he were reliving the murder all over again. "I didn't mean to—Thanis was my friend." Elvar's words broke off in a half-suppressed sob.

"I know," Bailthor replied, feeling guilty for having reminded Elvar of his crime. "He was mine, too. Thanis loved you like a brother; I'm sure he would have forgiven you, as I have." Then he took a breath, growing resolute once more. "But that doesn't change anything, Elvar. Trisic demanded justice, and I swore an oath to bring you back—alive—to account for it. You promised me you wouldn't resist."

Elvar grimaced and closed his eyes, as though the litorian's words were physical blows against him. "I did promise," he said softly, his voice unclear with the wetness burbling in his lungs. "So much I would have changed . . ." he said, staring into some unknown distance, his tone weak.

"As would I," Bailthor replied. "But what's done is done, and I have an oath. I won't fail another one," he added.

Elvar stared at his friend forlornly, saying nothing.

"We have to go," Bailthor said softly, gently reaching one hand out and taking the man by the arm, intending to steer him away from the cart and resume their journey.

Elvar began to nod, took one tentative step in the direction Bailthor tugged, but then he stiffened, shaking his head. He jerked his arm free, and Bailthor let go rather than injure the man further. "I don't care," Elvar said, his voice full of defiance. "Damn your oath! She might still live, and I must try to help her if I can."

"How?" Bailthor demanded, exasperated once more. "You can't even heal yourself!"

Elvar's eyes narrowed. "My rune may be fading, but I still feel its power. I don't know why I can't cure this damned lung-rot. Maybe it's a punishment, for . . . for—" And then his voice turned plaintive, his eyes pleading with the litorian. "I'm a runechild, a healer. I must try."

As if to punctuate the man's pleas, the woman beneath the cart groaned softly and stirred. Elvar's expression changed to a combination of surprise and impatience, and he turned back toward the wreck and wobbled in her direction.

Bailthor felt the resolve leave him then, felt cold dread in the pit of his stomach. He knew he wouldn't be able to talk Elvar out of what the man meant to do, and knowing the woman was alive quelled his desire even to try. They *did* owe it to her to help. But Bailthor feared he would never get Elvar to Trisic's manor house alive.

The litorian felt the weight of his oath press heavily upon him, the burden of his duty beginning to crush him. Suddenly, he was exhausted. Elvar would die before he could account for Thanis' murder, Bailthor would fail, and the third oath would be broken. He closed his eyes in resignation and let the despair wash over him.

Then Bailthor shook his head as though to brush away the doubts like cobwebs. Elvar's not dead yet, he insisted to himself. The litorian moved toward the cart, determined to see what he could do to aid Elvar—and hasten him.

The way the cart and horse were strewn in the ditch, it appeared that the woman and her bodyguard had been heading toward them along the road, away from Trisic's manor and the village of Daphe just beyond. She was not pinned beneath the damaged cart as Bailthor had initially thought. Instead, she lay sprawled beside it, face down, possibly tossed from the seat when the vehicle had careened off the road. One arm was bent at an unnatural angle, and the other was outstretched, the hilt of a small dagger still resting beneath her palm. A deep gash ran across her shoulder and down the ribs along her left side.

It was a godsend that the rhodin had left her alive. Bailthor wondered if she had even tried to put up a fight, or if her injuries from the cart crash had been too severe.

Elvar struggled to turn the woman over, but in his enfeebled state, he only succeeded in breaking into another round of vicious coughing. The man doubled over, collapsing on top of the woman, his own body wracked with spasms.

Bailthor reached out and gently lifted Elvar off the woman and propped him up against the side of the cart. "Just breathe," he said softly, trying to adjust the man's position so he could inhale more easily.

Elvar nodded and tried to contain his coughs. Finally, after a moment more of hacking, he drew a deep breath and let it out slowly. Then he nodded. "I'm all right," he said and gestured toward the woman. "Turn her over."

Bailthor complied, managing to get the woman face up. Blood, black and crusty, caked her mien and matted her hair. At that moment, she jerked up from the ground and wheezed, blood spraying from her mouth. Then she sagged back down, her breath rattling in her chest.

"Damn," Elvar said. "She's fading fast." He struggled to his knees, panting with the exertion, and moved toward her. He leaned over the woman, placing his hands against her wounds and closing his eyes.

Bailthor watched Elvar's face, noting the man's fierce concentration. "It'll kill you," he said.

Elvar opened his eyes again and looked intently at the litorian. "Probably," he said softly, staring at his counterpart. "But it's the only chance she's got."

Bailthor stared right back. "Will it make a difference for her?" he asked.

Elvar swallowed. "I don't know," he admitted. "There's little power remaining in me, in my rune. I'm almost spent."

"My oath," Bailthor said. "If you die now—"

"Is my life—the life of a condemned and sick man who's dead anyway—worth more than a chance to save her? Even for your oath?"

Bailthor looked at Elvar, and the feelings of helplessness cascaded over him all over again. The thought of a third failure made him grimace, made the knot in his stomach turn cold. He didn't know if he could live with the self-doubt, the humiliation. Already, he could feel the unwavering resolve seeping away, feel the inner strength of his conviction beginning to crumble and drain from his limbs. An oathsworn whose word meant nothing; that's what he would be.

But if there was a chance for the woman to survive . . .

Slowly, Bailthor nodded. "Do it," he said.

Elvar immediately closed his eyes again and began a chant, what sounded like a sing-song babbling, as he pressed his hands against the woman's chest. Bailthor watched as the man screwed up his face in concentration. He could hear Elvar struggling to keep the words clear, to keep the coughing from taking over.

At first, Bailthor wasn't sure he actually saw any change. There seemed to be a faint glow upon the body, almost imperceptible, but the litorian wasn't sure it was really there. Then, it grew the tiniest bit brighter, and Bailthor knew he wasn't imagining it. Where the man's hands pressed against the dying woman, the glow grew stronger, brighter, and her breathing strengthened and calmed.

The fur of Bailthor's mane was up before he'd realized something was wrong. Then he smelled it: the scent of rhodin, grown stronger. The litorian leaped to his feet just in time to spot one of the snarling, ram-headed beasts hurling a javelin toward him from the other side of the road.

Reacting on instinct and burning hatred fanned by that old familiar pain, Bailthor screamed a primal challenge and lunged up and away from the cart, spinning in mid-air to snatch the missile before it could strike him. As he settled to his feet again, the litorian saw three other rhodin moving in, closing on his flanks.

Out of the corner of his eye, he spied Elvar glance up briefly, but the runechild was not deterred from his work. Bailthor would need to keep the four raiders away from the human pair on his own.

So be it, Bailthor thought, satisfied, as he discarded the javelin. He rolled his head about in a circle, loosening the muscles of his neck and shoulders, muscles that had been tense with worry and doubt. Whatever the outcome of the journey, for the moment, at least, he was keeping to the oath. And killing the hated rhodin. His sense of determination had returned. Nothing could stop him. It felt good.

The first rhodin to try to close with Bailthor came in from the left, a big spiked club clutched in both hands. The litorian's eyes narrowed in feral eagerness as the club whistled through the air. He spun and ducked, getting inside the weapon's arc as it passed harmlessly behind him. In the same motion, Bailthor grabbed the creature's arm and yanked viciously down, twisting it around so that the momentum of the swing forced the creature's elbow to snap backward across the litorian's shoulder. The rhodin howled in pain as Bailthor continued to pull downward, thrusting his hip into the beast's midsection to pull it off balance, then throwing it several feet with another feral snarl.

The litorian turned quickly to see what new threat he faced. A second rhodin was charging him with a halfspear leveled at his stomach. The other two were moving toward the cart, toward Elvar and the woman, with blades in hand. Bailthor waited until the halfspear was almost to him, then he sprang into the air, kicking down with one clawed foot and out with another. The downward thrust caught the spear haft and embedded the blade into the ground. The sudden stop caused the rhodin's momentum to carry it up and over the pivoting haft— right into the litorian's other kick. Bailthor's heel slammed directly into the chin of the surprised rhodin, whose head snapped backward. Bailthor grinned in satisfaction to see the creature's eyes roll up in its head as it dropped. He snatched up the halfspear as he landed.

In one smooth motion, Bailthor sent the spear flying toward the nearest rhodin still standing and sprinted in the direction of the last of the four creatures. The spear did not score a direct hit, but it raked against the ram-headed beast's flank, drawing a thin line of blood. The rhodin screamed in pain and rage and turned back toward Bailthor, lowering its head to butt against him, but the litorian was already dashing past it and at the last foe.

The fourth rhodin spun to challenge Bailthor, but when it saw the malevolent battle lust burning in the litorian's eyes, it faltered and swung half-heartedly, dancing backward to avoid the flurry of punches it saw coming.

It was not quick enough.

Bailthor easily avoided the blade and snapped three quick, staggering blows to the rhodin's snout and throat, sending it stumbling backward, spluttering. Another well-placed kick to its midsection dropped the beast. It crumpled into a heap in the ditch and groaned softly, unmoving.

Bailthor spun back, bracing himself for an attack, and had the wind knocked out of him as the remaining rhodin, head lowered and horns thrust forward, plowed straight into his gut. The litorian went flying backward several feet and landed in an awkward heap, gasping for air and certain he had cracked several ribs.

The craven rhodin snorted in satisfaction, gathered itself for a second attack, and charged again, holding a short, thick sword somewhat awkwardly. The beast's first swipe with the blade whistled through the air toward Bailthor's head, and he barely managed to shift to one side as the tip thudded into the earth next to his ear. The rhodin drew back for another ferocious cut, and the litorian scrambled back madly to avoid the swing, with no time to regain his footing.

The rhodin came on, seeing a chance to finish off its dangerous foe. Bailthor was forced to roll and crabwalk back and forth to evade the strikes, each of which thudded powerfully into the ground. Every movement sent fiery pain up and down the litorian's side, his shifting motion jerking his damaged ribs horribly. The pain made him want to retch and left him gasping for breath.

On the next blow, instead of dodging away, Bailthor lunged back toward the rhodin. The sword nearly nicked him in the shoulder, but he slipped beneath the swing and kicked out, slamming his foot into the rhodin's ankle. He heard the satisfying crunch of bone grinding on bone and saw the beast stiffen in agony even as it toppled over in its own overbalancing swing.

Bailthor spun with his kick, keeping the momentum pressing and driving the rhodin's leg forward and down, forcing the beast to its knees. The litorian completed the turn to his stomach and shoved himself up with both hands, grimacing as he felt his ribs shift again. He stepped back to gauge the scene and see how everyone else fared.

The other three rhodin were still down where Bailthor had left them, but he saw that Elvar was slumped over the woman, in the grip of a particularly fierce coughing spell.

His breath coming hard in both exertion and clenching pain, Bailthor spun and raked a final crippling back kick into the rhodin's chest that sent it sprawling. Then he turned and trotted stiffly to the healer's side, listing slightly with his hand pressed against his ribs.

Elvar's coughing fit had not subsided, and when Bailthor crouched down to help the runechild to sit, he could see a mist of blood spraying from behind the hand that covered the man's mouth as the spasms continued.

At last, Elvar drew a single, deep breath and said, "Only . . . enough . . . for a little while. . . . Get her . . . help . . . quickly!" And he closed his eyes, slumping unconscious. His breaths were slow and sporadic, punctuated with a horrible gurgling.

The woman seemed to be resting easier, though Bailthor could see her wounds were still severe. He didn't know how much time either of them had. He wondered whether he could carry them both, groaning softly as each sharp breath sent little stabbing pains along his side.

And outrun the rhodin, he silently added, knowing that more of the band might chase him down before he could reach Trisic's manor house. The cowardly beasts always sought to outnumber their foes.

Bailthor's desperate musings were interrupted by a faint squeak from beneath the cart.

The litorian jerked his gaze toward the sound and spotted a small, dirty hand disappearing from view into the shelter of the overturned vehicle.

"Who's there?" Bailthor hissed, jumping to his feet and instantly regretting the sudden movement. He moved to the tilted vehicle and called more softly, "It's all right. Come out." He heard a soft whimper echo from beneath the cart, but there was no reply.

"Child," Bailthor said gently, trying to keep his voice down below a roar. "Do not fret; we're friends. We won't hurt you. I chased the bad creatures away."

After a long moment, the hand reappeared in the dirt beneath the cart, and then another. Slowly, a foot appeared, and then a second one, and finally, a little girl in a dress similar to the woman's poked her face out from the cart, peering up at the litorian.

Bailthor breathed a sigh of relief, thankful that she appeared unharmed. "It's all right," he reiterated, smiling. "I won't hurt you." He realized he was clenching his hands into fists and willed himself to relax.

The little girl looked uncertain, staring at Bailthor, but finally, she scrambled out from under the cart and stood up, looking silently at him. "Mama's hurt," the child said, pointing at the woman.

"I know," Bailthor replied. Painful images flashed to the surface of his thoughts again. The litorian's eyes narrowed as he considered the irony. He had not been much older than the little girl before him when he'd sworn that first oath. Just a child, insisting he could save his mother, too desperate, too frightened to see the truth. The fragile creature in front of the litorian, with her tearstained cheeks and the fear in her eyes, reminded him too clearly of that day.

Casting aside his own sorrow, Bailthor made up his mind. Elvar was right; he had to try to get them all to safety. He just had no idea how.

"We need to get her to a healer," Bailthor said. "Can you help me?"

The little girl nodded, looking unsure.

"Good," Bailthor said, thinking desperately. "What's your name?"

"Kieralla."

"All right, Kieralla, don't worry. Your mama is going to be just fine."

Kieralla nodded and squatted down. "Mama," she said. "Mama, don't die."

"Shhh," Bailthor said, moving beside the girl and turning her face to his. "Don't tell her sad things. Talk about happy things. Tell her how much better she's going to feel once we get her to someone who can help."

The little girl nodded again.

Desperately, the litorian looked over at Elvar. The man still breathed, but it was shallow and rapid and sounded ominously moist. The healer had very little time left.

Bailthor stood up and looked around, feeling useless. Despite his resolve, he could feel his energy ebbing from him, his inner power fading away as he realized he was letting go of his oath. Though he didn't care that he would fail Trisic, Bailthor felt . . . regret . . . that his word, his honor, would be suspect in others' eyes forevermore. That realization made him pause, made him bow his head as he admitted his failings. Then, spying the little girl who sat near his feet and held her mother's hand, Bailthor smiled gently.

Trisic will not get his moment of retribution; so be it. Someone else needs hope more than he needs vengeance.

Casting the remaining doubts from his mind, at last willing to live with the consequences, the litorian moved over to the cart, an idea forming.

Though it did not seem damaged, the cart was pitched awkwardly in the ditch, and Bailthor knew it would be a struggle to get the thing upright again. Snarling in determination, he grabbed the tangled cart harness and ripped it free of the dead horse. Then he jerked the cart a couple times, testing its weight and aligning it better for what he was about to do. With a mighty growl, he threw himself into the cart full force, knocking it sideways.

The first time, Bailthor couldn't quite roll the vehicle hard enough, and he staggered as a flood of pain radiated from his ribcage. But he ignored the throbbing and tried again. It tipped a little more, and with his next thrust he rammed his shoulder into the side of the cart and kicked with all the strength he could muster. The cart teetered on the edge of its lower wheel and finally rolled over.

Once the vehicle was right-side up, it was all Bailthor could do to get it up onto the road again, pulling the shafts and dragging it up the side of the ditch behind him, following the incline at an angle to lessen the steepness. When he finally crested the side of the road, he wanted to sag down to catch his breath, stolen from him by the fiery burning of his injury. But he didn't have time to stop. He rolled the cart back to his three charges, the little girl still huddled over her mother.

The woman still rested easily and, miraculously, Elvar still breathed as well.

Wasting no time, Bailthor hoisted the mother up and settled her into the cart. Then he lifted Elvar up beside the wounded woman. Finally, he boosted Kieralla up next to the two prone forms.

"Hold on," the litorian told the child as he ran around to the front of the cart and grabbed the shafts. "We're going to get you to help," he added over his shoulder as he began to pull.

The effort to get the cart rolling with three people in it wasn't as bad as Bailthor had imagined. Grasping the shafts tightly, he leaned forward and strained with all his might until he felt motion. Slowly, maddeningly slowly, he began to build some momentum. Finally, he was able to settle into a quick trot, though he had no idea how long he could maintain it.

"Will the monsters come back again?" Kieralla called fearfully from the back of the cart.

"No," Bailthor panted as he pulled. "And if . . . they do . . . I'll . . . chase them . . . away again." Talking made him lose his pace, and he snapped his mouth shut and resumed his exertions, timing his breathing and trying to ignore the insistent ache in his ribs.

It was well toward noon when Bailthor, still trotting despite the fierce burning in his side and an agonizing cramping in his trembling legs, crested the last hill and spotted Trisic's manor house, sitting on the outskirts of Daphe. When he staggered into the front yard, he was nearly blind from exhaustion, spots swimming before his eyes. He dropped the shafts, then fell to his knees, panting.

A shout came from the front steps of the house, and Bailthor could vaguely discern people running and hollering, but he heard none of it for the pounding in his ears. He wanted only to crumple to the ground right then, but he willed himself to stand and move to the back of the cart. Kieralla and her mother had already been removed, and several of Trisic's servants were just about to hoist Elvar off the cart, but Bailthor shouldered them aside.

"I must," was all he could manage as he lifted the man from the cart. Elvar was limp, and Bailthor could not discern any breathing at all. Wavering on his feet from the added weight, the litorian made his way inside the manor house. More than once, he nearly dropped Elvar, but somehow, he managed to stagger to Trisic's council chamber and push past the door.

Trisic sat at the head of a long table, one hand cupping his chin, brooding. His eyes were closed, and his silvery hair seemed disheveled. At Bailthor's entrance, the lord opened his eyes and turned his sorrowful gaze upon the intruder. His grey eyes widened—and darkened—once he saw the burden Bailthor carried.

The litorian set Elvar's form down on the table and dropped, the last of his strength totally gone.

"You!" Trisic said, his voice low and menacing. The lord stood and strode toward Bailthor, but his gaze was on Elvar's still form. "Now you shall account for the murder of my son! Now you shall pay for the—" He froze in place, sucking in one sharp gasp.

Bailthor closed his eyes. Elvar must surely be dead. Somehow, it didn't matter.

The litorian could sense Trisic turn on him, could feel the man's challenging stare, demanding to know how Bailthor could have failed in his oath.

Bailthor opened his eyes and, taking a fortifying breath, rose to his feet, slowly, painfully. When he reached his full height, he looked Trisic squarely in the eye. "It came down to a choice," the litorian said, feeling at peace. "A choice between granting you your vengeance, and saving the lives of others more deserving. He," and Bailthor gestured toward Elvar's corpse, "—and I—chose to heal rather than destroy. He surrendered the last of his life, and I abandoned my oath. Both of us, I believe, go to our graves content in the decision."

"Bah!" Trisic snarled, turning and stomping back to his chair. He slumped into it. "You let him talk you out of your duty. You lost everything dear to you for the sake of a murderer and a coward!"

Bailthor shook his head, wanting to make the man opposite him see. "To the end, he was a healer," the litorian insisted, pointing to Elvar's body, still lying on the table. "Despite his crimes, he sought to save those around him. Even me; he saved me from myself."

"And what of me?" Trisic demanded, leaning forward, his face flushed with rage. "What healing shall I gain, with no peace to be found? You promised me that Elvar would account for his crime. You failed. You are no oathsworn, and I feel no comfort now, because you made your choice!" He sat back, the rage on his mien replaced with anguish. "My son died at his hand," Trisic whispered fiercely. "So tell me; what healing did I receive?"

Before the litorian could answer, the door to the council chamber banged open, and Kieralla ran in, smiling.

"Grampa!" the little girl shouted, charging toward Trisic.

The silver-haired man's eyes widened at the sight of the child, still in her muddy and torn dress. He rose from his chair and scooped her up in his arms, giving Bailthor a bewildered stare as he hugged her tightly. "What happened?" he asked.

The litorian could only shrug, just as surprised that Trisic was related to his two charges.

"We were attacked on the road south," came a soft and wavering voice from the doorway.

Bailthor turned in surprise to see Kieralla's mother standing there, pale and held steady by two attendants.

"The road south?" Trisic exclaimed, looking bewildered. "But why? Where were you going?"

"I'm sorry, Trisic," the woman said, looking sorrowful, "but I couldn't stand to be here any longer. The pall that has fallen over this house since Thanis died was too much for me to bear. I grieve for my husband as you grieve for your son, but your thirst for vengeance shrouds everything here in a blanket of misery and regret. Kieralla needs a happier place. I was—" and as she paused, the woman looked down, her visage filled with sadness. "I was taking her away."

Thanis was married? Bailthor thought, stunned. *He had a daughter? He never told us!*

The litorian looked back at Trisic. The man's eyes glittered with the first tears of regret, and his mouth worked soundlessly, but he could not get any words out. He simply hugged Kieralla and swayed gently back and forth. The room remained silent for several long moments, as the weight of sorrow seemed to thicken among everyone there.

"I'm so sorry, Kaylie," Trisic said at last, his voice thick with emotion. "I didn't—"

"Shh," the woman, Kaylie, said softly, gingerly crossing the distance to embrace Trisic as well. "I shouldn't have gone," she added, crying. "I miss him, too." The three of them simply stood there, with Kieralla between them, hugging. Bailthor felt an urge to quietly excuse himself, to leave the trio to their moment, but he was too tired and in too much pain to make his way out of the chamber.

Finally, they parted.

"We were attacked," Kaylie said softly. "If not for—" and she turned to face Bailthor, her own eyes also shining with tears. "They saved us," she finished quietly, gesturing to both the litorian and Elvar.

Trisic turned back to Bailthor then, setting his granddaughter down at last. "Why didn't you tell me? I—" but he faltered once more, simply shaking his head in disbelief. "Your oath," he said when he'd regained his voice. "You abandoned it to save my precious girls." It was more a statement than a question.

Bailthor smiled gently. "I made a choice, as did Elvar, though we did not know who they were; Thanis never told either of us about them."

"But your oaths!" Trisic repeated. "Your word as an oathsworn is what makes you who you are!"

"It's all right," Bailthor said. "I see more good in what I did this day than in most of my oaths. And I see the good in what Elvar did. It was the right choice."

Trisic did not say anything for several long moments but continued to stare at Bailthor. Or rather, the litorian realized, at his forehead.

"It appears the land agrees, runechild," the silver-haired man said at last.

Bailthor blinked, uncertain he had heard Trisic's words correctly. He leaned forward to gaze at his reflection in the polished surface of the table and saw it—a graceful, curving symbol indelibly displayed upon his forehead. The land had found goodness in what he had done, and he had been given a new chance.

Runechild.

The word sounded odd in the litorian's mind, as if it were some sort of mistake. He rubbed gently at the mark. "I never would have thought . . ." he began, unsure what he thought. Suddenly, there was hope again.

"Perhaps Elvar wrought more good in his final act than merely saving my family," Trisic said, interrupting Bailthor's musings. "He helped you find a better path."

Bailthor nodded, considering his newfound possibilities. "And he saved Thanis' wife and child, perhaps making amends to the friend he'd wronged. And you?" the litorian asked. "What did he do for you?"

Trisic smiled, his eyes filling with tears once more, though they seemed to be tears of happiness. "He reminded me to appreciate all the precious things I still have, rather than lamenting those I do not." The man hugged Kaylie and Kieralla once more. "He healed me after all."

STAN!
SKIN DEEP

Sunlight rarely pierced the lush canopy of vegetation that hung over the hamlet of Simiir. But here, closer to the Sonish Sea, the jungle thinned, and pale yellow rays dappled the ground with pools of radiant warmth. Pashkin moved carefully, avoiding the sunshine as much as possible. He'd entered the Jungles of Naveradel by choice, forsaking the light of day for the twilight world of the rainforest. Now, ten years later, the sun seemed harsh and cruel—a light that burns those who dwell too long in it—and Pashkin had no wish to be burned.

Standing under a tree with thick, rubbery leaves that were larger than his bedroll, Pashkin scanned the surrounding jungle. He was a thin man, no taller than average. Wearing a tunic and leggings made of light cloth, he was dressed more like a farmer than a hero. Indeed, although he carried a sturdy longspear, Pashkin used it as a walking stick. He seemed to have only the barest concept of how to wield it as a weapon.

Still, no one who saw him standing there would argue the fact that Pashkin was a hero—a man with a great destiny. It was something in his eyes. Or, rather, it was the deep blue pattern around his left eye, the one that looked like a shooting star and sometimes seemed to shimmer in firelight. It marked Pashkin as a runechild and, therefore, as a hero. This marking was the reason he had come to the jungle in the first place, the reason he'd chosen to make a home in Simiir, and the reason he was now traipsing through the jungle searching for the wreckage of a slaughtered merchant caravan.

"Buck up, old son," Pashkin said aloud. "You're a Vekik-blessed runechild. Even the beasts of the jungle recognize that. You'll be fine."

He'd hoped that the sound of his own voice would make him feel more confident, but it was too thin and tremulous. The ambient noise of the jungle swallowed it like a lion devouring a rabbit. Pashkin took a long swig from his water gourd, scratched his cheek just at the base of his rune, and continued his trek.

"This is all part of the job. And a job," he reminded himself, "that you went looking for."

Pashkin still remembered the very moment he first laid eyes on a real runechild.

He was twelve years old and still living in Destimar's Flats, a small fishing village along the northern shores of the Aged Peninsula. Even as a youth, he dreamed of better things than the life of a fisherman. He saw every man and woman in the village toil endlessly with the sea—setting nets and traps in the shallows, sailing into the deep waters to catch blue scales in the spring and pink bellies in the fall, and spending every evening repairing boats and equipment damaged by the waves. Everyone and everything in town smelled of fish, and no one had ever thought there might be a different way to live one's life, let alone a better one.

The young Pashkin knew he was meant for more, but he had no idea what until the day she walked into town.

Her name was Misha. She arrived one summer afternoon and politely inquired if she might be able to perform some honest labor in exchange for a meal and some shelter. Misha was tall and powerfully built, had a flowing mane of fiery red hair, and carried a great axe strapped to her back. But the most striking thing about her was the mystic symbol emblazoned on her right cheek.

The village elders practically fell over themselves assuring Misha that she was welcome in Destimar's Flats. They would gladly feed and house her for as long as she cared to stay with no need for recompense. Misha, however, insisted that she not take advantage of the town's hospitality, and went down to the water every day. She had no real training or skill when it came to fishing, but she could lift twice as much as anyone in the village and was always willing to lend a hand hauling in lines, making repairs to hulls, or even cleaning fish and laying them out to dry.

At first young Pashkin thought Misha's face was tattooed—many people in Destimar's Flats had tattoos, usually gained on a journey to Sormere to sell dried fish. But those tattoos were crudely rendered images of whales and mermaids or the names of loved ones. Misha's marking was instead an abstract pattern of lines and curves—sleek and artful, as though her cheek were a canvas graced by a master painter's brush. Even more curious was the fact that, while tattoos were all cast in flat, dull shades of blue or sepia, Misha's marking was a vibrant purple.

His mother told Pashkin that Misha was a runechild—a hero destined to make the world a better place. The rune on her face was a gift from the gods. "It's how we can recognize the heroes in our midst," she said. "So we can show them proper deference."

Pashkin was skeptical. Certainly Misha was a hard worker, but a *hero*? There seemed to be nothing especially heroic about her.

At night, in the meeting hall, Misha would tell stories of her journeys. She'd been a good many places, particularly for someone who appeared to be no older than twenty-five. She'd visited the court of Gri-Taresh, the steward of Ao-Manasa, crossed the Southern Wastes on camelback, and braved the Wildlands of Kish to stand on the shore of the Rune Sea. And everywhere she went, it seemed, she found a warm welcome thanks to the mark upon her cheek.

Clearly Misha was an adventurer and a hardy soul. But, as near as Pashkin could tell, she had never actually done anything truly heroic. Still, she was treated like royalty just about anywhere she traveled.

The more he listened to Misha's tales, the more certain Pashkin became that he had found his life's calling. He would do whatever he had to do to become a runechild.

It is uncommonly easy for a person to get lost in a jungle, even when he knows where he's going. The undergrowth is so thick that it's rarely possible to travel in a straight line, and the trees grow so close together that the landscape changes radically every few hundred yards. The only thing a traveler knows for certain is where he is at that particular moment.

Pashkin was under the distinct disadvantage of not even knowing for certain where his objective lay. He knew that the caravan for which he searched was headed toward Simiir, and he suspected that they had entered the jungle at the northernmost tip of Sunrise Bay, because that anchorage was the most popular with the captains of merchant vessels. So far he had been following the meandering route of the Mipolo River—it was not the most direct route to the bay, but many traders used it because it was easy to lose one's way in the heart of the jungle, and the river eventually led to several settlements. As he neared the Misty Falls, though, Pashkin turned south and made straight for the coast.

It would be easier if the caravan had been expected. Then Pashkin might have known who was likely leading the merchants and what path they were liable to take. But a town as remote as Simiir was not on any regular trade routes. In fact, it often went a full year between visits from merchants. They would never have known this caravan even existed if one of its guards had not stumbled into Simiir four days ago, half delirious from exhaustion and covered with vicious wounds.

The guard was able to convey only the fact that some sort of giant leopard had attacked the caravan, then she slipped into unconsciousness. How long she'd been walking through the jungle and where the assault took place remained mysteries.

And so Pashkin walked carefully along what he considered the most likely path for the merchants to have used. At first the going was easy. In the deep jungle there was very little undergrowth. But now that he was nearing the coast and the sunlight broke through the canopy, the ground was covered in vines, ferns, and various shrubs. These plants grew extraordinarily quickly, so, even after so short a time, it was unlikely that any evidence of the caravan's passage remained visible. Pashkin poked his spear at every large shape hidden under a blanket of vegetation, hoping to find a cart or bundle or some other evidence of the missing merchants.

He'd been doing this for the better part of four days and, truth be told, was growing quite bored. He was tired, hungry for food other than trail rations, and felt as though he had a rash on his cheek. Only the fact that a tremendous leopard could be stalking him through the brush kept Pashkin focused on the matter at hand.

As he pressed past two towering palm trees and into a new grove, there was a flurry of activity. Birds took to the air, and all manner of small jungle creatures jumped, slithered, and crawled away from what seemed to be a large crate sitting in the middle of the thicket.

"You're going to have to be a bit more quiet, old son," Pashkin told himself. "Seems everyone in the Naveradel can hear you moving about."

He made straight for the crate, trying to make as little noise as possible.

Pashkin was still a good fifty yards from his target when he became certain he'd found the caravan. At his feet were the diminutive remains of a loresong faen dressed in a fashionable but practical outfit. His eyes were open, frozen in an expression of primal fear that, along with the numerous slash wounds on what was left of his body, told Pashkin everything he needed to know about his final moments. The faen had been mauled to death, then served as a meal for one or more wild animals.

More bodies littered the ground, Pashkin noticed as he drew closer to the crate. Most were faen merchants, but Pashkin also found a litorian and two humans dressed in the same uniform as the guard who'd made it to Simiir. It was a slaughter, and his hopes of finding anything more than the partial remains of the other members of the caravan faded quickly.

The wooden object Pashkin had spied turned out not to be a crate at all, but rather a merchant's covered wagon that had been knocked onto its side. Despite being knocked over with some degree of force (if the furrows in the ground were any in-dication), the wagon itself remained intact. The walls were scratched, both from the fall and apparently from some massive animal's claws, but they still held together, and the door to the interior was closed and locked from the inside.

"Sturdy construction," he observed as he circled around it. Pashkin rapped his knuckles appreciatively on the decoratively painted panels. He jumped nearly a foot in the air when something inside the wagon knocked back. Putting his ear to the wagon, Pashkin could hear a dry, weak voice rasping out what he presumed was a cry for help, but the author of the voice was too injured or too weak for the sounds to be comprehensible.

"Rallonoch's blessing!" he said, seemingly to the jungle around him. Then he cupped his hands against the upended wagon's side and shouted between them, "Hold on. I'm going to get you out of there. Can you unlock the door? Knock once for no and twice for yes."

A single knock came in reply.

"Damn it all. Are you hurt or is the door broken? I mean, knock once if you're hurt."

Again there was a rapping from inside the vehicle, this time fainter.

"Move away from the door," Pashkin said as he slid his longspear through the handle. "I'm going to pry it open."

Another soft rap came in reply.

Pulling with all his might, Pashkin felt the door start to give. Unfortunately, it was sturdier than his spear, which snapped in two and sent him tumbling head over heels into the brush.

"Reckon I'll have to do it the old-fashioned way," he said.

Grabbing the severely shortened end with the metal blade, Pashkin leaned in close to the door. He wedged the tip of the blade between the door and the frame and moved it about in a delicate pattern. He closed his eyes, listened to the wood creak, and felt the pressure of the bolt barring the door. Then, opening his eyes and smiling broadly, he gave a solid flick of his wrist, and the door sprang open.

"Some tricks you never forget," he said with a grin.

"Yes," said a faint voice from inside the wagon. "No matter how far you run, you can't escape your past, can you Pashkin?"

On his sixteenth birthday, Pashkin stuffed his few belongings into a backpack and left Destimar's Flats. Everyone who'd ever left town headed south to Sormere, so young Pashkin turned immediately west toward the bustling port city of Ka-Rone. Best to distinguish himself as quickly as possible from the life he was leaving. But the trip was long and his funds meager. Less than a month later, Pashkin wandered into Ka-Rone with his belly and purse equally empty.

But there was no work for a half-starved boy who still smelled more than vaguely of fish. Even at the wharf he could find nothing other than ridicule. Faced with the very real possibility of starvation, Pashkin allowed himself to consider every possibility open to him. Everyone else seemed to have money to spare, even here in the lowest quarter of the city. Would it really be such a terrible thing, he wondered, if he just "borrowed" some money from one of the passersby?

Certainly common thievery was not something a potential runechild should engage in, but if Pashkin did not improve his fortunes, he might not live long enough to earn an auspicious destiny. But he worried that he might jeopardize his chances of ever becoming a hero if he began committing crimes, even in the name of self-preservation.

In the end, his rumbling stomach made the decision for him. But Pashkin promised himself that he would only steal from someone who could afford the loss. It would be easy to cut the purse from a drunk passed out in the gutter, but those poor souls always seemed more desperate than he himself felt. No, Pashkin fixed his gaze on the shiny silk bags carried by the well-dressed women he occasionally saw strolling through the quarter. Clearly they had money.

So Pashkin hid behind a corner and waited until he heard the rustle of a bustled skirt moving closer. When the purse dangling off a graceful gloved wrist appeared, he grabbed it and turned to run. But the woman reacted quick as lighting, clutching the bag to her bosom and turning to face the would-be thief with fire in her eyes. Pashkin let go of the purse but continued to run, hoping to escape his botched felony. He didn't make it more than four steps before the handle of a dingy parasol hit him twice in the side of the head and then pulled his legs out from under him.

Lying on the ground, Pashkin stared up at the most beautiful woman he had ever seen. Her raven tresses perfectly framed her alabaster-skinned face, her deep brown eyes flashed with anger, and her lips were painted a red more brilliant than any rose. And on her cheek was an icon the color of sea foam—a heart. As the woman inclined her head to assess her prone captive, the heart seemed to turn greenish-blue, then cream, and finally back to its original hue.

"Forgive me, runechild," young Pashkin blurted out as he covered his eyes in shame. "I didn't know who you were."

"M-me? A runechild?" the woman's anger instantly turned to confusion.

Apparently, some onlookers found the statement exceptionally funny. They stopped and chortled like hyenas over a fallen stag.

"For a few silver coins she'll be the lost Queen of Devania if you like, boy," called out one onlooker, a burly man whose arms were covered with vulgar tattoos. He and his friends again burst into mocking laughter, then continued down the street.

Pashkin stared at the woman quizzically.

"You do me more honor than any five score other men on this street," she said. "But this mark comes from a bottle, not from the gods."

"A bottle?" Pashkin asked, still not understanding.

"She paints it on, lad," said a voice near Pashkin's ear. "Show him, Trina."

Pashkin turned to see a loresong faen standing behind him. Even lying on his back, Pashkin's eyes were nearly even with the faen's thighs. The tiny man straightened his very expensive waistcoat and smoothed his hair so that it accentuated the tapering of his ears.

When Pashkin looked back, he saw the woman dabbing at her face with a handkerchief. The heart was still there, but the cloth now shone with the same iridescent color.

"It's a cosmetic," the faen said. "A skin pigment of my own design. It captures the light and the imagination, giving the wearer an air of mystery and consequence. Only a very few special individuals ever become runechildren, but with the contents of this vial, anyone can show a message to the world."

"It's a lie," Pashkin said flatly. He dusted himself off and, when it was clear that Trina was not going to hit him with the parasol again, stood. He now towered over the newcomer.

The faen laughed, though not unkindly as the others had. His mirth seemed to come from having his secret so bluntly spelled out.

"So it is," the faen said merrily. Then he stood on his toes, cupped a hand around his mouth and whispered conspiratorially to Pashkin. "You will find the world is full of lies that people conveniently ignore, because they are so much more pleasant than the truth. And a lie that people choose to believe is always better than a truth they willfully omit."

Pashkin considered this.

"Besides," the tiny man continued, "the runechildren don't seem to mind. And no one would actually think my pigment was a *real* rune unless he was raised by a hermit—or had just been viciously beaten about the head and shoulders with an umbrella."

The faen winked and poked Pashkin playfully with his elbow.

"Come, my friend," he said. "I am Vael Mistcaller. Let me buy you the best meal in all of Ka-Rone. In exchange you can tell me more about yourself. Trina is notoriously difficult to take by surprise and, bruises not withstanding, you very nearly got away with all her hard-earned cash. I think that perhaps I have work for a lad with your particular skills."

———○———

Vael Mistcaller lay huddled toward the rear of the wagon. His right arm was wrapped across his chest, and he held tightly onto his left ribs. It looked as though he was trying literally to hold himself together, that if he let go he might fall into a thousand pieces like a craftsman's puzzle. The faen's left arm hung limply at his side. There were dozens of small cuts and bruises on his face and arms, and his face was pale and dotted with beads of sweat.

The scene looked as though some titanic infant had picked up the wagon, shaken it like a rattle, and then discarded it for a more amusing toy. All sorts of cloths, powders, dried meats, and bits of metal- and woodcraft were strewn about haphazardly. There were empty boxes, too, plus broken bottles and vials still vainly trying to retain the last vestiges of their former contents.

Vael held up what was probably the last unbroken bottle in the wagon. Its thick contents were a deep, rich blue that rippled with lavender as the light of day struck it.

"I saved one for you, lad," Vael said with a weak smile. "But I'm afraid the rest of your shipment was damaged in transit."

The faen tried to laugh, but winced at the effort. The laugh turned into a cough, which obviously wracked his tiny body with pain, causing him to cough again. When the vicious cycle subsided, Vael had spittle mixed with blood dribbling over his lip.

"Your jokes were never funny, old man," Pashkin said as he gently examined Vael. The faen clearly had two broken ribs and quite probably incurred some other internal damage; his breathing was labored and raspy, and his skin was unnaturally cold and clammy, despite having been locked in a sweltering wagon for several days. "Save your energy for something you're good at, like swindling jungle tribesmen."

Vael nodded.

"A fair point," he conceded, then his body was wracked with another violent fit of coughing. "Speaking of which, how are things in the village that the gods forgot? Is everything working out according to plan?"

"Oh yes," Pashkin lied. "Everything's just splendid."

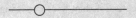

For nearly five years Vael and Pashkin worked together as Ka-Rone's most successful swindlers. They did a bit of everything—confidence schemes, robbery, smuggling, fencing, fleecing, blackmail, embezzlement, and occasionally even legitimate mercantile commerce.

One of their most successful cons involved Pashkin painting his face with Vael's magical cosmetic. Vael would play a disreputable merchant and join a caravan where, more often than not, several of the others were of a larcenous bent. A day or so into the trip, Pashkin would begin traveling with the caravan, playing the role of an ascetic runechild—a scholar and emissary who traveled the land at the expense of a great patron. Vael would lead the others in creating plots to fleece the runechild out of his money. In the dead of night, he would reveal their plans to Pashkin who would then be able to catch the crooks in the act. He would rant with righteous indignation and threaten to have the merchants arrested at the next city. Invariably they offered exorbitant bribes for Pashkin's understanding, and would turn in Vael as their ringleader. By this time Vael would have fled the caravan. Pashkin would take the merchants' money and go after his true tormenter. Just before leaving, though, he would always give an impassioned speech about honesty and fair play, ending with his fervent hope that the merchants had learned a valuable lesson. They always claimed they had. Pashkin was fairly certain, however, that not one of his victims ever learned the correct lesson.

"I'm always sad when it's done," Pashkin said after one such heist. He and Vael were sitting around a campfire appraising the gold and gems they had taken from a fat spice merchant.

"Yes, it's almost too easy," Vael agreed. "But we have to be careful not to poison the well."

The pair used this particular scam only sparingly. Although effective, it carried a greater than average associated risk. They feared merciless reprisal if they were ever caught abusing people's innate trust of runechildren. Reprisal not only from the wronged individuals and outraged general populace but, more importantly, from any actual runechildren that happened to be in the general vicinity. Thankfully, the scheme always made them enough gold so they could afford to take a few months off.

Pashkin sighed.

"Sure, the take's good," he said. "But I'd do this one for nothing."

He pulled a small hand mirror from his pack and inspected himself. Dressed in crisp white linen robes and with a stylized crimson crescent symbol emblazoned on his forehead, no one in the world would ever guess that he was not an honest-to-Vekik runechild.

"Don't be stupid," said Vael.

"No, really," Pashkin continued. "I've always wanted to be a runechild. Did I ever tell you that?"

The faen stopped counting and cocked an eyebrow toward the young man.

"When I left Destimar's Flats it was to go out into the world and make my mark," Pashkin said wistfully. "I was going to show what I was made of and earn a rune of my own—something no one could ever take away from me. Something that proved my worth in this world."

He lowered the mirror and looked away into the dark woods around them.

"I guess I've proved my worth, all right," Pashkin said. He paused, closing his eyes as a peaceful look settled over his face. "It's just that, when I walk up to a caravan wearing this outfit, it feels exactly like I knew it would. I'm always welcome. People who have known me for less than a day confide their deepest secrets to me."

"What sort of secrets?" Vael asked with a wide grin. "Anything truly lurid?"

"Piss off!" Pashkin spat as he got up and walked away from the fire. He stopped a little way into the woods with his back to his partner. "They trust me. And in return I rob them blind."

The faen shot to his feet and put his hands on his hips.

"You do no such thing," he growled. "You take money from someone who is more than happy to swindle his fellow travelers. You only rob from people who would cheat you to begin with."

"Don't you see, it doesn't matter!" Pashkin said turning back toward the fire. "I'm using a symbol of honor and duty to play on people's weakness. I'm taking my own highest aspirations and defiling them for the sake of a few gold coins."

As he spoke, the young man dragged his hands across his forehead, smudging the crescent and gouging shallow gashes into his own skin.

"More than 'a few,'" muttered Vael looking at the trove laid out around him.

"You know what I mean!" said Pashkin. A mixture of blood and pigment ran down his cheek like a tear.

The faen sat back down and rearranged the spoils—filling some pouches with coins and spilling the contents of others out onto the ground.

"We really did make quite a haul this time," Vael said after a while.

Pashkin did not answer.

"It's enough," the faen continued, "that we could actually consider retiring."

The young man narrowed his eyes.

"Retire?" Pashkin said with a chuckle. "What would we do then?"

Vael continued to shift coins.

"Well, I was thinking about sponsoring a merchant caravan," he said. "After all, if these cretins can make so much gold at this business, imagine what someone with my brains could do."

Pashkin stepped back into the full light of the campfire. The smudged makeup, blood, and flickering shadows made it seem as though his face was covered with scars, but his eyes were bright and wide.

"But I don't want to be a merchant," Pashkin said.

"No," Vael replied. "And I daresay you would make a singularly poor one, even if you had the motivation."

He stopped arranging coins and looked his young partner square in the eye.

"But you do make an extraordinarily convincing runechild," he said with a mischievous wink. "Have you ever heard of the Jungles of Naveradel?"

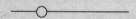

At first Pashkin would have nothing to do with Vael's plan. The faen wanted him to stay in his runechild costume, then the two of them would join a caravan headed through the Jungles of Naveradel. Vael would gather information about what sort of trading was done in the villages sprinkled throughout the jungle, and Pashkin would gauge the locals' reaction to seeing a runechild. More importantly, the young man would decide whether or not he could stand to live the rest of his life in a tropical rainforest.

"You want to pull a con on the natives?"

"No," Vael said rolling his eyes. "What have they got to steal?"

"Then I don't understand what you'll get out of this."

"Nothing," said the faen. "But you want to be a runechild."

"But I won't be," Pashkin whined. "I'll just be pretending."

"The locals won't know that," Vael said with a smile. "I'm betting they've never seen a runechild before. What's more, I'm betting that they never will. What runechild would come all that way?"

"Exactly!" Pashkin said. "So even if they *do* think I'm a rune-child, why would they believe I've come to join their village?"

"Why did the elders think that Misha woman would want to stay in your little fishing village?" asked Vael. "Because everyone believes that the place they live is special and deserving of protection."

Pashkin considered that for a moment. He remembered being heartbroken the day Misha actually left Destimar's Flats—he couldn't believe that she was abandoning his home. It didn't really matter that the village had no real *need* of her protection, nor that Pashkin himself had no interest in remaining there. Misha's actions seemed to say that the town wasn't worth staying for, and that had made young Pashkin feel worthless, too.

"But if I do this," the young man said finally, "I'll just be carrying on the lie. I'll never get to be a *real* runechild."

"Pashkin, you are the best friend I'll ever have in this world," Vael said, his voice quiet and strong. "I would do anything to spare you pain, but believe me when I tell you, this is as close as you will ever come to being a real runechild."

Vael was right. Pashkin knew it. He'd done too many questionable things in his life, taken the easy path for too long. The painted rune was the only one he would ever wear—this was the only way to achieve his life's goal. But the thought was too bitter for him to bear.

So, although he helped Vael find an appropriate caravan and joined him on the trek into the Jungles of Naveradel, Pashkin had no intention of actually putting the faen's plan into action. In the first place, he reasoned, the villagers would be too smart to fall for such a trick. They might not be worldly, but their connection to the land would let them see through the disguise where greedy merchants never could. In the second place, Pashkin could not live that sort of lie—not when it pertained to his heart's desire.

However, as Vael liked to tell Pashkin before any complicated scam, "You never know what will happen once the game's begun. Remember to put a smile on your face, keep your story straight, and work with whatever cards Mowren deals you."

The caravan traveled from village to village in the Naveradel. While the merchants were always welcomed, Pashkin was invariably treated as an honored guest. And when it came time for the caravan to move on, the villagers asked if the "runechild" would not consent to stay with them a while longer, offering him everything they had to give—shelter, food, livestock, and sometimes even slaves. Invariably he declined with a modest smile and hearty thanks.

Finally, the caravan came to Simiir, the final stop on its route. It was only a few days' journey from the coast, yet completely isolated. The people were as nice as any Pashkin had met along the way, and perhaps more in need of guidance than most. When the merchants began to pack their wagons, the villagers came to Pashkin and asked him to remain with them. They had very little to offer—even less than any of the other villages—merely a small hut to live in and a promise of food. All the merchants were flabbergasted when Pashkin told them he would not be returning with the caravan—all of them, that is, except Vael.

"Don't worry if you fail to live up to your own expectations," the faen said as the partners made their farewells. "You've always set them too high."

Vael left Pashkin with a small crate of cosmetic paint and promised to return with his own caravan in less than a year's time to deliver more.

"If things go badly," Pashkin said, performing his best imitation of the faen's wink and nudge, "I'll be swimming out to meet your ship."

But things did not go badly. Pashkin fell easily into the rhythm of life in Simiir. The people were generous, the land bountiful, and there was actually very little for him to do. The villagers were self-sufficient—hunting small game, gathering wild fruit, and tending a modest herd of goats. Pashkin was treated as the village headman, resolving the few disputes that arose between neighbors, officiating at weddings, and representing the village's interests when merchants or other outsiders arrived through the jungle. There were a few crises, such as when a withering plague killed off the entire herd of goats or a visiting alchemist burned down half the village. But it was in those times that Pashkin proved his value to the town, calmly discerning the best course of action and leading the people of Simiir through to safety. Although the townsfolk called him brave, Pashkin knew better—he was merely fighting to preserve his situation. If the town succumbed to calamity or moved, Vael would never be able to find him. And Pashkin knew he'd eventually run out of the pigment that allowed him to live the lie that his life had truly become.

Still, for ten years things went better than Pashkin had ever dreamed possible. Then came the day the wounded guard stumbled into town. He knew in his gut the caravan was Vael's—it had been at least a year since the faen's last visit. He also realized that this was the crisis that would mark the end of his tenure as village headman. For Vael was not the only person in the caravan who knew Pashkin. The guard, wounded and ailing as she was, remained instantly recognizable to him. Once she regained consciousness, she would never keep his secret.

"Misha?" Vael said incredulously. "That was *your* Misha?"

"Stop moving about!" Pashkin said. He carried the faen draped across his back as they hiked through the dense jungle, which was uncomfortable enough. But Vael's inability to control his habit of animated gesticulation during a conversation had more than once almost sent them both lurching to the ground. Pashkin found this both annoying for his own sake and worrisome for the sake of his charge's internal injuries.

The excitement at seeing his friend, and the distress over potentially ruining his longstanding charade, had seemingly allowed Vael to forget—or at least ignore—his wounds and exhaustion. Pashkin had given the faen all the water left in his gourd, done his best to set the tiny man's broken bones, and urged him to stay as still as possible, but to no avail. Eventually, all this activity would take its toll, and his friend would slip into unconsciousness and get the rest his body so desperately needed.

"Are you certain?" Vael said, leaning forward to see the look on his benefactor's face as he answered.

"What kind of question is that?" Pashkin asked. He stopped, shifted Vael back to a more manageable resting spot, and paused to scratch his own cheek. The itching was growing worse. "She's the reason I wanted to become a runechild in the first place. I'd recognize her anywhere. Besides, she's got the rune."

"So do you," Vael said.

"Not *a* rune, mate, *the* rune. The very same one she had when I was a lad." Pashkin set off again, still scratching at his cheek. "You can't fake that. She's the one, all right."

"What are you doing to your face?"

Pashkin laughed.

"Well, there's my *other* problem," he said. "Even if you had arrived safely, I'd have been leaving Simiir with you. It seems that your pigment isn't as perfect as you thought."

"What are you talking about?" Although Pashkin couldn't see the faen's face, Vael's voice told of his wounded look. No craftsman can stand to hear his work disparaged. "You're going to blame your problems with Misha on me? I never said it would fool a real runechild—"

"That's not it at all," Pashkin assured his friend. "Your cosmetic has been perfect through all these years. It just turns out that you can wear it only so long before it starts to eat away at your skin."

"It does no such thing!" Vael insisted. Before he could expound on the safety of his concoction, though, his agitation set him into another fit of coughing.

This wouldn't do. Pashkin knew his friend well enough to realize that the faen was well on his way to working himself into an apoplectic fit. He stopped and set his tiny passenger on the ground.

"Maybe the chemicals work differently here in the jungle heat," he said crouching next to his friend. "I'm not blaming you. But you have to admit that prolonged use of your invention is not supposed to cause this."

Pashkin spat on the hem of his sleeve and rubbed away part of the shooting star on his cheek. Underneath, the skin was the rich purple shade of a fresh bruise. Vael's coughing subsided with a horrified gasp. He reached out his finger and gently prodded the discolored skin.

"How did that happen?" he finally asked.

"It didn't 'happen,'" Pashkin explained. "At first I thought it was just a reaction from the mineral water. One of the village children slipped and fell into the hot spring, and I had to dive in after her. I'm usually pretty careful about not going swimming—I don't want the paint to wash off in front of everyone. Anyway, it stayed on fine, but the next morning I noticed a rash under the paint. It started small but kept growing and getting deeper."

"How long has this been going on?"

Pashkin thought for a second.

"That was pretty soon after the last time you were here," he said. "So about a year."

"Lad, it's been a full eighteen months since my last visit." Vael stared intently at the purple mark that perfectly matched the painted symbol.

"So, a year and a half," Pashkin said "It's hard to keep track of time here."

"I don't understand," Vael said. "Trina has worn this every day since before you ever thought about leaving that low-tide marker you call a home town. She does half of her work at the bath house, and she's never had any problems like this. Does it hurt?"

"No," Pashkin chuckled. "It just itches like mad whenever I cover it up. I've had to paint the star thicker the past couple of months to keep the discoloration from showing. You have no idea how worried I've been that someone would . . . would . . ."

"Would notice?" Vael finished. "Well, if they had any reason to suspect you, I guess they might, lad. But—"

With no warning, the brush to Vael's left exploded, and a mass of dappled golden fur pounced on the very spot where he was resting. It all happened so fast that he had no idea that anything was wrong until the dire leopard had swung both of its ham-sized front paws and taken a snarling bite with jaws large enough to swallow four faen at once.

It took Vael a moment to realize he was not dead—that, in fact, he was once again on Pashkin's back and they were moving away as fast as the human's legs could carry them.

"H-how did you . . . ?"

"I heard something," was all Pashkin said.

He carried them into a thicket of palm fronds, but they could hear the tremendous beast on their trail. It bounded onto five-foot-thick tree branches, making them bend and pop like a garden elm in a windstorm. Then it leapt to the ground, landing with such force that Pashkin nearly lost his footing.

"I take it that's what attacked the caravan," he said as he burst through the wall of foliage and emerged onto a small path that ran alongside the river. He hurdled roots taller than the faen he was carrying and kept running toward what seemed to be a wall of mist about fifty yards downriver.

"I guess," Vael said, voice high with terror. "It looks big enough to have knocked over the wagon—how many cats like that do you *have* in this jungle?"

"Too many," Pashkin answered and kept on running. The leopard was not behind them, but they could hear it plowing through the brush to their side. A low, menacing growl seemed all too close, and getting closer second by second.

"The river," Vael shouted. "Cats hate water!"

Pashkin kept running toward the mist.

"It's not a mouser. It's a killer, and it's got our scent," he said. "That cat won't give up until it's got us or lost us."

"So where are we going?" Vael could smell the leopard now—the musk of its fur, the stench of its breath. "Into that fog bank? Will that confuse it?"

"That's not fog," Pashkin said as the giant cat burst from the trees again, landing only a pounce or two behind them. "It's mist."

"Mist? Are we that close to the sea?"

"No," Pashkin answered, and only then did Vael notice that there were two roars in the air: one from the great predator about to spring on top of them, and the other from the thousands of gallons of water pouring over the cliff toward which they were running.

Three things happened in lightning-quick succession. First, Pashkin dove headfirst into the mist. Second, Vael shouted "waterfall!" at the top of his lungs, pulling out the final vowel sound for as long as he had air in his lungs. And finally, the leopard sprang after them.

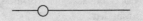

"That was your plan?" Vael said as soon as he could speak. "Leap off a cliff and hope you find something to grab onto?"

"It worked, didn't it?" replied Pashkin, his voice quivering. They'd felt the leopard pass overhead and heard its roar turn into a plaintive yowl as it disappeared into the mists. Then there was the sickening wet thud of something heavy landing on the rocks below.

"Did you know there was a tree here?"

"I thought there was a big one," Pashkin said apologetically. "Guess I was wrong."

He was holding onto a thin wisp of a branch sticking out from an otherwise barren cliff face. Miraculously, he was levitating in the air next to the branch, with Vael clinging to him for dear life.

"So you didn't know you could do this?" asked the faen with a tone so flat it wasn't really a question.

Pashkin slowly moved hand over hand along the branch, inching himself and his passenger gradually closer to the precipice. He was afraid that if he pulled too hard the flimsy roots would release their hold in the cliff wall, and he had no idea how long he could continue to defy gravity. "I *thought* there was a tree here."

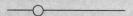

After shimmying up the cliff and back onto solid ground, the pair rested silently for an hour or more. A few times Vael seemed as though he were about to speak, but instead he simply took a deep breath, winced in pain, and looked over the edge of the cliff.

"You did it," the faen finally said. "You really did it."

Pashkin shook his head.

"I didn't do anything but save our worthless hides."

Vael stared dumfounded.

"What are you talking about?" he stammered. "Look at what you just did. You're not a fake anymore, my lad. You're the real deal—you're a runechild. We can throw away this paint for good and all."

Vael pulled out the last remaining vial of his cosmetic paint and prepared to throw it into the river. But Pashkin grabbed his wrist.

"Don't be stupid," he said. "I can't be a runechild. Look at everything I've done with my life. I'm going to need this until you're well enough for me to take you out of the jungle."

Vael smiled and nodded.

"Yes," he said. "Take me back to Simiir. Let's look at what you've done with your life."

The two glared at one another for a moment. Then Pashkin rose, hoisted the injured faen onto his back, and set off into the jungle, neither one saying another word. In fact, they didn't talk again until they paused atop a rise that looked down on the village. For a moment they simply stood there and enjoyed the smell of roasting meats. Then a shout rose up to greet them.

"They're back," came the excited call. "He's back! Pashkin has returned! He did it!"

"You really did it," Vael said smiling.

Pashkin considered for a moment.

"Well," he said finally. "Maybe I did, at that."

"You don't have to go back, you know," Vael added. "You can go anywhere you want now."

Pashkin paused again, scratching what remained of the paint off his cheek.

"If I leave now," he said, "I'll be an even bigger phony than I was when I arrived."

He smiled, shifted Vael to a more comfortable spot on his back, and began walking down the hill.

"Besides," said Pashkin, "I don't want to be anywhere else."

MONTE COOK

NOT WITHOUT COST

The snow down deep was solid enough to give a satisfying crunch with each step, but not enough to support Hvanen's weight. The snow above that was light and powdery, and getting deeper with each moment as big, thick flakes floated down from the night sky with the silent determination of a man interested in reaching a goal but in no particular hurry to do so.

Hvanen, however, did not have such casual luxury. If he didn't get to Garonton by morning, people would die. Many people. In his name.

He imagined that it was probably cold. Not interested in confirming that suspicion, he had mentally doused all sensation on his skin. Traipsing across the winter-wrought fields, however, was as alien to him as trudging through a marsh in the southern jungles. Like most verrik, Hvanen hailed from the hot, dry wastes of Zalavat. Not knowing much about the cold and snow, he supposed that going without any sense of the cold might eventually be dangerous. For all he knew, he could suffer frostbite. That knowledge would not alter his course or his actions, however, so he decided he was better off not knowing. At least for tonight.

People were going to die because of him. Hvanen could not bear the thought. For years he had fought for life, struggling against those who would so callously take it. Ending the life of another was the greatest crime one could perpetrate. Most of his race did not share his conviction—they thought of life and death as more practical matters. Perhaps the rune that had mysteriously appeared on his face like a birthmark or a tattoo when he was just entering adulthood had changed him.

Of course it had. He knew it had—every day he lived, every step he took reminded him of what the rune had done to him. He could hear the proof murmuring behind him.

His wound had stopped bleeding, but he could feel the venom in it seeping ever deeper into his body, ever closer to his heart. Each step he took pumped more blood through him—blood that carried a poison that would soon kill him.

Hvanen found himself longing for Rand's company, but that could never be. Hvanen would have appreciated the human's presence, even though he had not known him long. Not that Hvanen was alone.

He was never alone.

The verrik did not have to look around him. He knew that his eternal companions lumbered along behind him, although they would leave no path in the snow. If he concentrated, he would be able to make out what they were whispering.

So he did not concentrate.

Instead, he thought more of Rand and their first meeting just that morning.

———○———

The only human Hvanen had ever considered a friend was a short, squat fellow, perhaps entering early middle age, as those of his race measured their lives. Hvanen himself was probably only a few years younger, but verrik age more slowly than humans, and his bald head made him look younger still—like many Verrik, particularly those in his family, Hvanen shaved the hair from his head, his wine-colored skin smooth over his pate. Aside from the skin coloration, though, Hvanen could pass for a human male. Since humans came in many colors, he had always thought that, traveling north out of Zalavat and into the lands of the Diamond Throne, he would be easily accepted by the humans he found there. He had been wrong about that, of course. Humans—and to be fair, other races— found verrik unsettling for some reason. It was only one of a list of things Hvanen did not understand.

In Hvanen's case, the sense of unease might have come from the strange symbol emblazoned on the side of his face, sprawled like a spider across his features. The rune was dark purple in color, but it looked almost black against Hvanen's skin. He imagined most people assumed it was a tattoo, not that a verrik would ever bother with something as extraneous and nonfunctional as a tattoo. Humans never took the time to understand verrik, though, so that thought never occurred to them.

Rand had recognized the rune for what it was right away. When the dark-haired man walked into the livery early that morning stroking this thin, pointed beard, his eyes lit up at the sight of Hvanen. Rand himself was draped in runes and symbols, although none of them lay directly on his flesh. Instead, they adorned his long leather coat, the trim of his tough cloth trousers, and even his short vest and belt.

He approached Hvanen immediately. "A runechild?" His voice was soft but deep.

Hvanen considered the implications of his answer carefully. Although he had never met one, the short man's couture suggested he was a runethane. Such men commanded interesting and useful aspects of magical power through the creation of mystical runes. Most likely, he would look favorably upon Hvanen's unusual nature.

The human, clearly unnerved at the long moments that had passed with no answer from the verrik, took a different tack. "My name is Rand Yarrow," he said with a nod of his head.

"Yes," Hvanen said quietly. "I am a runechild. My name is Hvanen."

Rand's eyes sparkled, and he smiled ever so slightly. His next question was as abrupt and blunt as the first. "Why are you here in Garonton?" Hvanen had mistaken the human's candid questions for a refreshing level of forthrightness, a quality he missed in the time he had spent among humans. Instead, he knew now, it was simply excitement and keen interest. Still, these were qualities Hvanen could appreciate.

"We are here looking for a new horse to replace the one that died in an encounter with brigands on the road some miles back. We have business in Scarhold and little desire to go there on foot." Hvanen had already determined that the likely outcome of telling this human the truth would be beneficial rather than detrimental, but it was prudent not to reveal everything.

Rand looked around, but the only other person in the place was the overweight man who ran the livery. "'We'?"

No, Hvanen couldn't reveal everything. "I misspoke. I meant to say 'I'."

"I have a horse you could use," Rand said quickly. "Terril here's just been keeping it for me while I finish business in town." He motioned toward the livery man, who still had not looked up from the papers he was reading.

"That is not necessary. I have adequate funds." Something startled one of the horses. The creature whinnied loudly and stomped away.

Rand worked his jaw from side to side. He studied Hvanen for a moment, obviously considering something. Hvanen had met few humans who thought before they spoke. He found his liking for this fellow growing quickly.

"Look," Rand said eventually. "I've never had the opportunity to talk to a runechild before. I'd like to ask you some questions and perhaps learn a little something. I have my own interest in runes, as you can see. It would be a great honor for me."

The livery man jumped with a start, and looked around as if someone had poked him. Rand stared at him, obviously confused.

"Somethin' going on 'round here?" Terril rubbed the back of his neck and shuddered. "S'like somebody jus' walked over my grave or somethin'."

Instinctively Hvanen started to turn to look behind him, then checked himself. Ignoring the livery man, he asked Rand, "Would you care to accompany me to Scarhold? It's not even a day's ride."

Without hesitation, Rand nodded.

"It might be a bit dangerous," the verrik said, "but nothing I can't handle." He patted his scabbard confidently. But Rand was already calling out for Terril to saddle up his horse in preparation to leave.

Looking back, Hvanen knew that they both should have given their actions a bit more thought.

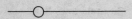

Seventy-five years ago, workers finished the fortress known as Scarhold. Built into the cleft of a rocky cliff that looked like a scar on the side of the rising Mount Garrold, Scarhold stood in defiance of what was then a terrible threat from raiders and rhodin tribes. Since that time, peace had wrapped the region like a blanket, and Scarhold—always more a fortification than a dwelling place—fell into disuse and, eventually, disrepair.

Over the last few weeks, Hvanen had been making his way toward the old human stronghold because he had been told that a murderer dwelled there. Not a murderer, he thought—a deposed tyrant, bereft of the power he once held. Hvanen felt no fear, for this foe was no warrior. He only feared what the man might do if he didn't intervene.

"When did you first gain the rune?" Rand rode clumsily along the overgrown path on his small brown horse. Hvanen rode a slightly taller, grey-backed mare. The trees on either side of the riders were brown and bare, having loosed their foliage onto the ground weeks earlier.

"When I was about fifteen years old," Hvanen said.

"What did you do to earn it?"

Hvanen considered the question a moment, and then nodded without looking at Rand. "That is not the way it works. At least, not usually."

"What do you mean?"

"No one, in truth, knows for sure where the power of the rune comes from. Some speculate that it has to do with the ancient dragons that left the realm for the west. Some think it comes from the gods. Or that the land itself has a level of awareness and intelligence all its own. Since we do not even understand the power's origins, certainly no one knows for sure why runes appear on the flesh of some but not others."

Hvanen glanced at Rand, who stared back intently, not attempting to conceal his eagerness. "I suspect," the verrik continued, "that the runes are tied to the very nature of the land itself. The power of the runechildren is the might of the land made manifest. Those who find themselves so marked are those who would use the power on behalf of the land. Somehow, the runes seem to know who should have them, and who should not. It is far less a reward than a responsibility."

"A burden, then?"

"That is not the word I choose."

"A manifestation of destiny?"

"Perhaps, although one doesn't need a rune to have a destiny. It is more akin to what I said before. A manifestation of power. A bequeathal of the right abilities on the right person at the right time." The verrik raised an eyebrow and glanced at his companion. "Do you find such words arrogant?"

"No," Rand said. "I don't think it's arrogant to simply understand the power you've been granted. Understanding what you can do and what you need to do, well . . . that's a kind of clarity I envy."

Hvanen felt no need to reply.

About a minute passed before Rand went on, "I guess I'm a fool for not asking this yet, but why are you—er, we—going to Scarhold? Does it have something to do with the rune?"

"We must find someone who hides within the old fortress."

"Who?"

"We shall soon see."

"Do you always avoid giving straight answers like this?"

"You find me difficult? I do not even know you, and yet I am allowing you to ask your questions and accompany me on a trip that I'd intended to take by myself."

Hvanen heard murmurs behind him, but as usual, he did not glance back. They didn't like it when he spoke as if they were not there.

"You're right, of course," Rand replied. "Forgive me. It's just that I am a straightforward person. I see the world with a mathematician's eye. When I create a rune, it's either scribed correctly or it's not, and thus it either works or it doesn't. I studied for years to learn how to craft a magical rune, to understand how and why their specific mystical shapes draw power from the ether. For you to not even know where the power of your rune comes from . . . well, it surprises me."

Hvanen considered the man's words carefully. He had put himself in an awkward position by confiding in Rand and bringing him along on this short journey. Hvanen told himself that he had examined the potential outcomes of doing so and thus no harm could arise from the decision, and something beneficial might. But the truth was that he was lonely for real companionship. He saw in Rand something of a kindred spirit, which he had missed in the months since he came up north.

Rand stared at his traveling companion, who rode silently next to him. "I don't mean to offend you, of course."

Still Hvanen said nothing.

"Would you like me to go?"

Hvanen turned. "No," he said, shaking his head. He even smiled a bit. "You need to forgive me, Rand. We verrik like to consider decisions carefully. That includes what we say."

"Ah," Rand nodded. "I'm afraid that you're not only the only runechild I've spoken to, you're also the only verrik."

"Well," Hvanen said, "perhaps we can learn a few morsels from each other, then. I've been traveling alone for too long."

He ignored the faint but harsh whispers behind him.

The two rode on the disused path for hours. Hvanen told Rand everything he knew relating to the enigmatic rune that graced his cheek. Rand related to Hvanen a little about himself. He explained that he had lived most of his life in the area, learning the art of magic and runes. He earned money using his skills to help the locals cure sick livestock, predict the weather, maintain the flour mill, and so on—he even entertained children with minor tricks and prestidigitation.

Without warning, the midday woods suddenly exploded with voices and clattering weapons and armor. People were racing toward them, cries of battle in their throats.

Two humans and a sibeccai, each clad in leather jacks with metal studs dulled from ill-care, charged from around a patch of thick brush. The sibeccai brandished a curved khopesh—a weapon unique to his people—and the humans bore spears. Of the two, the female held hers with some skill, but the male just barreled ahead, his long dark hair falling in his eyes.

They came from Hvanen's side, for which he was grateful. He wanted to keep himself between these attackers and his companion. He drew his longsword on pure reflex. He wasn't about to let his opponents' unexpected attack and longer weapons allow them the immediate upper hand. Instead, Hvanen used the advantage he gained from his high position on horseback to lean toward his attackers and swing with his blade just as the spear points came within reach. His powerful, single stroke cleft both spears in two and ended the humans' charge by knocking them both slightly off balance. Though he was very skilled and surprisingly strong, much of the credit for Hvanen's mighty blow was due to *Xiridil*, his grandfather's sword. Crafted of a nameless material found in the ruins of the ancient Vnaxians, *Xiridil* was far from a normal blade.

When his horse bleated out a startled cry and pivoted, Hvanen realized that the beast had no experience in battle. He could feel it attempting to rear, but he fought it and kept it down. He didn't have the time for this—the sibeccai was already next to him, slashing with his weapon. Hvanen brought his own sword around to parry the dark-furred warrior, but he was too slow. He lunged backward as the khopesh cut a thin gash across his chest, tearing his leather coat but not his flesh. His quick maneuver, however, sent him tumbling off the unsteady mount. He landed poorly on his back, the frightened horse's hooves stamping around him.

A shape of golden energy appeared around the sibeccai's long, almost canine head. It formed into a distinct symbol—a rune. But Hvanen could not spare the time to watch what happened next. The two humans were moving around the horse, drawing short blades. Worse, Hvanen had to guard his skull from the wildly stomping hooves. He rolled along the ground until he was off the path.

Hvanen managed to get to one knee before the human warriors were upon him. A sharp, quick stroke of his grandfather's longsword across the shins of the male sent him crashing to the ground. The woman stabbed at him but he avoided the blow. He threw his shoulder into her jaw as he got to his feet, knocking her back. *Xiridil's* pommel then came crashing down upon her head, knocking her senseless.

The startled horse ran down the path, back toward Garonton. Rand was still in his saddle, a short, curved blade of his own in his hand—although it was unbloodied. The sibeccai lay face-first upon the path.

"A well-timed spell," Hvanen said, checking himself for any serious wounds. "You saved me." Other than an ache in his neck from the fall off the horse, he seemed fine. And Rand was untouched.

"I doubt it," Rand said. "You're an amazing swordsman. Really full of surprises. I hardly noticed that blade at your side when we first met."

The moans of one of the wounded human warriors, still on the ground and probably unable to stand, interrupted them. Hvanen moved to the man and checked the cut across his legs. Serious—probably in need of bandaging—but not fatal.

"When did Xelhah dispatch you?" Hvanen asked the man as he pulled the fellow's woolen cloak from his shoulders.

The warrior didn't respond, but just scowled in pain and anger. Hvanen cut the cloak just enough to allow him to tear it into strips. Then, he wrapped the strips tightly around the man's legs to staunch the wounds.

"You're being awfully friendly to someone who just tried to gut you," Rand said.

"All life is sacred," Hvanen replied, looking in the warrior's eyes.

"You champion the cause of life," Rand said, "but you're no stranger to the use of that sword."

Hvanen looked regretful. "Sometimes I find that, to serve life, one has no recourse but to deal death." Then he turned to Rand. "Would you see if you can find my horse?"

Rand didn't move. "Xelhah—that's the guy in Scarhold?"

"Yes." Hvanen continued to bandage the warrior. "At least, I think so."

"He's there," the warrior said through gritted teeth. "He sent us out to kill you on the road. Before you could reach him."

"Are there more of you?"

"No, not that I know about, anyway. We just thought it would mean some quick coins. He said there'd be only one of you." The man winced as Hvanen finished his work.

"Nothing personal," the wounded warrior added.

"Nothing personal?" Hvanen asked. "You do not consider attempting to murder someone personal?" He looked behind him at the shadowy figures only he could see. They were, of course, making their own harsh but quiet comments. It would be nice, at times like this, to use his verrik-born talent of shutting off his sense of hearing, but he knew from experience that even if he did so, he would still hear the whispers.

The man didn't answer. He looked into the woods, and then at the ground—anywhere but at the verrik.

Hvanen stood. "I am sorry, Rand. I did not know I would be bringing you into such a battle. The man himself is no threat to us, physically, but I did not know about any hired mercenaries. I never thought that he would try to kill me— us—without even listening to what I had to say." He shook his head regretfully. "I had forgotten how lightly some people take killing."

He ignored the continued virulent whispering.

"You don't have to apologize. I can take care of myself. I still don't know what's going on here, though. Who's—"

"I will tell you about it. But my horse?"

Rand nodded with a smirk, then urged his mount back down the path. Hvanen stood over the three assailants on the ground and sheathed *Xiridil.*

Rand's rune-laced spell had only put the sibeccai to sleep. By the time he returned with Hvanen's mount in tow, the verrik had tied the hands of all three warriors behind their backs. The woman was still unconscious, but Hvanen was certain she would be fine in a few hours.

"I doubt this will hold them long," Hvanen said as they rode off down the path. "But then, we do not need it to."

"You're kind to your enemies," Rand said. "Is that a part of being a runechild?"

"As far as I am concerned, it is a part of being an intelligent, living being. But I do not think it kindness. I simply think there is no greater or more important force than life itself. I would not see that force extinguished lightly."

"I see. But who's Xelhah? Clearly he doesn't agree."

Hvanen sighed. "He is a verrik. A terrible man. He has little regard for life, or much of anything else, for that matter. I followed him up here when he left my land. I tracked him through the Southern Wastes and along the Bitter Peaks."

"Why?"

"He was a leader—a minor one—the master of a city. He brutalized those under him. Innocents died at his orders. He was eventually deposed, but he escaped."

"And so you're tracking him down," Rand said. "Revenge."

"No, I am not interested in vengeance or even, for that matter, in righting the injustice of it. Xelhah took with him a

259

spell scroll that could result in even more deaths. I cannot stand by and allow that possibility."

"He's a mage?"

"A wind witch. With the exotic spell in his possession, he can unleash death itself upon the wind. I had hoped to offer to spare him in return for the scroll. Without it, he would be able to cause no further trouble."

"But now..."

"Now I fear I have underestimated him."

They rode in silence for a while.

Rand cleared his throat. "So now what?"

"I must prevent that spell from being cast. Xelhah must be stopped."

"But you might have to... kill him, right?"

Hvanen ignored the harsh, whispered comments around him, thankful that Rand could not hear them.

"If I must." He glanced behind him and sighed. So much regret.

"Rand, you should not be here. I was wrong to bring you. This could be very dangerous. Those mercenaries before—they would have killed me if they could have. And probably you as well."

Rand nodded silently, but it was clearly not a nod of agreement. "Hvanen, everything I have ever heard about runechildren has led me to believe that they are blessed people—blessed with great powers and blessed with great purpose. Myself, I don't have any special purpose. That's why I approached you—why I sought you out. I'd heard there was a runechild in the area. I'd been looking for you for days. Then when I spotted you on the road on your way into town this morning, I had to follow you." The verrik raised an eyebrow quizzically.

"See, I understand the magic behind runes. I know what the books say. But I don't understand the reasons for it all. I don't know what I'm supposed to be doing." He smiled. "I figured that anything you're concerned with should concern me too. It's got to be more important—on a larger scale—than sitting in a room studying old tomes or performing tricks for the locals."

Hvanen said nothing.

"Don't send me back to town," Rand said, looking away.

"All right," Hvanen said finally. He looked around, not at his ethereal entourage, but wary of further attacks.

The dark sky finally brought the snow it had threatened for so long. It fell gently to the hard ground, the white dust quickly covering everything in sight.

"I've never been all the way to Scarhold," Rand said, "but I've traveled these woods before. Still, there's something about them today—something eerie."

Hvanen said nothing.

"Do you think it could be Xelhah's doing? I feel a cold prickly chill on my neck. I've felt it off and on for hours now."

Hvanen shook his head. "It is not Xelhah." The presence of a verrik sometimes made humans feel uneasy, but this was something more, the runechild knew.

"You sense it too, though, right? It's like we're being watched."

Hvanen considered telling his new companion that it was his curse to be always watched, but as he did, the cliff of Scarhold rose above the snow-covered trees in the distance. They were almost there. He pulled back on the reins and stopped his horse, looking around for trouble.

"You never told me how you've been tracking Xelhah," Rand said, also coming to a stop.

Hvanen simply put a finger to the rune on his face. Rand nodded with a thoughtful expression.

When Hvanen was certain there was no immediate danger, he urged his mount forward. The old path turned to continue straight toward the rocky cliff. Beyond the sheer face, the Bitter Peaks rose even higher. They crossed a small, snow-covered bridge that spanned a gentle stream not yet frozen over. Afterward, the land quickly grew more rugged, with grey and brown boulders tossed about haphazardly among the tall trees. The path no longer offered just the most convenient way to the fortress, but the only way. The terrain made Hvanen feel safer, for the land on either side of the path offered no easy means of crossing it without a great deal of slow effort—there would be no further ambushes from the woods.

Eventually, over the trees, the topmost tower of Scarhold came into view. They pressed on through the fading afternoon light and soon could see the entire fortress.

The cliff's face was cleft, and a stream emerged from the rock, the same stream they had already crossed once. Above the murmurs of the water as it passed into the daylight, and within the cleft itself, the builders had wedged a narrow fortress of stone. The entrance stood at the end of yet another span bridge over the stream. No other means of reaching the heavy wooden doors existed—the area beneath the fortress was open to allow the water to pass under. Two towers rose up from Scarhold, the taller of the two probably eighty feet, but neither reached the top of the cleft, which must have been close to one hundred twenty feet high.

The fortress appeared unassailable, and only now did Hvanen consider that he might have to do just that. It bothered him that he had not foreseen such a contingency, so he was relieved when, as they got closer, he could see that the wooden doors were rotten and the fortress walls were cracked. Moss growing in the cracks threatened to one day—perhaps sooner rather than later—topple the walls altogether.

Still, he felt unprepared for what lay ahead, and that was a feeling to which he was unaccustomed. All these months, he had planned on a one-on-one confrontation with his adversary—one in which Xelhah would in the end accede to his demands. Like the other mages Hvanen had faced, he expected Xelhah to surrender when confronted with someone strong enough to stand up to him. But if he had mercenaries lying in ambush for him in the woods, Xelhah knew he was coming and probably had other plans of his own. Hvanen wondered for a moment if his quarry was even in the fortress any longer, but the rune confirmed that he was. The magical link to Xelhah that he had established long ago felt strong now, stronger than it had been in months. Whereas until now it could only tell him his quarry's general direction, in such close proximity the rune's locating power became much more precise—it made the mark on Hvanen's face twitch ever so slightly. He wondered if Rand could sense it, but his companion seemed as oblivious to it as he was to the strange companions that followed them, always on the edge of Hvanen's peripheral vision, always murmuring just beyond the range of ascertaining what they said unless he concentrated on it.

Which he never did.

"So, what's the plan?" Rand's voice was just above a whisper. All else was quiet, except for the very gentle sound of the snowfall. The flakes had grown larger and more numerous in the past few minutes.

"I am going in," Hvanen told him quietly. "You should stay out here. If all goes well, I'll bring out the scroll and perhaps the man in a few moments."

"Look, Hvanen, I can help. I've got spells and runes. Give me a short while, and I can abjure the both of us with protective runes. We can go in together."

It was true that Xelhah could not possibly have counted on him coming in with magical protections provided by a runethane. Having Rand at his side appealed to him. It might make it all a lot easier and give him back the advantage he'd given up when they'd lost the element of surprise.

"Do it," Hvanen told him with a nod.

Rand rolled up a sleeve and began carefully tracing an intricate symbol on his forearm. He used only his finger, yet his movements left a mark as sure as any quill or brush. The mark glowed as if made of light. It was complex and took some time to create. Then Rand dismounted and urged Hvanen to do the same.

"This will be easier for me if we're both on our feet," the runethane said. After Hvanen got down from his mount, Rand took his arm and inscribed the complex rune of light on him as well. It was far more intricate than the rune on Hvanen's face. In comparison, his fleshrune was imprecise and simplistic—a stone created by erosion and natural events compared to a carefully constructed tool of straight lines and exact angles.

While Rand cast a few more spells in preparation for their encounter with Xelhah, Hvanen tied the horses to a tree. The animals would remain exposed on the path, but there wasn't much he could do about it. He still believed they wouldn't be in the fortress long.

Once they were ready to go, Rand drew his blade. Hvanen put a hand on his sword arm. "Not yet. We should go in with at least the hope of settling this without a fight."

"He's already sent people to kill us," Rand replied.

"So perhaps now he knows he has no hope."

The early darkness of winter was drawing the afternoon to a close. The snow on the bridge was turning to ice, making it slick. They walked carefully across it, glancing momentarily at the running water thirty feet below them.

The doors into Scarhold were not only rotten, but hanging slightly ajar. The two of them passed through them and into the dusty, dim entry hall beyond. The quickly fading daylight slanted in through high-placed, narrow windows. It was just as cold inside as it had been outside.

"Xelhah, I know you are here!" Hvanen shouted. "I have come for you, but you know that already. I want the *death's wind* spell."

Silence.

"No one else has to be hurt this day, Xelhah. But the chase ends here."

Silence. Hvanen did not even hear the usual harsh whispers around him.

First came the odor. Although faint at first, it grew much stronger very quickly: an oily, noxious smell of burned metal and rotting flesh like dead fish. Then, the deepest shadows in the place began to move—churn, in fact—like a mouth ready to spit something out.

And it did. As the two watched in silence, the darkness vomited forth a horrible creature that at first appeared to be a black-scaled serpent. The terrible, alien face atop a winding, serpentine neck bristled with long teeth like those of a viper-fish. As it came fully out of the shadows toward them, they saw that its body was like that of a bulbous, hideous spider, with far too many spindling legs skittering along the stone floor.

Hvanen knew a powerful summoning when he saw it. *Death's wind* was not the only strange and exotic spell Xelhah had discovered. This conjured creature was nothing less than a venomous slassan, one of the terrible legacies left behind long ago by the demonic dramojh—a race that had ruled over these lands for a thousand years of tyranny and horror.

With a flash, his longsword was in his hand. He heard Rand intoning a spell. However, the monstrous thing possessed surprising speed. It charged them, lashing out with its mouth open. Hvanen slashed defensively at the side of the thing's head, barely managing to parry its attack.

Rand finished his spell, and a flash of blue fire lanced from his fingertips to the creature. Unfortunately, the flames washed across the slassan's scaly skin as harmlessly as a gentle splash of water. Hvanen hoped the spell at least distracted the creature as he lunged at it with a powerful stroke of his blade. It sliced into flesh and drew greenish-black blood, but the slassan did not appear greatly hurt.

It did, however, skitter backward, its multiple legs moving so rapidly Hvanen could not keep track of them. A brief halo of dark, magical energy formed around its head. It stared intently at him, then flung back its head with a whiplike motion. As it did, an invisible force wrapped around *Xiridil*. Then, before he could react, Hvanen's sword was yanked out of his hand and flew across the room into some dark corner.

Hvanen glanced back and saw Rand draw his short sword. Hvanen noted that the weapon glistened with a magical rune that ran down the blade, gracefully following its curve. He yelled a shout of protest as Rand darted forward to join the creature in physical combat.

Rather than panic, Hvanen attempted to attain a sense of calm. He closed his eyes. The verrik reached deep within himself, into his mind, his spirit, and his devotion to his ideals. He drew upon that devotion for strength and power, calling upon the cause of life itself to grant him the means to meet this challenge.

After what seemed an eternity, he felt his plea answered. A tingling in both hands grew quickly into a quivering force he could barely hang onto. He opened his eyes and saw a shimmering, pulsing blade of light in his right hand and an equally potent shield in the other. His exultation melted from him, however, at the sight of Rand already on one knee, barely fending off the blindingly fast strikes of the slassan's serpentlike head.

Hvanen loosed an incoherent howl and leaped toward the melee, his new weapons full of puissance and powered by his own conviction. On his first blow, the blade bit deep into the creature's neck. Now it was the slassan's turn to howl—a shriek of pain and anger.

The beast stepped back again, into the deep shadows of the ever-darkening room. Again sorcerous power flared around its head like fire, but this time the magic coalesced into a terrible bolt, like a stroke of lightning that struck the ground between Rand and Hvanen. The heat of the resulting burst of energy was terrible, scorching both flesh and leather armor. Hvanen's conjured shield sheltered him somewhat, but the force of the blast knocked him off his feet, and he skidded across the cold floor, a pebble kicked haphazardly by a boot.

Rand lay motionless at the slassan's feet.

Hvanen flung himself upright, ignoring his pain. In fact, reflexively, he cut himself off from any sensation in his flesh. Now was not the time to feel anything. A ringing in his ears blocked out the slassan's horrible screams as he pushed himself toward the beast.

It pivoted to face him, away from Rand's body. Hvanen slashed wildly with his conjured sword at the beast's head, but the slassan recoiled and avoided each blow.

Hvanen took a shaky step forward.

The creature's neck arched, its head directly above Hvanen. It prepared to strike. Hvanen used the opening to thrust the point of his weapon into the base of the slassan's neck.

The monster's head struck down like a cobra, but Hvanen stood his ground, driving the blade in deeper. The slassan's mouth gripped his shoulder, slicing easily through his thick leather coat. Teeth sank into flesh, but so did blade. And Hvanen still allowed himself no feeling. The keening of the slassan indicated that the creature had no such immunity.

The slassan's bite loosened. The creature died.

As it did, it faded into wisps of shadow and oily stench, returning from wherever it had been conjured. The wound it inflicted and, Hvanen groaned inwardly, the venom it left behind in that wound, remained.

But there was no time to think about that now. As hurt as he was, Hvanen hurried to Rand, who lay only a few steps away. His magical sword and shield faded away like dying embers.

Rand was very still.

Hvanen picked up the human's head gently, cradling the back of his neck. It was wet with blood.

No!

He did not speak Rand's name, or attempt to shake him awake. There was no need. All verrik possess a modicum of telepathic sensitivity, related to their talent to selectively turn off their various senses. Hvanen could sense that no thoughts lingered within his friend's mind.

Hvanen was silent as he laid Rand back onto the ground. Around him, he heard the unkind murmurs of the others. They hated him so much—and for good reason.

But Hvanen did not spend any time thinking about them. He thought only of Rand. He had known the man for a single day—a few hours, really—but they had already formed the foundation of a strong friendship. The future of that friendship, which had never really existed except in Hvanen's mind, was stolen from him.

Worse, far worse, Rand had clearly been ready for so much more in life. He had trained and studied and learned much of magic. He hungered for knowledge and desired to do something meaningful. Had this journey been meaningful? So far, it would be difficult to say yes.

"He would not have died if you had not come here."

Hvanen whirled toward the voice.

A figure entered the room from deeper within the fortress. Slight of stature, the man had long white hair hanging straight down from his harsh, angular face. He wore a heavy woolen cloak and had a bag slung over one shoulder. Like Hvanen, his skin was a deep, vinaceous color. A verrik.

Xelhah.

Hvanen forced himself to his feet. Xelhah gesticulated with a sweeping motion of one arm. An invisible force, like a concentrated blast of air, knocked him back to the ground. The blow stole his breath and he lay on his side, gasping. He still felt no pain, but that did not exempt him from the effects of the punishment.

"Hvanen," Xelhah spat. "You have dogged me for months, never letting me rest. Never letting me regain my footing. I am not some prey meant only to flee. I am a man of power and import! I am destined for greater things than spending cold nights hiding in ruins, wondering when you will finally find me. Things are not as they should be."

He was already at the door. Hvanen wanted to get up, but he was spent, barely able to breathe.

"You call yourself a champion of life, but you have left me with a life of nothing but strife and misery," Xelhah said. "You fear this spell so greatly," he said, clutching a tattered scroll of vellum in one hand. "I can think of no better way to repay you for the last few months than to cast it."

"No!" Hvanen could not manage more than a wheeze.

"And I can think of no better place to cast it than in the center of Garonton, where it can do its work with the greatest . . . efficiency. If I don't miss my guess, nary a soul in that place will survive this cold, miserable night."

No. Please.

"So many lives lost tonight," Xelhah smiled down at Rand's body sardonically. "All because of you, Hvanen."

Hvanen struggled to his knees.

"Live with that, if you can—if your pain and guilt are not so great as to make life unbearable." He grinned evilly. "Ah, can you imagine it? A champion of life forced to take his own." Laughing, Xelhah passed through the space between the rotten doors.

Hvanen wondered if Xelhah's curse was premature—the slassan's poison would most likely kill him long before he could suffer enough to contemplate suicide.

Small comfort.

He collapsed to all fours, still trying to get his breath. In the distance, he heard the horses voicing some protest.

Rand was dead. Because of him.

Still on hands and knees, Hvanen crawled across the room to the exit. He looked out into the snowy dusk. He gazed across the bridge and into the woods.

As he feared, the horses were gone.

Hvanen sat on the stone floor and prodded his wounded shoulder. He felt nothing, of course, and so he lowered the mental block that kept his nerves from sending information to his mind.

He cried out in agony. He wounds were even worse than he'd thought.

Rand was dead.

Xelhah got away.

Because of him.

The figures around him were mocking him now. Their whispers came louder than ever. They called his name. They laughed.

"Shut... up!"

He looked at them. There were six of the figures, barely visible in the near-dark room. He knew their faces, though. Each one. They were quiet now.

Hvanen closed his eyes.

He could not allow more deaths this night. He could not allow Xelhah to end more lives in his name. He had to follow him. But how?

Perhaps, even on horseback, Xelhah could not make much better time than Hvanen could on foot, because of the snow. Assuming that Hvanen half-ran all the way back to town and never stopped to rest. He could not do such a thing on his own—no man could. Even if he wasn't wounded, exhausted, and poisoned.

But he still had one resource.

If ever there was a time to call upon the power of his rune, this was it. If the magic that infused it—infused him—truly was some sort of legacy from an earlier time, granted to those who might persevere against threats to the land, then it was designed for just such a situation as this. He had to reach Garonton.

He held a hand to his face, allowing one finger to trace the pattern of the rune. He didn't need to see it. It had been a part of him for so long, he knew each line and every curve. Hvanen closed his eyes tighter still and thought only about the rune. He called upon it to strengthen his connection to the lifeforce of the land. He begged for the power of the land to work with the strength of his own devotions and allow him the ability to serve both.

He felt the warmth of the rune on his face. The sensation spread down his neck, to his shoulder and to the rest of his body. It was followed quickly by a gentle balm of coolness. His body relaxed.

The rune channeled strength into his body. With this new energy, Hvanen opened his eyes and stood. His hands shook. The blows he had suffered, even the bite on his shoulder, barely registered, though he knew the venom was still there. His limbs and back soon throbbed with energy. Rather than feeling exhausted, his body was eager to move.

Hvanen quietly thanked his rune, and whatever power had given it to him.

Before he could go anywhere, though, he retreated back into the darkness of the entry hall. Careful not to step on Rand—or go anywhere near him, in fact—he moved to the back wall and felt around on the floor until he found it.

He walked back to the door and into the dim light with *Xiridil*, his grandfather's sword, held tightly in both hands.

"I will come back for you, Rand."

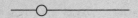

The long night of winter was dark, but the moonlight's reflection on the snow allowed Hvanen to follow the path
through the woods and out into the open fields toward Garonton. Even with the snowfall, he could trace Xelhah's tracks—or
rather, the tracks of the two horses. The fact that the snow had
not entirely obscured the prints suggested that he couldn't be
too far behind. That knowledge kindled his determination. He
never once stopped to rest. He never slowed.

Sword still clutched in his snow-covered hand, Hvanen
struggled forward. Every step was an effort, but he forced each
one to be as quick and forceful as the last.

In the distance, he saw the lights of Garonton. The tracks
led straight there.

When he entered the confines of the town, he did not slow.
Xelhah had told him where he was going.

The streets were understandably empty. It was a cold night
of heavy snow. The town was quiet, although here and there he
passed a building from which he could hear voices, laughter,
and in a few, music.

Life.

In the center of town, not far from the livery where he had
met Rand just that morning, Hvanen saw his horse, and
Rand's as well. Both were tied to a post. They looked weary
but uninjured. No one else was around—Xelhah was nowhere
in sight.

Hvanen stood at the edge of the town's central square. Although he had pushed himself past the point of exhaustion, he
forced himself to hold his breath. He remained very still and let
the quiet night wash over him. He heard distant noises from
within the houses around him. He heard the snow fall gently
on the windless night. He heard the figures that lurked behind

him whispering to each other, and to him, but even they could not block out the sound he sought.

He heard Xelhah intoning the foul words of the spell from the scroll.

Such a difficult spell normally would be beyond the abilities of a witch like Xelhah. However, the corrupt mage who'd created the spell long ago, for a terrible purpose no longer known, had inscribed it upon the scroll to make it easier to cast. Fortunately, since it was so complex, it would take Xelhah some time to complete the casting.

Hvanen had a chance.

He tracked the sound of Xelhah's voice, chanting words in some tongue unknown to Hvanen. Around the side of a large, two-story structure Hvanen followed the words, and then he saw the footprints in the snow. They led to a ladder against the stone wall of the dark building. The words came from above. Finally sheathing his sword, Hvanen climbed.

He was halfway up the ladder when Xelhah's words ended.

The spell was finished. *No!* Hvanen forced himself to keep climbing. As he did, the snowflakes began fluttering around him. A wind began to blow. Its intensity grew.

Hvanen reached the top, the flat roof of one of the taller buildings in town. From here, he could see over almost every rooftop in Garonton. He could also see Xelhah, who was just now pulling out the scroll from where he had tucked it into his belt.

It dawned on Hvanen that the spell Xelhah had just cast was not *death's wind* after all. The night had been too still for the witch to cast his horrible sorcery. He first had to conjure a wind before it could take hold and inflict its horrors. He wasn't too late.

Hvanen wasted no time with words. He drew *Xiridil* and walked across the snow-covered rooftop.

Xelhah looked at him in surprise. "How?" He shook his head, his mouth agape.

Hvanen gave no answer.

The wind was strong now, pulling at Xelhah's cloak and hair, as well as Hvanen's coat. The loose, powdery snow was easy for the gusts to pick up and churn into the air. *Xiridil* flashed as Hvanen drew it back.

Xelhah motioned with his hand and grasped into the wind, catching hold of a gusting breeze and pulling a sword of his own out of it—a sword made of frigid air. He parried Hvanen's initial blow, but it was only the first of many.

Xiridil was a potent blade, but the conjured sword of wind was its equal. It churned the air around it, blocking each of Hvanen's stokes. Xelhah smiled.

"You move. I counter the move. I stay one step ahead. This seems to be the way of things, Hvanen."

The wind around them was increasing, although it seemed to bother him much more than Xelhah. Conditions were only going to get worse.

Hvanen lunged left. Xelhah moved to parry the blow with his windblade. It was merely a feint, however. Hvanen brought *Xiridil* quickly around to the right. Still, Xelhah was fast, and his sword moved like the wind itself. If Hvanen had been trying to strike at his foe's heart, Xelhah would have countered his strike just like the previous blows. But the runechild had other plans. He brought his sword around wide and sliced at Xelhah's other hand—the one holding the vellum scroll. It was a wild slash that only just barely caught the back of the man's hand. A minor, negligible wound at best, except that, reflexively, Xelhah's hand opened and he let go of the scroll.

The wind grasped the vellum like a raptor snatching its prey and carried it off into the night. In a flash, it was gone.

Xelhah cried out in surprise and horror. He lowered his windblade as he watched the scroll disappear.

Hvanen did not hesitate. He thrust his sword at his startled foe.

Xelhah collapsed at the end of the blade once wielded by Hvanen's grandfather. The runechild winced, knowing what came next. His face flashed with a dark burst of energy, his rune suddenly squirming like a spider. With a terrible scream that Hvanen knew only he could hear, Xelhah's spirit left his body and appeared like an apparition just a few paces behind him.

With all the rest of them.

These were the six men and women Hvanen had been forced to slay in the name of life—all of those who had left the champion no option other than to take from them what he felt was most precious. Now there were seven. The spirits all whispered at the appearance of another in their ranks. Their murmurs sounded venomous and cruel, as they always were, and Hvanen did his best to ignore them, as he always did.

This was the yoke the rune forced him to bear—the price he had to pay for the power it granted him. He did not know if other runechildren had such burdens, but he did.

"Yes," Hvanen said, knowing that no one could hear him, but picturing Rand's face as he said it. "Sometimes one must deal death to serve life. But not without cost."

He left Xelhah's body atop the roof. The conjured wind was already dying down. Soon the corpse would be covered in snow. Once back down on the ground, he spent the rest of that cold night looking for the terrible spell scroll. He eventually found it and sat down in the snow between two buildings. He promised himself that when he was done, he would find a healer in this town who could help him deal with the poison.

It took some time to get a light, but eventually he produced a spark with flint and steel. While he watched the scroll curl as it burned, he thought about the long, lonely return trip to Scarhold to bring Rand's body back for burial, just the seven—no, eight—of them.

He ignored the whispered voices around him, like he always did.

WOLFGANG BAUR

Wolfgang Baur lives in Seattle with his wife Shelly and their dog, a feisty Tibetan spaniel. He contributed to the Beyond Countless Doorways *sourcebook from Malhavoc Press and is currently at work on two novels.*

RICHARD LEE BYERS

Richard Lee Byers is the author of over twenty fantasy and horror novels, including The Shattered Mask, The Black Bouquet, *The Dead God Trilogy,* The Vampire's Apprentice, Dead Time, *and the bestseller* Dissolution. *His short fiction has appeared in numerous magazines and anthologies.*

MONTE COOK

Monte Cook has written more than one hundred roleplaying game products, including coauthoring the 3rd Edition of the Dungeons & Dragons® *game. A graduate of the Clarion West writer's workshop, he has also published short stories and two novels:* The Glass Prison *and* Of Aged Angels.

BRUCE R. CORDELL

Bruce R. Cordell is known in the roleplaying game community for his many adventures and rulebooks. Recently he's had the opportunity to write some stories sans game mechanics, including the novels Oath of Nerull *and* Lady of Poison.

ED GREENWOOD

The creator of the Forgotten Realms® *fantasy world, Ed Greenwood is an award-winning writer, game designer, and columnist. The Canadian author has published over one hundred books, six hundred articles and short stories, and several bestselling computer games.*

JEFF GRUBB

Jeff has written fourteen novels, over twenty short stories, and more game products than you can shake a stick at. A founder of both Forgotten Realms *and* Dragonlance®, *he often vacations in other domains. Jeff lives in Seattle with his wife and coconspirator, Kate Novak, and his cat, Emily.*

MIRANDA HORNER

Miranda Horner loves to play games, edit games, read books, write for fun, and work on needlework. She lives in the Kansas City area with her husband Shaun and three cats.

WILL MCDERMOTT

Depending on who you ask, Will McDermott is best known as the author of the novels Judgment *and* Moons of Mirrodin, *editor-in-chief of* Duelist® *and* TopDeck® *magazines, or simply "Dad."*

MIKE MEARLS

Mike Mearls was born and raised in Pelham, New Hampshire. He works as a game designer, disproving his teachers' claims that reading books about giant robots, dragons, and space aliens during study hall was a waste of time.

THOMAS M. REID

Thomas spends his days in the Texas hill country writing fiction, including such novels as The Sapphire Crescent *and* Insurrection. *He enjoys time with his wife Teresa and sons Aidan, Galen, and Quinton, and their cat. Check out his website: <www.thomasmreid.com>.*

LUCIEN SOULBAN

Lucien Soulban has contributed to seven fiction anthologies and has written for video games and over ninety roleplaying game products, in addition to developing White Wolf's Orpheus® *game. Lucien lives in beautiful Montreal.*

STAN!

Stan!, the creative vice president of The Game Mechanics, Inc., has been writing and illustrating professionally since 1982. He lives in Renton, Washington, where he eats nothing but meat and cheese. Visit him online at <www.stannex.com>.

KEITH FRANCIS STROHM

Author of the novel Tomb of Horrors *and several short stories, Keith lives in Washington state with his wife Marlo and their dog Osen.*